Return to Abo
A NOVEL OF THE SOUTHWEST

———=))(((○)))((=———

Sharon Niederman

University of New Mexico Press ❦ Albuquerque

© 2005 by Sharon Niederman
All rights reserved. Published 2005

09 08 07 06 05   2 3 4 5

Printed in the United States of America

LIBRARY OF CONGRESS CATALOGING-IN-PUBLICATION DATA
Niederman, Sharon.
  Return to Abo : a novel of the Southwest / Sharon Niederman.
    p. cm.
  Includes bibliographical references and index.
  ISBN 0-8263-3720-1 (cloth : alk. paper)
  1. Women journalists—Fiction. 2. Real estate development—Fiction.
3. Mothers and daughters—Fiction. 4. City and town life—Fiction.
5. Divorced mothers—Fiction. 6. Aging parents—Fiction.
7. Teenage girls—Fiction. 8. New Mexico—Fiction. I. Title.
  PS3614.I356R48 2005
  813'.6—dc22

                                      2004021274

Return to Abo is purely a work of fiction. While many of the settings do in fact exist, many of the names used are common in the region of New Mexico described, and history, legend, and actual stories stimulated the author's imagination, none of the characters portrayed in this book bear any resemblance whatsoever to any person living or dead.

Book design and type composition by Kathleen Sparkes
This book is set using the Palatino family
body text is Palatino 10/15
display type is Utopia

For their generous and blessed help, inspiration, encouragement, and guidance with the writing and publication of this book, I thank with all my heart: Max Evans, Demetria Martinez, Miriam Sagan, Charles Henry, Sarah Lovett, Julia Goldberg, Carolyn Gilliland, Irma Bailey, Eloise Henry, Linda Davis, Mercedes Cravens, the Neeley family, Muriel Pounds, and Mabel Renfro.

I also want to express my gratitude to the Chuckwagon CowBelles and all the ranch women who have with kindness and patience welcomed me into their kitchens and shared their stories with me over the years.

Sharon Niederman
Albuquerque, New Mexico
June 2004

San Francisco,

March 1999

MAGGIE TOOK THE MORNING OFF FROM WORK to tackle the list of annoying but necessary errands on her to-do list. While she mentally patted herself on the back for her excellent progress, her cell phone rang. She rummaged with her right hand for the annoying instrument, buried under the pile of plastic-sheeted dry-cleaning, bags of groceries, and postage stamps, while keeping the wheel steady with her left. She caught the cell on the sixth ring.

It was a woman's voice. "Maggie! Help me!" Stunned by the caller's desperation, she took a few seconds to register the panicked voice as Ramona's. Although she couldn't make sense of the words, her friend's terrified shouting punctuated with out-of-control male howls sent all the message anyone needed. With reflex speed, she punched 911, rattled off directions to Ramona's apartment for the dispatcher, and maneuvered her Subaru Outback into a highly illegal U-turn. Scouting for whatever openings she could find, she changed lanes to gain seconds as she charged through the rush-hour traffic, her urgent need to get to Ramona's overriding her instinct for self-preservation.

Last week, after her bylined investigation of domestic violence in the city broke on the front page of the morning paper, Maggie received all sorts of calls, from women thanking her to angry men calling her a liar and much worse, to an independent producer who wanted to shoot a made-for-TV docu-drama. He name-dropped big-league actresses, one older, one younger, to cast as her and Ramona. Meanwhile, local TV stations picked up on the story, running features on the evening news, as if the brutal consequences of domestic violence were suddenly big news. She hadn't just touched a nerve. She'd grabbed a hold of that sucker, yanked it out like a rotten root, and exposed it for all the world to see.

Producers and directors all wanted to meet Ramona, the young woman whose story had moved the city. Readers wanted the personal, they needed a private tour of Ramona's particular tragic world. Maggie felt so passionately about the story that as soon as she'd lined up her stats and quotes, it practically wrote itself, the words cascading out of her fingertips.

As Maggie made a sudden stop at a red light, her thoughts were interupted by the sound of oranges rolling onto the car floor. She'd gone underground and lived in a shelter for victims of domestic violence, so she had plenty to say. Posing as a wife on the run from a brutal, estranged husband, she'd met Ramona, a recent arrival. Using her best put-the-subject-at-ease interviewing techniques, Maggie quickly discovered she and Ramona were from the same state—New Mexico. The beautiful black-haired girl with the sculptured face was from up north, Taos Pueblo, in fact, while Maggie hailed from a small ranching community that was actually the geographic center of the state. Ramona had never heard of it, but sharing their place of origin, which they both loved and both fled, twenty years apart, created a fast bond.

"I wanted to be an artist," Ramona told her. "And I wanted to see the ocean. That's why I came to California." She had left at seventeen, before high-school graduation. Maggie had waited to graduate but didn't dare leave without her college scholarship in hand. Ramona had the clothes on her back and some turquoise jewelry left after she bought a one-way Greyhound ticket. Nevertheless, they both had to get away from their native state, which felt more like a big small town going nowhere. Ramona called it "the Land of Entrapment."

Ramona wanted to tell her story. Maggie had been clear about who she was and her mission at the shelter, but learning Maggie's identity as a reporter hadn't stopped Ramona's outpouring of confidences. Her face swollen with bruises, Ramona needed to tell other women it was possible to break free from a violent drunk who believed it was his right to come home and beat you for no reason and rape you in front of your child. There had to be a better way, but you could only find it when you made up your mind to walk out.

That's what Ramona kept telling herself in the months and weeks before she made her run for it. Nobody could help her but herself. She had to do it. She had to protect Sammy from him. Rick had violated the restraining order, and he would do it again, with more fury. Finally, one day after her lunch shift at a Market Street café, she got the courage to call the hotline number she'd been studying every day on the bus ride home. The shelter people told her what to do, and she followed their directions to the letter. Miraculously, it all seemed to work.

While Maggie lived in the shelter, she met many women whose stories broke her heart, but none more than Ramona's. The girl had left the known world of her pueblo and run straight into the arms of the devil. Her innocence, her complete lack of guile or discernment, set Ramona up for the first guy who set eyes on her. Rick was twenty-eight, a long-haired navy vet with a job as an aviation mechanic, and he promised her the world. He knew how to sweet-talk her, how to treat her in bed, and how to push her around. They moved in together, and before long Ramona became pregnant. Even before the baby came, she was spending nights crying into her pillow, telling herself, "He doesn't mean it. He really loves me, I know he does."

Separated from the world in an all-woman environment, a kind of nunnery where they prayed together and ate together while listening to Bible verses read aloud, Maggie and Ramona became the best of friends. Maggie offered her genuine sympathy, and she answered Ramona's questions with the wisdom of a woman two decades her senior. Maggie knew it was unprofessional to cross the line by befriending Ramona, but she found herself helping the girl every way she could. She gave her money, clothes, promises—of rent, tuition—whatever she needed. She babysat Sammy. Never before had she permitted herself to become so involved with a subject, nor had she even been tempted. She knew all along she could weave a great story out of Ramona's experience, and she wanted to get as close as she could.

Maggie swerved around a double-parked delivery truck. There was no other way to get to Ramona's except through this obstacle course. The sun's bleached glare did little to lift the morning fog. Downtown traffic stalled her progress. Was there a fender-bender up ahead blocking the way? She snapped on the radio for a road report. World tensions weren't improving, and neither were her chances of getting to Ramona in time to do any good. As she waited her turn to pass through a four-way intersection, a lone protestor waved a poster of Our Lady of Guadalupe while he inscribed the sign of the cross over every passing car. Was his gesture a blessing or a warning? The picture of Our Lady reminded her of New Mexico, where the image could be found in nearly every house, and statues of the Virgin erected in upended bathtub shrines blessed the flowerbeds and vegetable gardens. Ordinarily, she'd have parked the car and jumped out to interview the protestor. She might have found a story, some human interest that articulated an undercurrent of life in the city—if the guy wasn't a total wacko out to predict the imminent arrival of Doomsday, the Apocalypse, or some other millennial catastrophe.

It'd been far too long since she'd been home to New Mexico. The letter from Momma she'd received last week reminded her of that fact, as if she needed to be reminded. She'd responded as usual by sending a check.

It wasn't as if she didn't have enough to handle right here. Things at the house had gone to hell since she'd been working on this story. She promised herself as soon as it was over she'd make it up to Hannah. Her daughter, twelve going on seventeen, was behaving particularly defiantly these days. The minute she put on a training bra, she became a total brat. It wasn't just a matter of pleading to wear eye shadow and lipstick. No, their fights were about body piercing and tattoos, painful, permanent scars Maggie didn't understand. She'd given up on the ever-changing hair colors, from fluorescent pink to toxic green, all acceptable to Hannah so long as she wasn't wearing any color that appeared in nature. She had no idea how she was going to handle the teen years ahead. Maybe she should just ship Hannah off to her grandmother in New Mexico and wait out the storm. Lucy would set her straight in short order.

And whenever she tried to talk with Paul about Hannah, his perpetual distraction turned into a solid stone wall that she had neither time nor energy to break through. They'd kept up the minimum civility necessary to run the household and inhabit it together during this tense spell. Then, when she'd found that love note from his legal intern, she surprised herself by not feeling much more than annoyance, as if he were an adolescent boy in need of a reprimand for a troublemaking prank. Still, when she'd brought it up, as reasonably as she possibly could, the fight they had into the night woke Hannah and maybe the neighbors, too.

Almost there, just up the block, Maggie saw the flashing lights of the cop cars, parked three-deep, blocking the street, while sirens wailed and ambulance and fire trucks careened around the corner. A crowd was already gathering in front of the three-story once-grand Victorian where Ramona lived in a dull apartment that could have been pretty, with green plants in the bay window, bright flower boxes, and the trim painted ice-cream colors. Word traveled fast in this working-class neighborhood. Maggie parked alongside the ambulance, slammed the door, and sprinted to the house. A silver-headed woman dressed in black, carrying a basket of tomatoes on her arm, stood looking up. She pointed upward as Maggie approached. "Very bad," she said.

The door to the apartment steps swung wide open. As Maggie raced up the staircase three shots blasted the chaos. She never made it to the top. An officer stopped her and sent her downstairs to wait with the others. Moments later, two EMT's came out the front porch steps carrying Ramona on a gurney. Please, God, let her still be alive, Maggie prayed. Let her live. "Out of the way, ma'am," the EMT told her, pushing past with his load. "What's going on?" she asked. "Crazy guy shot up his girlfriend and kid," he spat back at her. "He turned the gun on himself, and it was too late for the little boy."

She must have done some fast talking and flashing of credentials, because before she knew it, she was helping load Ramona into the ambulance, and then she was sitting beside her as the vehicle sped to the hospital, lights flashing and sirens blaring as cars moved aside for them.

Maggie held Ramona's hand. "It's going to be all right, baby," she said, smoothing a strand of dark hair off the girl's forehead. Ramona was still conscious, bleeding heavily from the shoulder, as the EMT inserted a line into her arm. "Maggie," she whispered, her eyes misting over. "Look after Sammy for me."

"Of course I will, baby," she lied. "But just until you come home. You're going to be fine. I'll help you get everything back to normal and stay with you until you're better." She bent and kissed her gently on the cheek. The EMT shook his head. Maggie held her hand until they reached the hospital, when the EMT pried Ramona's slender fingers, the fingers of an artist, already growing cold, from her grip.

Southeast of Albuquerque

January 2000

ONE

A BAD THING ALWAYS BRINGS SOME GOOD. *No hay mal que por bien no venga.* That's what Elias, who could recite a *dicho*, a timeworn Spanish homily, for every occasion, always said. A scruffy, weathered man in a brown plaid jacket and a dusty black Stetson that made his ears look too big for his face, he'd share his wisdom as he leaned on a fencepost, gazing at the sky and puffing on a hand-rolled cigarette.

Maggie smiled as she recalled his gap-toothed grin and the way he made up stories in Spanglish. He'd see how far he could get with his tall tale before she realized he was only pulling her leg. By the time she was nine or so she caught on, and after that she let him think she believed his yarns about talking cows and windmills that spun so fast they rose off the ground, scaring the cows away. Elias respected horses and dogs highly but didn't think much of the intelligence of a cow. When he finished his tale he'd slap himself on the knee and howl. Elias loved to laugh at himself, no matter how many times he'd told the story.

But as she drove the twisted, fractured back road faster than she had any right to, Maggie wondered what good could possibly come out of this blasted cold January day. She clutched the wheel of her rental car and kept her foot firmly on the gas pedal as she swung in and out of the curves that climbed the Manzano foothills southeast of Albuquerque. Anybody who intended to abide by the posted speed could just get out of her way.

Elias's funeral was set for eleven A.M., only an hour away. A considerable stretch of rollercoaster road lay ahead. There had been talk about fixing this narrow two-lane years ago when Elias taught her to drive out here. As chewed up as ever, the blacktop remained the public health hazard she remembered. She accelerated as much as she dared, glanced in the rearview mirror, and watched for a flashing red light.

When her mother called with the news about Elias, Maggie booked the first flight available out of San Francisco, at sunup that morning. As always, Lucy had given it to her straight. "Elias is gone, Maggie. Yesterday. He was out back chopping wood when it happened. He went just like that. Doctor said it was his heart. You know he was never sick a day in his life. Just took his herbs if anything bothered him and he'd be fine."

He would be buried in the *camposanto* behind Our Lady of Sorrows, where he'd attended mass faithfully all his life. And now her mother, not at all well herself, would be by herself on the isolated ranch six miles from town. Maggie could hear the unspoken thoughts of Monte Alto's old folks as she walked in today: *"Gone to San Francisco. Whatever for? Leaving Lucy like that. And after all that woman has been through. Hard as she's worked to keep the place going all this time."*

A part of her agreed with them. Sometimes, lately, it was hard to remember exactly why she had gone away.

Trapped in the shadowy canyon thick with piñon and juniper

Return to Abo

that gave way to dense Ponderosa pine on the left and wind-hewn yellow sandstone cliffs on the right, Maggie maneuvered over glaring patches of black ice. Handmade wood crosses draped with faded plastic flowers, *descansos* that marked poor souls' final touch with earth, stood along the roadside. Many of the crosses marked the sites of fatal car wrecks, the result of hormones mixed with boredom and spiked with booze.

Suddenly, she reached the summit. The way the land opened up at that moment was always a surprise. It unfurled into the enormous ochre and violet blanket of the plains, and she could see farther than she'd ever thought possible. All the way to Oklahoma? To Texas? Hell, she saw straight into another world, to some kind of Promised Land. Ghosts of distant mountains hovered on the edge of her vision. They'd tempted plenty of others, in search of gold and glory, to cross the dry Jornada del Muerte. The dead man's journey.

A lonely white Penitente cross on a hillside overlooked dismembered, rusted-out trucks parked alongside splintered board houses with sagging roofs. Crumbling adobe walls, enclosing nothing, leading nowhere, rose up out of meadows of dried brown grasses. The shrine of the bathtub Virgin, her arms outstretched amidst the rocks, offered solace and understanding to all. Windmill blades, so beloved by Western landscape painters, spun round and round, like the iridescent carnival pinwheels twirling on the graves. A hope for water, a hope for heaven? As she passed the mutilated tires, the broken-down trailers, the tilted For Sale signs that littered the roadside, she knew the only thing worse than what people had done to the land was what the land had done to the people. Both were scarred by the never-ending battle between them.

Like it or not, she was home. She was from someplace, and this was surely the place her soul recognized and longed to roost in.

Maggie drove through the cluster of tiny villages that clung to the roadside as wondrously as chamisa that sprouted from rock crevices, drawing its nourishment from cold stone. Each had its eighteenth-century church, supported by rock-pile buttresses, built by loving, faithful hands out of rocks, mud, and logs—whatever materials villagers could scrabble from the earth. By now, most everyone was related somehow. Families who had lived out here for generations greeted one another every Sunday, asking after the newborns and the ailing elderly just as their great-great-grandparents had. In addition to its church, each village had its gas station, variety store, and school. That was about it.

On the outskirts of Monte Alto, Frank's Texaco was still open. The wind rattled Pepsi cans past this store where you could buy firewood, Bisquick, and beans, enough to keep going.

She remembered RuthAnn Vigil, a few years ahead of her in school. RuthAnn, a girl who wore lots of green eye shadow and teased her hair into a flip, used to hang out at Frank's. She'd go up to truckers and say, Please, mister, get me out of this goddamn place! Then, one day, she disappeared. Such a pretty girl, they used to say. Stories came back for years. Folks visiting kin at Thanksgiving said they'd spotted her in Colorado Springs. Or she'd been seen at the mall in El Paso. One thing was sure: she never came home again.

She slowed as she drove the dozen blocks of Main Street. There'd only been about four thousand people living here when she'd been growing up, and now it looked even smaller than she remembered. Monte Alto, the mountain the town took its name from, was big only in comparison to the surrounding landscape. The village had come into existence with the railroad, and its fortunes rose then fell with those of the Atchison, Topeka & Santa Fe line. The Kowboy Kafe's red neon "Open" sign was still on, illuminating ice-glazed Main Street like a headlight running off a weak battery. The last picture show had closed up here a long, long time ago; collapsed letters on the Kiva Theater marquee jumbled an indecipherable title. The box office window was nailed shut. Dawson's Hardware and Feeds, Bauer's Grocery, the Rexall, and the Seven Cities Saloon looked like they still might be going concerns. The VFW where Glen Campbell—*the* Glen Campbell—used to play Saturday nights sat padlocked, a skin of white paint peeling from the stucco, revealing the corroded brown flesh of its structure beneath.

She turned at the north end of town and found a parking space behind the other cars around the corner from the church. She looked in the mirror. Sure enough, dark shadows framed thick-lashed hazel eyes that today had decided to show green irises rimmed with gold. She ran her fingers through wavy black shoulder-length hair and touched up her lipstick. Wrapped in her down storm coat, scarf, and gloves, she walked to the cemetery.

Her heartbeat quickened as she stepped inside the wrought-iron gate and picked her way among the headstones framed in low white picket fences that were the custom here. More faded yellow and pink plastic flowers, placed here unknown seasons ago, decorated the graves. She moved toward the crowd gathered in the far corner.

The sky was a smoky gray marble, the color of a headstone. Vague clouds drifted behind a translucent milky screen. An unearthly silver glow reflected onto the bowed dry grasses and twisted cholla branches in nearby fields.

The priest stood over the grave, reciting from an open book. Maggie entered the circle of drab-clad mourners to take her place beside her mother. The crowd of two dozen breathed a collective gasp, however, as all eyes watched her take Lucy's arm. In her royal-blue coat she was as conspicuous as a peacock among a flock of sparrows. She stumbled over a loose rock and almost lost her footing. Lucy bowed her head. The crowd followed suit, as if taking a cue from the conductor.

As the padre intoned the service, Maggie glanced around. She struggled to connect names with faces. The ladies of her mother's Wednesday bridge club were here. Elvira, Lola, Ruby, Mercedes—they hadn't changed at all that she could see, except Mercedes now toted an oxygen tank. With their silver hair, gold-rimmed glasses, and faces wrinkled like tissue paper, the bridge ladies seemed the same indeterminate, ancient age as always. Many of the town's storekeepers had turned out as well. Their character—born in tough times, matured during years of hardship—was distinctly visible in the permanent set of their jaws and their deeply furrowed brows.

She didn't recognize any of Elias's people. He had no family of his own that Maggie knew of, nor any world beyond the ranch. They had become his family, and today people had come out in the cold to pay their respects to Lucy as much as to the man lying in his coffin. Elias had been their hired hand, but even so, he had the village's respect as the man of the ranch.

Elias had always been there for her, though, no matter what she'd done or left undone. Maggie counted on the gentle smile that turned his eyes into sparkling half-moons and his soft-spoken words.

She looked up. Low clouds of a January storm gathered force. If they were lucky, those clouds would break today and there would be snow by afternoon. If not, as was more likely the case, the cloud cover could hang suspended for days, weeks even, while ranchers' fears of another dry year dominated thought and conversation in Monte Alto. Two decades of West Coast city living hadn't erased her memory of that particular hopelessness, nor of the endless struggle to coax life from a land that stubbornly withheld it season after season. Descended from homesteader stock, folks here knew how to hang on and make do. They remembered when times were really tough, growing up in dugouts, walking to school in windstorms.

Only a fool would call this too dry, too windy land beautiful. Either the land made you tough enough to stand it, or you left. Clearly, Maggie didn't have what it took. Her mother, Lucy, knew it too, hard as she'd fought to change her daughter.

As she scanned the crowd, Maggie saw one person she remembered well. For a flicker of a moment, she met the eyes of Roger Dawson, her old high school boyfriend, her first love. He was still what you'd have to call a handsome guy, but from here it looked like the sparkle she'd loved in him had been extinguished, blown out by the cold winds of too many Monte Alto winters. He held the posture of someone paying attention, but his distant expression communicated that his mind was elsewhere.

And across from Roger on the other side of the circle stood Tommie Herrera, her best childhood friend. For years Tommie had faithfully sent Maggie Christmas cards. Maggie hadn't returned with any of her own, and eventually, the cards stopped arriving. Roger and Tommie had suffered a terrible tragedy: three years ago, their only son, Jesse, had been killed in one of those awful wrecks out on the highway east of town. Tommie appeared to be in better shape than her husband. In a well-tailored suit and heels, with a good haircut and careful makeup, Tommie looked downright fashionable, at least for this crowd, decked out as they were in zippered Sears jackets, Stetsons, and sturdy black winter coats they'd worn to church the past twenty years. No sense buying a new one so long as the one you had still had plenty of wear in it. As Maggie studied her, Tommie sent her a nod of acknowledgment.

The priest droned on. At her side, her mother shifted her weight. Yesterday, Lucy's voice had sounded the same as always—

level, sensible, in control. But what did Maggie expect? Of course her mother would remain dry-eyed despite the loss of her lifelong partner. Whatever her emotions might be, she was not about to share them with her daughter. Or anyone. Lucy saw no point to indulging weepiness. She'd never had a minute to sit around feeling sorry for herself, and she didn't have any respect for those who did. It was her attitude of mind over heart that had made the difference, she'd tell you. The only reason their ranch had survived while so many others had gone under was because she had the sense to know what was important and what was unnecessary to the task. Maggie understood her mother's instinct for survival, but she couldn't always go along with its unforgiving dictates.

Her own voice had shaken as she fought back the tears that came when she heard about Elias. "How are you doing with all this, Momma?" Grasping the phone, she found a chair and fell into it.

"I'm going to be fine. Got to make Elias's arrangements."

Maggie didn't trust her own ability to make it through this funeral without going to pieces. She hadn't been home in over two years, but Lucy and Elias were never out of her thoughts. What was the truth about their long relationship? Maggie would love the answer to that one and plenty more, but she knew better than to ask her mother personal questions.

Lucy must have shrunk during the past two years; the crown of her black-veiled velvet pillbox hat only reached Maggie's shoulder. How odd. Maggie remembered looking up at her mother. Lucy stood straight-backed as ever, wrapped, it seemed, in a cloak of her own remoteness, absorbing the priest's every word. Her arm, under Maggie's grasp, felt fragile as a doll's. Her bones might be thinning, but her will, and her ability to intimidate, never would. Sooner or later, Maggie would have to tell Lucy what was going on in her life. She didn't look forward to the conversation. Mechanically, she recited the Lord's Prayer along with the crowd.

One by one, shovelfuls of stony earth hit the coffin that lay at the bottom of the open grave. Tears filled Maggie's eyes. Thank God for Elias's warmth and humor. She'd never taken the time or made the opportunity to tell him all he'd meant to her. She'd left so soon and been gone so long. Through her tears, Elias leaned against the fencepost, rolled another cigarette, and smiled down at her.

TWO ✢

With her mother tucked in on the front seat beside her, Maggie turned the car toward the ranch. They drove without speaking. Her claw-like hands twitching, Lucy knotted her damp hanky and occasionally cleared her throat. She reached up, unfastened her pearl hatpin, removed her black pillbox, and placed it on her lap, punctuating the finality of the day's events. To break the tense silence, Maggie remarked, blandly, "It's good so many people come out today." She cracked the window and inhaled the January morning scent—skunk and cold.

"That's true." Lucy stilled her nervous hands by folding them in her lap. She turned and gazed out the grimy window at the bleak landscape, shutting Maggie out, choosing to remain alone with her thoughts.

Would it be this way when her mother went, too? A phone call, a rushed flight to New Mexico, no chance to say goodbye? While she was wrapped up with her San Francisco life, this place seemed distant. It existed for her only on the edge of her mind, almost too far in the past to remember, populated with characters and events she'd just as soon forget. She kept the land and the people who clung to it fenced off. Monte Alto was ancient history, quaint and backward, stuck in time.

Yet, the place haunted her whenever she was away from it, so she never felt completely at home anywhere else. Then, when she did return to the land, she became preoccupied with getting away. She kept looking at her watch, as if she were watching a slow movie, wondering how much longer until the end. Divorcing her husband had been a piece of chocolate cake compared to the eternal contradictions Monte Alto inflicted. Aside from the squabbles and inconveniences Paul was prone to cause, once she'd made up her mind divorce was the best decision, their separation had brought her more peace than she'd had any right to expect.

There was no triumph in this homecoming today. But over a dozen years ago she'd come this way bringing her baby daughter Hannah home. The entire town had come out to see them, loaded with crocheted pink and aqua bonnets and booties. Maggie was so busy tending her new baby, she didn't have time to fester in her usual discontent. Serving up pie, showing off her chubby, adorable grandbaby, Lucy looked as happy as Maggie had ever seen her. Maggie had done it right that time, even if her now ex-husband Paul hadn't made that trip with them. He was a Motor City boy, and these big spaces made him twitchy. All that land with nothing on it, he'd say. The emptiness was some kind of affliction to him, and she could understand his discomfort. Back then, he'd told her he had a big case to prep for and couldn't get away. Now she wondered what he'd really been up to.

When she'd arrived, Elias had lifted Hannah up on the saddle and circled the corral with her baby. Hannah didn't mind her first time on a horse one bit. So he came for the child each morning. "See, 'jita?" he winked. "Just like you—she'll learn to ride before she starts to walk."

That was the family legend, anyway: "Maggie could ride before she could walk," as if to explain why she'd rather be on horseback than anywhere else. She'd heard it recounted so many times she didn't know if it was true or just a story. Now Maggie never rode. She hadn't been on a horse in years.

Seeing this place again—that enormous, free sky alive with constant motion, arching over empty space dotted with mysterious wreckage of the past—touched her heart and imagination. That's how the place affected her. She felt shut out most of the time, but out of nowhere an occasional beam of illumination suddenly broke through, warming her soul with its beauty, and she was hooked again. It continued to wait for her, then required she recognize and contend with it, making the same demand it had made of her mother and three generations of her family. They had each obeyed the call, however, while she had made her refusal quite clear. She'd left and created a life as different from this one as possible. And for two-plus decades, her beautiful, useful creation had held up very well.

She drove out of town past the rodeo grounds, where ranchers used to turn out every Sunday to compete for prize money, eat barbecue, and drink beer, and where, every Fourth of July, cowboys came from all over this country to compete in the Maverick Club rodeo. Now the split-wood fences they'd built were beyond repair; tumbleweeds piled up around the fenceposts. She swerved to avoid a lacerated road kill as they passed the deserted Happy Trails Motor Court. Approaching the abandoned McNitt place, she spotted the old yellow school bus Alice used to drive.

At the six-mile marker south of town their small ranch came into view. Her grandparents had homesteaded here, built a dugout and proved up on their stake. Lured from Oklahoma by the promise of free land, they'd had plenty of company. Too late and the hard way, people found out that the 160 acres the government offered wasn't enough to sustain a family. That kind of acreage just couldn't support sufficient cattle sales to be called a living.

But somehow, their family got by, raising chickens, keeping milk cows, selling eggs and butter and cream in town for spending money. They planted fruit trees, tended a big vegetable garden, canned and dried their fruit and produce. They had plenty to eat, and they always had a turkey or a hog to butcher. They worked long hours day in and day out, and they kept their complaints to themselves.

Grandpa, something of a water witch, had a well drilled not too far from where he sited the house. That precious water source made all the difference in their ability to survive on their land. "You know how good our well is," Grandpa always said. "It'll hold up, and it'll hold our family together." He piped water to supply all their needs right into the house.

But many of their neighbors couldn't abide the hardship of living in a dugout then getting dusted out. They were forced to sell, one by one. The ranches that remained, like Lucy's, were the inheritance of those who'd had the gumption to stick it out. As the others departed, those who stayed bought up the surrounding claims cheap. "Sometimes they'd settle for a team of horses and a wagon, anything to get them across the state line," Grandpa said.

Maggie turned at the mailbox, just an old bucket someone had rigged by welding on a lid and a latch. She got out of the car and worked the tight barbed wire over the fencepost to open the gate. She got back in and drove through, then got out again and shut the gate. Today for the first time, when she drove up to the ranch there would be no welcoming wave and reliable smile from Elias. The slight yet surprisingly strong man in a worn brown plaid jacket buttoned up to his chin, hat pulled low on his forehead, wearing a two-day grizzled beard and beat-up dusty boots, was gone. A blast of cold wind rocked the car. Windy enough to make whitecaps in a washtub, Elias would have said. Maggie turned up the heat, but she couldn't stop the trembling of her hands.

She drove over a yellow cattle guard, then bumped across miles of washboard road to the house. The ranch house faced west for a view of Monte Alto, granting the family witness to its moody beauty. A windmill not far from the house insured they'd have the water they needed from their well. In back, two miles to the north, lay the Abo Pueblo Indian ruins, in ancient times a thriving trade center beside a tributary of the Rio Grande. Then five hundred years ago, the Spanish came and enslaved the Indians, who built the red sandstone cathedral of San Gregorio. The façade of the three-story Spanish mission ruins still stood, faintly visible from the porch. Drought, famine, raids, and disease drove the Tompiros out more than four centuries ago.

To the east lay flats once rich with nutritious grasses where her grandfather's herds had grazed, and where, against all odds, Lucy and Elias had continued to run enough cattle to keep calling the ranch a ranch. In the old days, they'd run fifty head, and in decent years, they grew a meadow of good vega grass, provided their stock with hay all winter. With their forty acres of corn, they'd been able to keep their horses well fed, too. That, with chickens and a few sheep, and somehow they'd gotten by. They never got ahead, but they were able to live self-sufficiently, didn't have anyone else to answer to, and so they considered themselves blessed.

In recent years, most of the cows got a bad weed and died, the others walked off, and now the land lay still. Maggie had heard of ranchers getting rich off their land. She didn't happen to know any. Squeezing a living out of dry grass, coping with the whims of weather, and constant aggravation over the price of beef wasn't Maggie's idea of a life, but for her mother, it was the only way. Some folks didn't care what they sacrificed, so long as they had their land and with it, their honor. Although they didn't understand the bond, they never questioned it. They did exactly what they'd been raised to do. But others now seemed to be in the position of the homesteaders they'd displaced, waiting until developers offered them top dollar for their land and their water rights. Then they'd pack up and head out in their battered pickups faster than jackrabbits chased by coyotes.

Though neglected, the house, surrounded by cottonwoods, was still beautiful, both spacious and cozy. Made of adobe bricks with a tin roof, it had been built by hand and built to last by people who had time and materials, craft and an eye. They'd created a thick-walled architectural anomaly, a house built of native materials stretched and shaped to suit their memories of the East. It needed major work—paint, plaster, windows, probably a roof—work Lucy couldn't afford on her meager Social Security check. But it still looked more like home to Maggie than any place she'd every lived.

She looked at her mother, so pitifully diminished, shrunken into her black coat, in a trance of her own making. In the tarnished locket of Maggie's memory stood a robust woman who lifted hundred-pound feed sacks out of the pickup bed. She'd been a woman who pulled a calf from a cow's womb, then carried the wet thing into the kitchen and set it in front of the wood stove, her arms bloody up past the elbows. Then she kneaded ten loaves of bread and set them to rise, all before it even got light. That Amazon could not have become this frail, white-haired old lady. Lucy had suffered a small stroke two years ago, when Maggie saw her last. But she insisted to her daughter she was completely recovered, getting along just fine. "No need for you to waste a minute worrying about me," she'd said.

The slam of the car door rattled the cold day like a gunshot. No border collie, smarter and sweeter than any dog ever, ran out to greet them. And steady Elias, with his kind welcome and broken-toothed smile, wasn't there to wave from the corral. Maggie looped her arm through her mother's, and the two of them made their way across the gravel driveway, up the porch steps to the front door. Lucy moved slowly, on unstable, wobbly legs stiffened by arthritis. Her stride, all her life so brisk and confident, was now reduced to a step-by-step search for the next bit of level ground.

Inside the chilly house, Maggie tended the fire in the Home Comfort stove that sat in a corner of the big kitchen. She added kindling, blew on the embers until the flame revived, then fed the stove a chunk of cedar from the woodbin.

"I'm tired, Maggie. Think I'll go lie down a while," Lucy said. She put her hands on the kitchen table and pulled herself out of her chair. Her limited repertoire of movement was quickly becoming obvious. Once inside the house, Lucy allowed herself the use of her cane. Leaning heavily on it, she laboriously tapped her way down the hallway to her bedroom at the back of the house.

When Maggie heard the bedroom door shut, she filled the kettle and set it on the stove. She sat in the Mission oak rocker, brought, as she recalled, by wagon from Oklahoma, its red leather seat cushion torn and in need of reupholstering. Green gingham-checked curtains, cracked linoleum, scarred oak kitchen table, paint darkened by wood smoke, ticking wall clock—everything was exactly the same, permeated with the familiar scent of yeast and apples, dryness and cinnamon that existed only in this room. Had the place always been so quiet? While she sipped a cup of hot tea, she noticed the three-foot-long snakeskin nailed to the wall across the room. She shuddered.

Maggie remembered her mother whipping to death any

rattler that dared come near her house. One chilly morning, when Maggie was a child, a snake crawled into the old adobes, looking to make a mouse its breakfast. Lucy took the frayed old horsewhip with the black handle from its hook inside the pantry. She lashed at the snake over and over, hitting its head as it coiled and rattled. Maggie had been frightened and thrilled that Lucy would rather whip the snake than shoot it. She knew her mother was capable of winning any battle with a snake; nonetheless, the reptile terrified her. She saw how much Lucy enjoyed the kill. She put everything she had into delivering as much harm as she could possibly inflict on the creature, as if its death, caused by its desire to seek a bit of warmth and shelter, was well deserved and would purge this house of its troubles. Her justified fury rode every whirl of the whip. Even after the hellish rattling ceased, Lucy continued cracking the horsewhip, possessed, her eyes gleaming with a terrible light. When the snake finally lay still, she took the broom and with a few brisk strokes, swept its three-foot length out on the back porch steps.

In the cold morning light, Lucy grabbed Maggie's arm and dragged her out the back door. Black diamonds glittered along the creature's back. Maggie wasn't sure it was really dead. "Here," Lucy said. She wrapped Maggie's fingers around the cold pistol handle. "Shoot," she commanded. Maggie hesitated. "Shoot, I said!" Lucy stood over her and raised the whip. "Or do I have to teach you how?"

Maggie pulled the trigger. The screams she had stifled tore out of her like siren wails without end. Lucy, still standing over her, whip in hand, slapped her across the face, one more sharp crack. Maggie felt the sting, touched her cheek and stared at her bloody fingertips. Her mother's face showed pure contempt. Maggie sank to the ground sobbing, her arms wrapped around herself, rocking back and forth.

"Clean that up." Lucy was pointing at something. Maggie looked down and saw she had peed on the floor. "When you're through, go to your room and wash your face." Lucy wiped her hands on her apron. She returned to the kitchen sink and continued cutting biscuits. Maggie fetched the wash bucket, got down on her knees, and wiped up her own mess. She stayed in her room until after lunch, the one mercy Lucy permitted her. That afternoon, while Maggie did her chores in the barn, her mother skinned the snake and nailed her trophy to the kitchen wall. They never discussed what happened, although Lucy repeated the story of the snake killing over and over to anyone who'd listen, recalling that day as one of her finest. She reveled in the praise she received for her courage and strength from whoever heard the tale.

Now Maggie needed air. She pulled on her coat. As she hiked to the old cottonwood a half-mile back of the house, she passed Elias's empty bunkhouse. At that moment, her heartache was so strong that she'd have given a year of her life for the glimpse of him calmly leading a pony into the barn. Tears blurred her vision as she continued along the narrow stony path.

The land told you its story, if only you knew how to read it. Old-timers hereabouts could read the land the way a perceptive individual read the lines on a person's face and told you what kind of generosity or weakness or stubbornness to expect. They could tell you how deep the water table was by the kind of grass that grew on top.

In early spring, spikes of scarlet Indian paintbrush carpeted the ground and dainty purple asters bloomed in summer. Here, just out of the shadow of the splintery old windmill Grandpa had built, she had brought her dolls, her pretty gold and turquoise stones, her arrowheads and potsherds, her salamanders and turtles. It's where she secretly thought Daddy could hear her, and where she hoped she might sometime hear from him.

The wind creaked in the cottonwood's branches. That was the sound of La Llorona, the lady who went through the forest crying for her lost children. Some said La Llorona was the spirit of Malinche, the Indian princess who'd betrayed her people by helping the conquistador Cortez. When he returned to his wife in Spain, she'd done away with her half-breed children, and she cried for them every night. So the story went, a tale used to frighten children into staying away from the woods, a dark fairy tale to keep them safe.

A stalled hawk beat against the wind—feathers and desire. It caught a thermal, then glided down through a window of blue, circling to the ground. When it flew up again, its prey, a small rabbit, twisted in its beak.

Blue-violet Monte Alto stood guard in the west, solid and serene. The sun released a faint mountain perfume of dry sage. Maggie picked up a smooth oval stone, put it in her pocket, and faced the wind.

"Damn this place!"

She listened to the wind blow. It wasn't Daddy's voice that came to her. It was her mother's.

It finally looked like we were going to get rain, after those clouds had been gathering for what seemed like most of August. I was four months pregnant. I could still fit in the saddle easy. As the storm was building, you could smell the rain in the air. You could see it falling all around you just everywhere, those big gray fountains far away. Your father said, "I'm just going to go out and check the cows before it storms."

It got dark as night, but it was only four o'clock in the afternoon, and the lightning was flashing everywhere. There came a tremendous crack of thunder, louder than the rest, and a bolt of lightning that lit up the sky like a bomb. Then it started to hail, stones big as baseballs. And then the rain came. He didn't come back and he didn't come back, and it was ten o'clock at night, and I knew what happened. I knew what had hit him. I saddled my horse and went out to find him. My horse stumbled right on him. I found him in the dark. Right there, where the lightning hit him. I had to leave him there to go for help. And I had to tell your grandfather what happened.

And it was time to sell those cattle. So I had to find a buyer and get them shipped. So I did. I got to work the day after we buried your father. Your grandfather, he went that winter. So I was all alone when you came, except for Elias.

We were like a team of oxen, him and me, pulling this old place through the drought. Only reason we didn't quit was we didn't have the good sense to admit when we were licked. You used to see rows of beans growing all the way to Claunch—you're too young to remember. That drought lasted ten years, and that was the end of those bean fields. Folks just packed up what they could carry and headed to Socorro, Albuquerque, or Las Cruces—any place where they had a relative or any hope of finding work. The only ones who stayed didn't have the money to leave.

You know, that was the last good storm we had for a long, long time.

The singsong twang of a TV preacher greeted Maggie when she returned. She rubbed her cold fingers and warmed her hands at the fire. Then she walked down the dark hallway to her mother's bedroom. She moved warily, fighting the impulse to bolt at each step until she reached the threshold. She rapped on the closed door. "Momma? Can I fix you a bite to eat?"

Receiving no answer, Maggie opened the door a crack. A sickly smell wafted out to greet her. Slumped in bed in a man's plaid robe, Lucy dozed. Her hands rested on pinked pieces of quilt fabric. She had fallen asleep mid-stitch, the needle between her fingers, her mouth a dark pink open bruise.

The murky light of the bedside lamp revealed dust and disarray. Maggie fought the urge to sweep her arm across her mother's nightstand and banish the jumble of half-empty medicine bottles and used Kleenex. The hodgepodge of quilts on the cherry-spool bed hadn't been straightened in quite a while. Dead leaves piled under the Boston fern on the wicker stand. Worn Max Evans and Louis L'Amour paperbacks lay on the bookshelf. Maggie prowled the room, picking up scattered woolen underwear, *Readers Digest*s, and teacups scored with grime.

She turned off the TV and stood in front of her mother, whose blue-gray eyes shot open. They registered confusion, then focused into astonishment. "Maggie. What are you doing here?"

She shook her mother's chicken-wing shoulder. "Momma, wake up. I came in for Elias's funeral. We've been together all day—remember?"

"Of course." Her mother rubbed a hand across her eyes. "I must have been dreaming. Let me look at you." She drew herself into a sitting position and adjusted the robe that had fallen open. "You've been away a long time."

"Looks like a twister came through here."

"I'm restless as a cat, Maggie. Not sleeping good. So I doze all day."

"Have you talked to Dr. Patterson? Maybe he can give you something."

"I've got enough pills to open a drugstore."

"So I noticed." Maggie folded her arms. The wide silver bracelet set with a huge chunk of old turquoise, the one Grandpa traded hides for at Taos, gleamed at her wrist. She'd always worn it. The stunning bracelet was the one thing Grandma had left her. "So, how are you, Momma?"

"I'm getting along. I'm managing."

"Momma, you had a stroke."

"That was over two years ago. The last time you were out. It was only a little one, Maggie. I'm recovered now. Dr. Patterson said I could get along fine. Plenty of folks much worse off than me." She pointed out the window. A lone antelope, its hide a fleck of burnished gold, sprinted across the bleached field against a sunset of brilliant crimson and orange. "Besides, there's something else." Maggie couldn't take her eyes off her mother's twitching fingers, with their grotesquely swollen knuckles.

Maggie shivered. She searched the room for a shawl, something to wrap herself in. "What's that?"

"You'll probably say I'm just an old fool." She lowered her voice and spoke as though to herself. "Probably think I've gone batty."

Maggie drew a deep breath. What she said, and how she said it, was crucial. "I'm concerned about you—especially now—on your own out here."

"Well, no need." She leaned forward. Her breath expelled in a sour gust. "I have it on higher authority," she whispered. "It's not my time yet. Elias—it was his time. He knew it was coming. But it's not mine. The Lord gives you a sign." The room darkened as twilight deepened the sky to smoky indigo.

"Not everybody gets a sign, Momma." She sighed, remembering Ramona, and folded a towel she picked up off the floor. "Not everybody gets to make their peace." Dragged out of this life against her will and before her time, taking her child, what peace could Ramona have known?

"You make your peace as you go along," Lucy said. "You have to do that every day."

"How about Elias, Momma? Did he make his peace?" She tugged a Kleenex from the box on the nightstand, wiped her eyes, and blew her nose. "I'd sure like to know he did."

For the first time all day, her mother looked at her directly. "I believe he did, child."

"How do you know?" Maggie crumpled the Kleenex and tossed it in the wastebasket.

"Not too long ago, about a month back, he came to me, you know how he did whenever he walked in the house."

"He took off his hat and held it over his chest. Whenever he came in, he acted like he was asking permission to be here." Maggie never understood the relationship, and now anger colored her words. With a child's clarity, she had sensed some sort of bond between her mother and Elias, a bond that excluded her and was never explained. She had been angry at her mother then for the barrier she put up against this warm and generous man who waited at the back door to be invited in. Lucy lived by a private code that both included and excluded Elias at the same time; and, the awful thing was that Elias abided by this code as well. What had really gone on between her mother and the hired hand?

"I hear the judgment in your voice, Maggie, but Elias came from a different generation, and his manners were learned in another place. He did as he was comfortable," Lucy said. "Anyway, we sat down at the kitchen table and he handed me a list of his possessions and his wishes for them."

"A will?"

"Yes, his will. He said, 'Lucy, if anything ever happens to me, I want you to take care of this. Will you do that for me?' 'Well sure I will,' I told him. 'Don't be worrying about that.' I took the will and showed him where I was putting it, in the dining room cabinet, in case he wanted to come get it and make any changes. He thanked me and got up to leave.

"'You're not feeling poorly, are you, Elias?' I asked him. 'No, ma'am. I'm just fine as can be,' he told me. Then he left. I didn't think anything of it at the time," Lucy said.

"You think he had a premonition?" Maggie asked.

"Whatever you want to call it. He knew his time was near and he wasn't afraid. He'd done what he came to do. He was a very religious person, you know. I'm sure he'd talked it over with the Lord."

Maggie patted her mother's dry hand, a map of blue veins. "I wonder how you'll keep this place up without him."

Lucy picked up her quilting and began jabbing her needle in and out. "It's a thousand wonders how this place holds up as it is." She sighed. "At least he went quick. The merciful way. One minute out back chopping wood, the next minute gone, just like that." Her voice tightened, a fiddle out of tune. "Lord knows, I miss him already."

"I can help out some," Maggie said.

"Do what you can until you have to get back."

"I don't have to get right back," Maggie said.

"What do you mean?" Lucy asked, her needle stopped mid-air.

"Momma, I've lost my job at the paper."

"You mean you got fired?"

"Not exactly. Ads are down, so pages are down, so they reduced the staff. My job was one of those cut. Downsized, they call it. The newspaper business just isn't the same." If she had her way, her mother would never know the reason why she was no longer at the paper. After Ramona's death, she couldn't cope with it any more. She'd lost the ability, and the will, to chase stories and write them.

"But you've had that job better than fifteen years!" Lucy's features sharpened, leaving her face no room for understanding.

"That's right. And some people who got let go along with me were there twice as long."

"We're not quitters, Maggie." Lucy spat out each word.

Maggie stood. "I didn't say anything about quitting, Momma. I've just got to take some time to figure out my next step."

"And just how do you intend to pay your bills while you're doing all this figuring?"

"Don't worry." Maggie, searching for a distraction, unwrapped the cellophane from a lemon drop and popped the hard candy in her mouth. "They gave me a nice buyout package." At least that part was true. Her editor, understanding perfectly well that Maggie had become disabled, fought to make it happen.

Lucy grabbed the cane propped by the side of the bed and shook it. "Don't you let what happened scare you off. You're as good as you ever were."

"Thanks for your vote of confidence, Momma. But I won't be unemployed long. I've got a couple of offers I'm thinking over." Even if that were true, she didn't know how she could possibly walk into another newsroom. Thank God she'd been sending her mother a few hundred dollars every month. What had Lucy been doing with the money? Maybe that's what kept this place going.

Lucy muttered as she stitched. "Over and done. Best thing you can do is get back on that horse after he throws you. It's foolish to go and give up a career you've worked so hard for."

"Momma, I know *you'd* get right up on the horse again. I don't intend to give anything up. I just need some time out right now. I've got a little saved. Plus the settlement from the divorce. I want to think carefully about my next move and make sure it's the right one for me." Maggie's head began to throb. She felt a sick headache coming on. Where was her Advil?

"It's the doing that'll cure you, my girl. The world is full of people who'd rather 'think about it.' Thinking too much only gets you in the devil's hands."

Maggie tried on a smile. "Well, speaking of doing, seems a while since anybody around here made a trip to the dump. I still know how to haul trash."

"Who's looking after Hannah?" Lucy stitched a white quilt square. A green and yellow tulip was blooming in her hands. A quilt pattern was a wonderful thing. You knew exactly where you were going and how to get there.

"Paul has her back in Washington."

"That big a separation can be awfully hard on a child."

"I like it about as well as I'd like walking across Death Valley in my bare feet. Trouble is, it's the best I can do for now. Hannah chose to be with her Dad this year."

"You let the child choose for herself?" Lucy's eyebrows rose in shock. "Do you honestly think she knows what's best for her?"

"I think letting her choose for herself *is* what's best at her age, Momma," Maggie answered evenly.

Incredible. In less than five minutes, her mother had succeeded in compiling a list of her failures. Busted career. Busted marriage. Abandoned child. Undoubtedly one or two other flaws needed attention. She'd be hearing about them soon.

Night had fallen. Maggie went to the window and pulled down the shade. "So what do you say, Momma? Now that I'm unemployed, I can stick around for a while and help you out."

Lucy held up a finished quilt square, eyeing it for smoothness and even stitches. "I don't think so, Maggie, but I thank you for your offer."

Maggie folded her arms. "What do you mean? It's obvious there's work to be done around here. I can set things to right for you, help you get on track after losing Elias."

"I mean just what I said. Thank you but I can take care of it."

"I don't understand." Maggie's voice rose to an angry whine. She exerted herself to remain calm.

"I know what needs to be done on the place." Lucy would never admit she was failing or needed help. She'd pretend she could carry on as usual, even if her stubbornness brought about her own end. All right then. Maggie had long ago learned the futility of opposing her mother's conviction.

Lucy said, "You need to get home and back to work. Staying on here would only be a waste of your time."

She controlled her voice to a low pitch. "All right, Momma. Whatever you say. I'll pack my bag and be on my way day after tomorrow." She'd return to her empty apartment, to food she barely tasted, to friends she forced herself to see, and to the cold, foggy city she wandered, searching for the sign that would restore meaning to her life. She wouldn't have minded staying a while. Caring for her mother—and for this place—would take her mind off her own aimlessness. Now she was thrown back on herself with the additional worry over her mother's diminishing condition.

"That'd be fine." Lucy folded her quilting. "If you don't mind, I'll say goodnight now."

"Goodnight, Momma." Maggie placed an obligatory, obedient daughter's kiss on her mother's temple. She walked to the door and closed it behind her.

THREE

MAGGIE PUSHED OPEN THE DOOR of the Kowboy Kafe as the bell jingled a welcome. Tinged with the odor of flapjacks and green chile, the café smelled as familiar as her own skin. She slid into her old place, the red vinyl booth in the back under Eddie Aguilar's diamondback rattler. "Captured at Gran Quivira, August 9, 1956," the snakeskin caption said. Proprietor Lorraine Neeley hadn't changed the decor any. Rusty horseshoes and fire-blackened branding irons still hung on crooked nails. Burnished plywood brands of every ranch in Blue Grama County covered the wall like a hieroglyphic code, spelling out a long, complicated story of land ownership, acquisition, loss, and intermarriage through the generations.

If Monte Alto was a museum of her past, the Kowboy Kafe was its premier gallery. Here she and Momma had treated themselves to fried chicken baskets when they came to town on Saturdays, back when every store in town was busy. When she was growing up, Saturdays were the chance to get out and socialize, to take a break from a hard, unyielding routine. She and her girlfriends met after school at the café to discuss their favorite topic, boys. She must have heard every variation of inexplicable male behavior known to womankind on this spot. In this cozy, overheated booth, whispers rose to hysterical giggles and broken hearts were patched up with consolation, fries, and the world's best chocolate malts.

Good thing no one was coming to her for advice now. The experience of intervening years had taught her to appreciate, or at least accept, the single state. And so far no one had come along to try to talk her out of it. Although from the moment she opened her eyes she missed Hannah terribly each day, she had to admit that most of the time, she didn't mind having her North Beach apartment to herself. Mainly, she liked the early morning stillness, with no chatter and no TV news, and her view of the bay as the fog lifted, with no arguments with Paul to clutter it up. No longer was she burdened with the nagging feeling she'd done something wrong or offended somehow—been too outspoken, too opinionated, too late, or too careless—and had to fix it. For the first time in her life, she was setting her own schedule, following her own rituals, and living on her own. And she found a certain peacefulness in this new arrangement.

She took her time waking up, then she sat on her comfortable, battered leather sofa with her coffee cup, watched the view, put her feet up, and just breathed for a while. Although she didn't understand the process, she knew this time alone was essential to repairing herself after Ramona. Shortly after the girl's death, Ramona had come to her in a dream, actually wearing wings and a crown of flowers. She assured Maggie she was happy and in a better place. The dream seemed so vivid, so very real. Maggie had woken up rested, fortified by her first unbroken night's sleep in weeks. She tried to superimpose this image on the vivid, bloody memories that continually intruded on her peace of mind.

She would never forget Ramona, and every day as long as she lived, she would blame herself for the girl's death. If only she hadn't written the story, or hadn't written it so graphically that it drew that kind of attention. Of course, there was no way to prove Rick had been enraged by it, and of course Maggie had altered Ramona's identity to protect her. But still.... She would never forget the look on the faces of Ramona's mother and father when they came to claim their daughter and grandson.

She knew she had to "move on," much as she disliked that expression. She tried writing but gave up after spending hours scowling at the blank screen, her fingers weighted as if paralyzed. Her ideas floated away, thoughts that initially made sense refused to connect coherently, and her insights gelled into trite clichés. Writing was all she knew how to do, and now she couldn't even do that. She'd picked up a few course catalogs, but nothing appealed to her. She had to find a way to rebuild her life, but so far, all she was capable of doing was prowling the city, searching for herself in the face of every passerby, placing one foot in front of the other on a path that remained invisible.

A familiar but forgotten voice chimed through her thoughts. "Well, now, Maggie, you're a sight for sore eyes. Come all the way out here from San Francisco to see us, have you now? Real sorry to hear about Elias's passing."

She looked at squat Lorraine, as tall as a ten-year-old girl but with the body of a full-grown woman. Long fringe studded with shiny silver and turquoise conchas decorated the pink-shirted front of her plump bosom. The once-brown sausage curls hugging her head had turned to steel gray, and a network of fine lines crisscrossed her face. But the half-moon smile remained untouched by time, an expression fastened on as securely as the horseshoes nailed to the wall.

Lorraine loved to talk. She saw everyone and heard everything.

And she loved to share the news. She poured it right out like coffee from the pot. "How are you, Maggie-girl?"

"Maggie smiled back. "I'm doing okay, Lorraine. How've you been?"

"We're getting by, dear. The cows ain't chewed off all the grass, and the wind ain't blown us away." She laughed, squinting her tiny eyes, and filled the white mug with dark steaming brew. "Just made a fresh pot.

Lorraine studied her. "You look real nice, Maggie. Yes you do. As pretty as ever. I always said you were the prettiest girl in town. But you know that. Kind of thin though," she said, her eyes bright behind her bifocals. "If I may say."

"I've lost a little weight. Not sure what my size is anymore." Maggie knew all about the dark smudges under her hazel eyes and the deepening lines at the corners of her mouth. It took more and more effort to present an acceptably pretty face.

Maggie looked at the wall crowded with snapshots of kids on horseback. She spotted her sixteen-year-old self astride a good-looking quarter horse, wearing the blue-spangled outfit Momma had made her, with the hat they'd ordered from Monkey Ward over her long glossy black hair. That day she'd won her buckle as High Point Girl in the Junior Cattlegrowers Rodeo.

Lorraine continued chatting. "Haven't seen Lucy around in quite a while. Seems like she quit coming in a ways back. How's she doing? Elias's going hit her pretty hard?"

Lorraine's question touched off anger and sadness, themes echoed by the unforgiving cold, gray day and the whole business of being back here. How could Lucy reject her offer to stay and help? Plus, she needed Lucy, and a purpose, just as much right now. Maggie shook her head. It wasn't right and it wasn't natural for a mother to treat a daughter no better than unwanted company. "She's having a tough time, I'm afraid."

Lorraine reached out her freckled, pudgy hand and patted Maggie's arm. "Sure she is, honey. But we all know how life goes on." Lorraine sighed. "We've lost quite a few this winter." She bobbed her head. "Pity about Elias. We won't see no more like him, I'm afraid." She shifted her weight and smoothed her apron. "Still working for that big paper, Maggie? You sure done us proud out there."

Maggie gripped her coffee cup so tight it seared her hand. "No." She shook her head. "No, I'm not working at that paper any more."

"Well, it's just a job, honey. Anybody with your brains and talent—oh yes, talent—can go out and get you another one. You ain't no empty stall." Lorraine laughed, a low machine-gun stutter.

"Sure, Lorraine. I'm just between jobs right now." Lorraine was an expert at bringing up subjects Maggie didn't want to talk about, like her employment and marital status. If she'd been so bold as to venture out into the world, to become a deserter, she damn well better have made good before she showed her face around here again. Her unemployment and divorce would give the town gossips plenty to cluck about.

Although she already knew every item on the menu, she scanned it again. "Can you bring me some breakfast?"

"Can we? We can bring you a breakfast like you can't get out there!" The eager smile was back. "How 'bout some huevos? Red or green?"

"Sure. Red. Over easy."

"Comin' right up, dear." Lorraine paused. "I bet your momma's real pleased to see you, honey."

"I suppose she is," Maggie answered slowly. "She's got a lot on her mind right now."

"Don't want to worry you. But I did hear that the church

ladies been lookin' in on her. Elvira Orme brings by her medicine from the Rexall."

"How old is Elvira anyway?"

"She won't give her age, but they say she'll be ninety-two this year. Still driving that old Mercury of hers. Her mind's as sound as mine is. Still likes her root beer floats, one a day. You be sure to give your momma my best, you hear? Not too many around like that Lucy. Tell her we miss her. We want to see her back in town, right quick!"

"I'll do that, Lorraine. I'll be sure to tell Momma you were asking for her." Maggie replaced the menu in the chrome stand. The cry "Order up!" came from the kitchen over scratchy country music on the radio. Lorraine turned and bustled off.

On the other side of the café sat two wiry old fellows in dusty Stetsons, their faces withered from sun and tobacco and Jim Beam. One was hooked to an oxygen tank. They moved in slow motion, as did everyone in this place. Maggie poked around her memory for their names. Elmo. Elmo Upchurch—he was the one with emphysema—and Lamar Hansen. Brothers-in-law. Worked all their lives at the dairy. Made the best peach ice cream. Elmo caught her eye and tipped his hat, ghostly, through a quill of smoke. Were their wives at home, or were they gone by now?

While she waited for breakfast, Maggie silently rehearsed lines she was preparing for her mother: "But Momma, you're not well. You need care. You need good doctors. You can't stay out here by yourself. Time to sell the place, move into town and hire a housekeeper."

How could she convince her mother when she couldn't convince herself? Lucy would never leave the land Maggie's grandparents had homesteaded and the thick-walled house they had built out of their own ground. Momma had been born there, and Momma's two sisters and a brother had died there. The steps of four generations had worn a golden patina onto the pine-board floors. The adobe walls created a peace and security like nothing else. All the ribbons they'd ever won hung in the living room, and they had a mantle full of trophies. Grandma's Haviland china still sat locked in the china cabinet, overlooking the long oak dining table Grandpa had made. If she'd hung on this long, through the Depression and the big drought of the 1950s, she was not about to allow herself to get booted off by a well-meaning misguided prodigal daughter.

Lorraine bustled over and set down a steaming platter of huevos rancheros. "Here you are, darlin'. Range delivery."

Maggie dipped a piece of fresh, homemade tortilla into the blazing crimson sauce and took a bite. Her tongue burned and her eyes watered. "God, this is good, Lorraine," she murmured.

"Well, sure it is. Did you think I'd forget how to make my red chile?"

"Of course not."

Maggie finished her breakfast and paid the check. She reached in her purse for her list of errands—bank, grocery store, hardware—zipped her jacket, and headed across Main Street, empty except for a couple of battered pickups.

She stood at the doorway of Dawson's Feed & Hardware. The front window still served as town bulletin board. The hand-lettered signs could have hung there for twenty years or been taped up yesterday: Rotary roast beef dinner Sunday night; auction of household goods Saturday at the Old School House; Red Angus, 3 year old bull, 63 pound birthweight, $800, see Dwayne.

She gripped the horseshoe handle, pushed, and stepped inside. Feed, fertilizer, kerosene, and wood smoke—old smells and the heat of the potbelly stove hit her head on. Rattlesnakes still dozed in their glass cage behind the auto-parts section. As she passed their cage she heard a hiss. The wooden floor creaked under her boots, just as it had when she'd come in here as a seven-year-old, holding the hand of the rancher Elias Romero. Uncle Albert Dawson's mounted trophy heads still crowded the walls. Deer, rabbit, javelina, bobcat, elk, fox, mountain lion, coyote, Barbary sheep—Uncle Albert had shot every species of wild animal known to the country. He'd even got an ibex, on a once-in-a-lifetime hunt in White Sands. He loved nothing better than to tell you how he'd bagged the critters.

He spent winters scheming how he was going to get the last black bear on Monte Alto. But that one got him instead. And that bear still went free, according to sightings that came in over the years. A storm had come up, the earliest snowfall they'd had in years, and it took the search party a week to find Albert and bring him back. At least he went doing what he wanted, they all said, an observation that paid tribute to the man's righteous life.

Maggie roamed the aisles, the only customer. While the old sights and smells remained, the store had been brightened up considerably. A fresh coat of paint, new lighting, and well-stocked shelves kept it up with the times. Yet the updates hadn't put a dent in its character. She found the washers and faucet handles she needed. She picked up the copper globe shaped like a fish. She placed the items on the high oak counter and stared up at a glass-eyed buck.

The Fox News announcers, in dark suits, shouting at one another about the stock market, had replaced the gab of old-timers wearing suspenders and chewing tobacco. Were the Spit 'n Whittlers who'd gather 'round this stove to share opinions on the price of feed and the price of politicians all gone?

She heard Roger's voice in the back room, talking to a customer on the phone. The timbre of that voice that took its own time, pleasantly deep with a slight drawl that ran through it like honey, had once aroused pure joy in her. She could have listened to that voice read the phone book and thought it was the most fascinating recital she'd ever heard. That voice could have told her frogs had wings and she'd have believed it. He stopped talking. She heard him hang up. The Fox News commentators rattled on. She waited.

His long jeans-clad legs carried his six-foot-two frame gracefully forward and Roger Dawson set an armload of boxes down on the counter. His straight black hair, streaked with silver, hung over his forehead to one side, not quite falling into his eyes. He wore it braided like an Indian's. A tarnished amulet, a silver feather, hung on a chain around his neck.

This man could still turn heads. As a boy he had been so handsome, like Montgomery Clift, only better. Women couldn't help staring. Walking at his side, Maggie had watched as they dismissed her, imagining themselves in her place. He never seemed to notice.

She had been so sure of him.

She noticed that scar on the left side of his forehead from the Sunday a bronc threw him like a sack of flour at that long-ago Ranchers' Day Rodeo. She'd driven him an hour to Socorro while he'd bled in the seat next to her. Head wounds bleed a lot, she kept telling him. She finally got him to the emergency clinic, where the doc sewed him up with seventeen stitches.

She had her scars, too, only hers weren't quite as visible.

"Maggie!" he exclaimed. "Good to see you. Too bad it takes losing somebody to get you back to town." As he stepped out from behind the counter to greet her, he knocked over the pile of boxes. Tiny silver tacks spilled out and rolled all over the floor. "Will you look at that," he said. "See what happens when a good-looking woman walks in? You'd think by now I'd have learned to keep my mind on business."

"I bet you say that to all the girls around here," Maggie replied.

"You know me too well, don't you?" he came back, with a grin. His cowboy charm was irresistible. It also provided a convenient cover. Behind his amiable, natural way with folks, he was free to think and do as he pleased, always sure of being granted plenty of leeway. As a young man, Roger had always gone to the edge. He rode farther, drove faster, moved quicker than anyone else. She shuddered as she remembered how he had pushed her edges, too. "Momma and I appreciated your coming to the funeral yesterday," she said.

"Wish I could have stayed to talk afterward. But I had to get right over to a county commissioners meeting." He reached into a corner for a broom and began to sweep up the mess. He paused and looked at her. "I'm sorry about Elias, Maggie," he said. "I know you'll miss him. We all will."

"Thank you," she said, looking into his cobalt eyes. But for the gauntness of his features and the fine lines that radiated outward from the corners of his eyes and mouth, he looked much the same, this man who had broken her heart. There had been times she'd wanted to die, and other times she'd wanted to kill him for what he'd done. All her prayers and dreams that he'd come back to her had been a waste of time.

Right after the accident, Lucy had sent her the obituary of Roger's son, Jesse, clipped from the newspaper. The boy, only seventeen, had been killed one night in a wreck on the highway just outside of town. Maggie had intended to send a note. She'd tried to compose it in her mind. But her words never sounded right. She kept putting off writing the letter. Somehow, she never got around to it.

"I was so sorry to hear about Jesse," she said. "I've been wanting to tell you that for a long time. You'd think somebody who makes her living writing could say it right, but I never could find the words."

A log cracked. The fire in the woodstove flared.

"He was a great kid," Roger said. "I wish you could have known him. He loved horses. Wanted to be a vet. You'd have been one person who really understood him." He swiped the floor with the broom, then stopped and faced her. "It's been a rough time, Maggie." His voice broke. "Losing him."

"How is Tommie doing?"

"Guess you haven't heard. Tommie and I split up, Maggie. After Jesse died, she had to get away from Monte Alto. And from me, I guess. It'd been coming on for a long time, but losing Jesse brought it all into focus."

"Where is she? Where did she go?"

"She's up in Albuquerque working at St. Joe's in the intensive care unit. From what I understand, she's doing okay."

"She disappeared before I could talk to her yesterday," Maggie said. She paused. "So now you're the mayor. That must keep you busy."

"Busy and then some, between all the meetings and the store." He rang up her purchases. "That do it for you today, Maggie?"

"That'll do it. I'm just going to try and make a few repairs around the place before I head back."

"Head back? You just got here. Monte Alto in January—there's a vacation trip not too many get to experience."

She smiled. "I've seen the place in January before, you know."

"The town's grown some. I'd be happy to show you around. What do you say. A personal guided tour by the mayor. Usually charge people fifty cents for that, but for you, it's on the house."

"I appreciate the offer, Roger. But I have to get back to San Francisco."

"That's too bad." He began ringing up her purchases. "Another time then." He handed her a brown paper bag.

"Another time," she said. "Good to see you, Roger." For a moment, her palms rested in his warm, much-larger hands. Those hands of his. So many nights, when they were young, she had run her fingers lightly up and down and around those hills and valleys of tendons and pulses, making the journey last as long as she possibly could. She had traced the lines on his palms: the heart line, the fate line, the life line. She had wanted them all.

She took her purchases from him and walked to the door. She turned around. He stood in back as he watched her leave. "I'm so sorry about Jesse," she said, again. Then she left.

FOUR

GRASPING A HEAVY SACK OF GROCERIES in each arm, Maggie walked up the sagging porch steps of the neglected ranch house. Paint was peeled and faded, grime coated the windows, and the sense of abandonment hovered. If she had her way, she'd hire someone today to tend to the repairs. The painting, plastering, and caulking the house cried out for could keep a handyman busy for weeks.

But it wasn't her house, and it wasn't her call.

She reached down and tried the front door handle, twisting it to the left. With the toe of her boot, she pushed the door open. Lucy still didn't lock her doors—another problem on a growing list over which Maggie had no say-so. Anybody could walk in, any time day or night, and walk out with everything on the place. But try telling that to Lucy. Maggie could be irate, concerned, and as right as daylight, but let her make any suggestion, however sensible, and all she'd get for her trouble is a great big "mind your own business."

As soon as she pushed the door open, she smelled something burning. The scorched odor of a pot that had sat too long on the stove and boiled out permeated the air. Acrid smoke wafted through the living room.

"Momma?" she called, as she plowed through the front rooms to the kitchen, trying to keep the groceries from spilling. She made it, just barely, to the kitchen table and set the bags down as one ripped down the side. Cans and boxes clattered out onto the big oak table. She caught a bottle of pickles before it rolled over the edge. "Momma? Where are you?"

Under a charred saucepan a blue flame flickered. She ran to the stove and turned it off. Thank God she'd returned before Lucy burned the place to the ground! Whatever her mother had been cooking had alchemized into an unrecognizable, blackened mess that would require heavy-duty scrubbing.

Maggie strode down the hall. "Momma, what're you doing? What happened? You left something on the stove!"

She heard a cry that sounded like a cat trapped behind a wall. Retracing her steps, she followed the sound back toward the kitchen. She stopped and listened to the pitiful, angry-edged whine. This time, the sound spoke her name. She followed it around the corner to the pantry.

Her mother lay on her back on the linoleum floor in an oddly twisted position, her face splotchy, her hair practically on end. "Maggie! Thank goodness you're home." She extended an arm in her daughter's direction. "Here—help me up."

Maggie knelt beside her mother in the shelf-lined room, just a closet, really, barely big enough to hold them both. "Hold on. Let's make sure there's nothing broken."

"There's nothing broken," her mother spat. "What is wrong with you? Just give me a hand up, will you?" Maggie had been stunned by the sight of her mother helpless on the floor, and she was not prepared for the woman's fury. Automatically, she did as Lucy commanded. Offering her hand, she pulled her mother into a sitting position. Lucy puffed hard with strain. "Get me my cane, will you? I left it outside the door when I came in here."

Maggie handed her mother the cane. "What happened here, Momma? How long have you been like this?"

"Nothing happened!" Lucy snapped. "I came in here for some baking powder and tripped over that infernal step." She brandished her cane in the direction of the three-inch step down from kitchen to pantry. "Ought to have fixed it years ago!" She shunned Maggie's offer of her hand and struggled to straighten her frame by grabbing hold of a pantry shelf.

"There, now," Lucy said, wrenching herself upright. "That's better." She shook herself. "Too bad about that buttermilk pie I was fixing."

"Looks like I got home just in time. You were working on burning the house down."

Lucy waved her away. "No such thing." Leaning awkwardly on her cane, Lucy thumped across the kitchen floor. She pushed open the faded gingham window curtain and peered out at the sky. "Looks like that sun is trying to break through, don't it? He just might do it by afternoon."

"What happens when you fall and there's nobody here to help you get up, Momma?"

"You saw how I did. I always manage to get myself up. I brush myself off and get on with it. There's no worker's comp or leave with pay to collect."

"So this isn't the first time you've fallen." Maggie saw it now. It wasn't just interference from Maggie that Lucy resented. Her mother feared Maggie would have her put away.

Lucy poked her cane in Maggie's direction. "Don't you go playing any of your reporter tricks on me."

"I don't have to trick you. I can see with my own eyes what the situation is."

"There is no 'situation.' Don't make a mountain out of a molehill," she said, her voice tight. "Everybody trips once in a while. Even you."

Maggie took a seat at the kitchen table. "Come here, Momma. Please sit down and talk to me." She spoke calmly, as if to a child, and patted the chair beside her.

Lucy cocked her head toward Maggie's gentle voice. She leaned heavily on her cane and began to move across the room. She took two steps before her knees crumpled under her. Maggie rushed to break her fall but couldn't reach her in time. Lucy collapsed on the floor, again.

"That's it, Momma," Maggie said. "That's enough. It's lucky you didn't break your hip."

"I don't know what happened. It's like my right side went numb on me."

Maggie studied her mother carefully. "Any headache?"

"I've had a blasted headache all morning."

"What else?"

"My leg feels like it went to sleep. Tingling sort of."

"Momma, don't move. I'm getting your coat and taking you to the doctor, right now." Lucy was describing classic symptoms of stroke, Maggie knew that much. The quicker she could get her mother to medical help, the better her chances.

Within the hour, Maggie and Lucy sat before Dr. Patterson, his thinning gray hair disheveled, his white jacket wrinkled and in need of laundering, in his office located in the side room of the 1920s brick house where he lived alone. His wife had died of cancer years back, and his children had moved to Phoenix, where they had good jobs and families of their own. A late-middle-aged man whose soothing voice contradicted his harried appearance, his was the only medical authority acceptable to Lucy. He had practiced medicine in Monte Alto for more than thirty years—Maggie remembered his house visits when she'd come down with strep—and was on intimate terms with the ailments of his elderly patients, many of them lonely widows and widowers, single ladies and bachelors.

His office shelves were jammed with disordered papers and files, books and manuals, as well as pharmaceutical samples for arthritis, blood pressure, cholesterol, and insomnia. These he dispensed freely to those in need who often could not easily afford the expense of such medications. His generosity and patience, as well as his monopoly on the medical profession in Monte Alto, kept people flocking to him and singing his praises. They wouldn't dream of seeking another doctor in Socorro or Albuquerque.

In an age of debunked physicians, Dr. Patterson retained his demigod-like status. Lucy's friends were, to a woman, his true believers. There was nobody like him. He was a real old-fashioned gentleman who knew his business, they all said. "He really listens to me," Lucy always said. Whatever prescription he scribbled on his white pad was dutifully filled at the Rexall. The combination of attention and medication made them feel better, until the next time. What would they do without him?

The doctor spoke. "It's a good thing your daughter acted so quickly, Mrs. Chilton. After observing you, I feel safe in saying what you've had is a TIA."

Lucy sat with her hands folded primly in her lap. "What's that?"

"It's a small stroke."

"A stroke?" her voice caught. "I've had a stroke?"

"It's a passing situation. No permanent damage will result. Not serious."

"What does it mean?" Lucy had conquered the quiver in her voice, but she sounded as small and defenseless as she looked.

"It may mean something—or nothing. You may experience similar incidents again. Perhaps it's a signal of problems that might arise sometime in the future."

"That's a nice way of telling me I'm about to be paralyzed or worse, isn't it, Doctor? Next you'll be ordering me to take to my bed and patiently wait for my just reward."

"Not at all. I'm changing your medication." He scrawled a few lines on a pad. "Start taking these three times a day."

Lucy looked at the indecipherable message on the piece of paper. "What is it?"

"A standard blood thinner is all. It ought to keep the problem under control for the time being. I want you to call me in a week and let me know how you're feeling." The doctor folded his arms. He was accustomed to handling argumentative patients, and he just about always won.

"I don't understand," said Lucy, the slightest quaver coming into her voice. "All's I am is worn out from the last few days. Until then, I'd been feeling perfectly fine."

"You've been under quite a strain," he said. "Stress can bring these things on. I want you to take it easy for a while—but I know that's asking a lot. I wouldn't be too careful, if I were you, Mrs. Chilton." He looked in Maggie's direction. "What are your plans, Maggie? Did you just come out for the funeral, or will you be favoring us with a longer visit?"

"I'm available to stay. I'd like to."

"Well, that's good, then." He closed the cover of the black book on his desk and folded his hands on top of it. "That solves a lot of problems."

Lucy spoke up. "She needs to get back. She's job hunting."

"Now Mrs. Chilton." His voice sounded as though he'd just

oiled it. "It'd be better if you had someone with you for the time being. Until we see how this new medication works out."

"I'm perfectly able to take care of myself!" Lucy said.

"No one said you weren't," said Dr. Patterson. "But your daughter has offered to stay a while. Surely you can use the time to visit."

Lucy spoke in a fury. "You two have been conspiring!"

"You know that's not the case, Mrs. Chilton," said Dr. Patterson mildly. "What's family for? If your daughter couldn't stay with you, we'd have to make other arrangements. With strangers. You are not to be on your own until you're feeling better."

"You heard what the doctor said, Momma. Thank you Doctor." She stood and pulled on her coat. "Let's go home, Momma."

"Maggie?" he said, as they reached the doorway.

"Yes, Dr. Patterson?"

"You call me any time. Day or night's fine. Ask me any questions you have, anything unusual. Are we clear on that?"

She understood him perfectly. She would be on the lookout for any changes in Lucy's health—her sleeping, her eating, her walking, her moods. "I'll do that," Maggie said. "Thank you, Dr. Patterson." She thought about shaking his hand, then checked herself, considering how the gesture might appear to her mother.

Maggie helped her mother on with her coat, a kindness Lucy accepted without fuss. She looked pale and worn out, as if she'd lost her starch. In slow motion, she scuffled out the door.

Maggie's heart buckled at the sight of her mother looking so old and defeated. Behind her sympathy for the woman's suffering, another feeling welled up, surprising her: relief. Now she'd be able to give Lucy tender loving kindness, staying alert to whatever she wanted or needed. And touched by the effort, as anyone would naturally be, Lucy would respond in kind. Maggie dared glimpse a sunny future with the two of them chatting and laughing together. Finally, she might begin to build a decent relationship with her mother.

"Let's get home and make some supper, Momma," Maggie said. She took her mother's arm and led her out the door, keenly aware she needed to learn the proper way of handling a fragile old woman.

Back home, Maggie lit the stove and set the kettle on for tea. She rubbed her fingers and held them near the warmth of the fire. Then she went into the pantry and got to work. She pulled the string of the ceiling light bulb and brushed away a cobweb. The little room smelled of cloves and dust. She could still remember how everything was arranged on the shelves covered with yellow-checked paper. But the canisters of flour and sugar were almost empty, and the shelves were no longer packed with jewel-colored Mason jars of fruits, vegetables, and preserves. Those full shelves, along with the woodpile Elias collected all summer off the mountain, had meant they'd be fine no matter what. Maggie scavenged among the few tin cans to find the fixings for supper.

In an hour she called, "Momma, supper's ready. Do you want me to fix you a plate?"

Supper was beans and rice and salmon patties. Lucy picked at her food while Maggie chatted: "Tomorrow I'm taking that load of trash to the dump. I'm itching to get started with some caulking, too, and lay down weather stripping on your doors. Cut some of the draft in here."

"It's good to have you here, Maggie." She reached across the table. "I guess God knows better than we do what's right. It's lucky you were here today."

For now, this was as near as she would get to a thank you from Lucy. For years, Maggie had longed to be closer, but she could never figure out the right way to get through to her mother. Every time she reached out her hand, she met the same stone wall. Eventually, she'd given up and just stayed away. But she'd been careful to send nice gifts, and photos of Hannah, and call on holidays. With just the two of them, it would be different from now on. Maybe everything that happened back in San Francisco had happened for a reason, so she could be here now.

"Thanks, Momma." She took a deep breath. There never would be a right time for the question on her mind. The sooner it got out on the table, the better. With Elias gone, Lucy might even be open to the idea. "Momma, did you ever think about moving into town?"

"No, I did not. Ever."

"Momma, listen." Maggie sat down hard. She looked her mother in the eye. "You could sell this place and move into town. You'd never have to worry about money again. If anything happened, if you ever got sick, you'd be right where you could get help."

"Sell my place to some California real estate developer with more money than God? I'd sooner put a torch to it. I can't believe I'd ever have to say such a thing to you. What do you think we've worked for all these years? Where are your feelings for this land? What kind of a child have I raised?" She pushed herself up from the table, her crone's face drained of color. "Why Elias, he understood perfectly. He knew I could never leave this place. I could depend on him to stay here with me, so neither of us would ever have to leave." A vague soft look flitted across her face. Maggie stared harder into her mother's eyes, but she couldn't find a trace of that momentary softness on that face that hid all those feelings under a stony surface.

"As long as you're in my house, this is the last I want to hear about leaving," her mother declared.

The old woman turned and walked away, stiff and determined. Her cane tapped a measured beat down the hallway. Once again, Maggie wondered what had really existed between her mother and Elias. She couldn't imagine what kind of understanding or closeness they could possibly have shared during their lifetime together, but that brief hint in her mother's eyes sparked her determination to find out.

The bedroom door slammed shut. Maggie covered her face with her hands and sat that way until her arms fell asleep. She shook her numb hands and went upstairs. When she switched on the light in her old attic room, she saw the blue cornflowers floating on a field of pink stripes. At the single window, yellowing organdy curtains drooped, the starch long gone out of them. Raggedy Ann gave her a one-eyed smile from atop the mound of quilts on the high, white-painted iron bed. She used to curl under those quilts listening to owls calling at night. Maggie caught a whiff of cedar and lavender sachet. This room was still a perfect hideaway.

She climbed on the bed and reached for the black rotary phone. First she canceled her flight for tomorrow. Then she called her housesitter to explain she'd been delayed. Her watch read just past seven. It was two hours later in Washington, D.C., but in the East that wasn't too late to call.

"Hi, Robin. This is Maggie. Can I talk to Hannah?"

"Oh. Hi Maggie."

Maggie had heard that men searched until they found a second wife just like their first. Not Paul. He'd run as hard and fast as he could straight into the waiting arms of Maggie's opposite, a woman with perfect hair, perfect make-up, and the perfectly ordered life of an interior decorator.

"Is Hannah awake?"

"I'll go check."

"Thanks, Robin," Maggie answered.

She smoothed the top quilt, a faded Lone Star made of feed sacks. Instead of fairy tales, Momma used to tell her about the ladies who made those quilts. Grandma Vera Mae was known for her tiny, even stitches, eleven to the inch, and for her prowess as a hunter—she shot six antelope on her way out from Oklahoma, then jerked the meat.

Someone picked up the phone, and she heard breathing on the other end of the line. "Hi, Hannah darling."

"Hi, Mom," a voice said cautiously. Her voice was already deepening out of its childhood lilt. Hannah had been a quiet baby. She smiled and watched, never spoke baby talk, just one day came out with perfect sentences.

"Were you all tucked in?"

"Not really. I was just brushing my teeth."

"Good girl. Gotta keep those choppers bright." Her words clattered like coins falling from a purse. "What's going on in your part of the world?"

"Nothing much. I'm going to be in the school play." Hannah sounded dispirited.

"What are they doing?"

"*Our Town.*"

"I'm sure you'll be wonderful. I'd love to see you in your play. Will you send me pictures?"

It was bad enough that Hannah had chosen to live with Paul. How many nights Maggie had lain awake, fretting as that painful decision played over and over in her mind. Yet, if she put herself in Hannah's shoes, she could understand it better. She'd been an absent mother for too long. Strive mightily as she had to find a balance, her work had come first; at least, any time she had to work late, or miss a school activity, that's how it must have felt to Hannah. This arrangement was only temporary, she told herself. In a year or two, Hannah would be back. She'd learn her father wasn't as perfect as she thought. Maggie counted on it.

"Sure, Mom," Hannah said. "Thanks for the check. For my birthday."

"You're welcome, honey." She wanted to put her arms around her daughter.

"I'm not sure what I'll spend it on. Just go to the mall, I guess."

"Whatever you want is fine. I'm not even sure what your size is anymore. Or what you like. I want you to get something you like."

"I will."

"So how's school?"

"It's okay. I like the math teacher better this term."

"Your friends?"

"We hang out. Whatever. It's pretty boring."

"You know, Hannah, I'm back here in New Mexico for a while. With Grandma Lucy. How'd you like to come for a visit, maybe over spring break? That's coming up pretty soon, isn't it?" She tried to keep her voice light. "In about a month?"

"I'm supposed to go with Daddy and Robin and Emily to Delaware then."

Of course. Maggie should have known. They'd be going to Rehoboth Beach. To Robin's parents' house, for an early spring vacation at the beach.

"Well, maybe I could talk to Daddy. Would you like to come out? I could show you how to ride."

"I don't know, Mom." She hesitated. "I've already taken riding lessons here in Rock Creek Park. Don't you remember?"

"I guess it slipped my mind. Look, you don't have to decide right this minute. Just think about it a little, will you, hon?"

"Okay."

"Okay then. Good night, baby. I love you."

"I love you too, Mom."

TV commercials showed you how easily you could be connected to someone two thousand miles away. Just push a few buttons. They never talked about how you could be disconnected by a little click, just as fast.

I'm not about to lie to myself, Maggie thought. I miss Paul. I miss the skin of his back at night and I miss the eggplant with garlic sauce and I miss our fights. We were good at those.

Hannah couldn't know about the note Maggie found in the closet, from the twenty-two-year-old summer legal intern, telling him he was the most wonderful thing that had ever happened to her and that she couldn't wait to be with him again. She couldn't know that discovery came at her lowest point, when, after losing Ramona the way she had, she'd most needed her husband's love and support. When she'd brought the matter up to Paul, he'd simply said he wanted a divorce. "Look Maggie," he'd said. "It's over between us. It has been for a long time." He offered no excuses.

Paul walked out on her. Soon after, he married the woman he'd hired to decorate his new Washington office. And Hannah had chosen to go with him and be part of his new family.

Now, in her old room in her mother's house, she buried herself under the quilts, under all that fine, enduring, patient pile of warmth. Maggie squeezed the double wedding ring quilt made by Daddy's Aunt Lorna, who'd taught in a one-room schoolhouse at Willard, then married a rancher, Leroy Bishop. Six weeks after the wedding, a bull gored him in the field in back of the house. Leroy knew his stock; nobody could understand how he'd gotten so badly mauled. After the funeral, Aunt Lorna saw him walking out in the field, dressed in his wedding clothes. She never married again. Maggie wept for her, for herself, her mother, and for all the women in her family who'd lost and suffered.

Exhausted and cried out, she got up and went to the window. It'd been a long time since she'd seen the stars arrayed so brightly, or even remembered they were up there, watching. "I'll get Hannah back," she whispered to those distant lights. "I swear I will. Just watch me," she told the stars.

FIVE

MAGGIE NOW KNEW HOW HER MOTHER LIKED her eggs (over medium), when she wanted her tea (10:30 A.M. and 3:30 P.M.), and which soap operas she faithfully followed. All week, dedicating herself to meeting Lucy's approval, she'd dusted and mopped and scrubbed. She knew the proper performance of these household tasks was vitally important to her mother, plus she had an agenda of her own. Maggie figured if they could avoid arguments and the bad feelings that hung around afterward, maybe they could really do some talking. A bright and shiny kitchen seemed to be the way to her mother's heart, and Maggie would take any way she could get. And maybe if she cleaned enough, she could wipe out or at least dilute her San Francisco memories.

This daily performance threw her into an unfamiliar and somewhat disoriented emotional state, an earlier time that had never been. She'd finally become the good girl, the daughter her mother wanted—practical, hard-working, who kept her problems to herself and didn't ask challenging questions. What good would it do to rake up the past, anyway?

Maggie opened the front hall closet and pushed her arms through the sleeves of a brown plaid jacket hanging there. The scent of pipe smoke enfolded the woolen garment softened by wear. As she slipped it on, Elias's presence wrapped her like a warm hug, and, for a moment, she felt herself embraced by the sense of security and peace knowing him had brought her. In the pocket she found a silver key, a half-empty packet of tobacco, and the little tally book he'd used to record his observations of daily ranch activities

The jacket fit her well enough, even though Elias was at least a foot shorter than her and his shoulders broader than hers. Well-woven and warm yet light, it made a good protection from cold spring winds. She liked the way it set off her jeans and black turtleneck, and even better, she liked how it felt.

"Momma, I'm going to town for a little while." Her mother sat propped up in bed reading a Tony Hillerman mystery. "Anything I can bring you?"

Lucy looked up from her book and gave Maggie a hard stare. "What's that you're wearing?"

Maggie held out her arms. "Why surely you know. Elias's old jacket, Momma. It's perfectly good and warm. No sense giving it to Goodwill. I'll just keep it."

She placed a mark on her page and put the book down on the bed. "You'll do nothing of the kind. Take that jacket off right now."

"Momma!" Maggie's voice registered her dismay. "What's the harm in it?"

"Just do as I say!" Lucy commanded.

"Why argue over this? There's no point letting a perfectly good jacket go to waste."

"You'll do what's right and take it off this minute," she fumed. "Put it back where you found it. That jacket doesn't belong to you."

"I'm sorry, Momma. I had no idea wearing this jacket would upset you so." Reluctantly she peeled off the jacket, hung it in the closet, and left. So much for playing the good girl.

———◈———

Maggie sat in the Kowboy Kafe and reflected on her time here. By keeping busy with lemon polish and pine cleanser, she'd put off making decisions about her own future. She didn't feel ready to resume a full-time job either reporting or editing, although she felt fairly confident her former boss would give her another chance if and when she wanted one. But she had no idea what else to do. She'd wait and see what Dr. Patterson had to say at the next appointment.

In the café kitchen, silver clattered over the scratchy voice of Buddy Holly singing "That'll Be the Day." Lorraine, all in pink today—fuzzy pink sweater, pink stretch pants, pink rosebud earrings, and pink satin ballet slippers—chalked up pie flavors on the blackboard, her corkscrew curls jiggling.

"Last week you looked like you needed a dose of vitamins, girl," Lorraine told Maggie as she filled her coffee cup. "But now look at you! You got some color in those cheeks!" she crowed. "This good clean Monte Alto air is just what a city girl needs, am I right?"

Maggie had to smile. "You could be right about that, Lorraine."

"Not that I'm saying you looked bad, mind you."

"Of course not."

"You couldn't look bad if you tried, child." With a pudgy finger, Lorraine rearranged her glasses on the bridge of her nose. "Been back to see any of your old friends yet?"

"Haven't had a chance. Too busy looking after Lucy."

"I'm gonna send an apple pie home with you. You feed her a slice of that! Fix her right up."

"I'll do that," Maggie said. "Thanks, Lorraine."

Lorraine shouted the order for huevos rancheros over her shoulder to the kitchen, then moved on to the next booth.

Maggie picked up the crumpled *Monte Alto Independent* lying on the table. The headline story was about Mayor Roger Dawson's upcoming meeting with the county commissioners on land development policies. Of course future development was tied to water, or rather, to the lack of it. There was a debate about the accuracy of the hydrologist's report. Another expert's opinion was called for. Another story focused on the drought—were they in a twenty-year, a four-hundred-year, or a fifteen-hundred-year cycle? People knew it had to rain sometime. The question was, could they hold out until it did? Or would they take the easy (and perhaps necessary) way and just pack it in?

Maybe the time had come. Maybe it just wasn't feasible to try to live off the land the way her family had for generations. Maybe it was just too damn hard, and maybe there were just too many old people like her mother, whose time out there was up. She wanted her mother's last years to be comfortable and secure, and she didn't want to have to worry about Lucy so far from the care she needed. Selling the ranch would provide for Lucy's old age. She refolded the paper and continued reading.

Roger had gone into politics like his dad. Everett Dawson had been the town's most beloved leader. Sitting on the school board or in the state legislature, he'd somehow managed to keep everybody happy, yet there was never a question about his honesty or his devotion to his family. There'd been talk about him making a run for governor, Maggie recalled, but the time was never right. The reigning governor, a powerful rancher known for his quaint turn of phrase and almost magical ability to show up at every local rally serving barbecue, was a savvy, folksy politician who never forgot a name. A die-hard Democrat able to woo Republican hearts, he was considered unbeatable.

Everett's were big shoes to fill, and his reputation opened the way for his son. That's the way it was done out here. Folks wished old Everett was still around, but if he wasn't, they figured his son was the one most likely to get the job done, so long as he hadn't been caught committing any felonies and had the good sense to remain mostly sober in public.

Maggie sipped her coffee and leafed through the *Independent*. The local weekly had improved considerably. It was cleaner, with larger type, lively writing, and to her surprise, quite readable.

"Maggie, Maggie, Maggie," sang a familiar voice. There stood a woman with bright blue eyes and a haircut birds could've nested in. She wore a red jacket with a ten-foot, lumpy, hand-knit purple scarf wrapped around her neck. "Guess you didn't see me when I waved to you from my little pickup this morning on the road. You looked preoccupied."

Maggie had no recollection of the encounter. She blinked as she searched her memory for this woman's name.

The diminutive woman unwound her scarf, laughed, and opened her arms. "That's all right. You wouldn't be high-hatting me. Give an old lady a hug."

Maggie let herself be enveloped in the woman's fierce grasp. She inhaled Tide and Jergens lotion. "How are you, Mrs. McGrath?"

"Fine as frog's hair and twice as silky! But don't go Mrs. McGrathing me. It's Ivy to you now, Maggie." Her old high school English teacher tilted her head and turned on her famous x-ray vision. Maggie knew she'd been read to the last page.

"Hey, Lorraine, you call this coffee?" Ivy shouted in a voice that had no idea it belonged to a little old lady. "How am I supposed to put out a newspaper on this pond water?"

"Be right there. Making a new pot. Double strength and all for you. Nobody else can stand it that way. You can just float your spoon in it."

"You're putting out the paper now?" Maggie asked Ivy.

"Well, you don't have to sound so surprised. What'd you expect—I'd devote myself to Stitch 'n Chatter or doin' good works for the church guild? Honey, I've done my share of good works. Wasn't about to lean back in that old La-Z-Boy and flip on the TV, either. Soaps, talk shows, the six o'clock news. What's the difference? It's all war!"

Maggie leaned back in the booth and smiled, finding herself more amused, and interested, than any time since she'd come to town. "Most people your age think about retiring, not taking on a new career."

"You know what George always said? 'We ain't gonna re-tire— we're gonna be-tired.' Guess I took him to heart on that one." She slurped her fresh hot coffee. "I was a good wife. I listened to George bellyache about the *Independent* all those years. Thought I'd heard it all. When he died, nobody beat a path to my door to take it over. So I appointed myself publisher and editor-in-chief. Wasn't about to let everything he'd worked for go down the drain. It's my rodeo now, I said."

Ivy placed both elbows on the table and leaned forward. "Won an award from the state press association last year. Then I picked up the grand prize for reporting." She snorted. "Think it did anything for circulation? Not a chance. Only way we keep going is the few stores left gotta have someplace to advertise. And of course, there's always money to be made in obituaries around here."

"Congratulations." Maggie traced the circle of her saucer with one finger. "What was your story about?"

"The *Independent* broke the story of the year, don't you know." Ivy rubbed her hands together and chortled. "Those boys at the paper of record, you should have seen them gnashing their teeth that they got beat by the likes of me. That paper of record is more interested in preventing lawsuits than old-fashioned, for-real reporting, so what do they expect?" Ivy practically jumped up and down on her seat. "I investigated those kickbacks going from the contractor to the county commissioners to get a Wal-Mart's built. Big money went under the table!" Ivy slapped the table top so hard the coffee spilled in small waves over the sides of their cups onto the table. "Girl, we stopped that Wal-Mart!"

"Good work there." Maggie feared Ivy wouldn't be too pleased if she knew she was flirting with the idea of convincing her mother to sell the ranch—maybe to one of the despised out-of-town developers.

"Oh, it's only a temporary reprieve. They'll be back." Ivy took another slurp of coffee. "But we're ready for 'em now. We're organized." She paused for breath. "I tell you, those boys from the paper of record didn't much care to see a little old lady walk away with the blue ribbon. Age has its good points. One of 'em is it takes no time to convince everybody you're harmless. Quite an advantage when it comes to getting a story. Common sense is what it takes." Ivy emphasized her point with another whack on the table. The knives and forks jumped. "And sticking with it. Refusing to take no for an answer. And knowing where to put the quotation marks. Quotation marks, you know, were my business for thirty-six years." With her triumph told, Ivy seemed to wind down. But she was only coming up for air. "But why am I telling you all this? You know better than anyone what journalism is all about."

This woman, however old she was, had more energy than she did twenty-five years ago. "And what would you call your business now?"

"Gossip, girl. Gossip and whose cow got out on the road." Ivy's voice gained velocity. "And what that crooked so-and-so who got himself elected should have done if he had brains that did more than rattle around like two bb's in a boxcar." Her eyes gleamed the way they used to when she got going on the *Grapes of Wrath*. "Talk is about all most people around here can afford, anyway." She gulped half a cup of blistering coffee. "And my penchant for troublemaking is what keeps me going. The busier the better, I say. I can stay up later, get up earlier, and work anybody under the table!"

Maggie smiled. She remembered that day, senior year, when Mrs. McGrath asked her to stay after school. "That's a beautiful essay on *Jane Eyre* you turned in, Maggie," she said, her hands folded on top of her big oak desk. "You have real insight into the characters, and you express yourself very well. You have an excellent feel for the language."

"I enjoy writing," Maggie responded, somewhat embarrassed by her teacher's praise.

October sunlight played shadows on the walls, decorated with orange crepe-paper pumpkins, black cats, and cardboard skeletons. "You've got all A's. And your SAT's are at the top of the class. Have you thought about going away to a really good college, Maggie?"

Leaves smoldered in nearby fields. "I'm planning to go to State. That way I can come home from Las Cruces weekends and help Momma. It's the best ag school. Besides, she couldn't afford to send me away."

"Are you sure you want to study agriculture?"

Maggie nodded. "Maybe range management. I want to learn everything I can about how to make a ranch work." Outside, the Monte Alto marching band practiced "Everything's Coming Up Roses."

"Isn't Roger going to State?"

"Yes ma'am. He's going to major in business."

Her teacher handed her a brown envelope. "I've sent away for some scholarship applications. Will you fill out that one from Berkeley? That's my alma mater. No better place to get an education. You never know."

Berkeley. California. Might as well be Bombay. Nobody from Monte Alto High had ever gone to Berkeley. Couldn't hurt. She'd never get in.

"Yes, ma'am," Maggie answered.

"I'll expect you to have this in to me by Monday."

"I never thanked you properly for helping me win that scholarship," Maggie said, finally.

"You more than deserved it. And you used it very well. Berkeley, cum laude. Columbia Journalism School. *Chicago Tribune.* Investigative reporter for the *San Francisco Chronicle.*" Ivy glowed as she reeled off her student's resume. "Don't look so surprised. I've kept up with you, young lady. I'd say that's plenty of thanks for any English teacher from the tules." Ivy sent her a level glance that Maggie couldn't avoid.

"Wish I could live up to my own reputation." Maggie looked down and stirred her coffee, ashamed of her teacher's praise. "But I'm not doing any writing at the moment."

"What do you mean?"

"If you were a friend of mine, you'd say I was between jobs right now. If you weren't, you'd say I was unemployed."

"So? You're looking around for a better opportunity. What happened?"

"Ads and circulation keep dropping. They had to let go of a few people, make the people who still have jobs do their own job plus the one that just got vacated." There was no way she was going to tell Ivy about Ramona and how she'd lost her nerve. Truth was, she couldn't sit in front of a computer without feeling sick.

"What a joke. Here they've got the best reporter in the world, and they just let her go without so much as a howdy-do."

"Say, they didn't just throw me out on the street and make themselves look bad. They gave me what they call 'the package.' Enough to last me a few months while I 'relocate' myself."

"I bet the offers came pouring in the minute others found out you were available."

"Not quite pouring." That was an understatement. None of the few jobs available was going to come her way. "But I have a few possibilities I'm looking over," she bluffed.

"Well, honey, your ego's got to have taken a few bumps and bruises on this one. But believe me, I know you, and I know you'll land on your feet and show them all up!" Ivy patted her hand. "You just take your time and decide what's best for you."

Ivy had fought the board of education. She'd insisted on teaching books some people in town wanted removed from the classroom. They tried firing her. They'd accused her of being un-Christian and anti-American. But she'd fought and won.

Ivy got a gleam in her eye. She ran her fingers through her bright silver hair. "Say, Maggie. Here's a thought. I can always use somebody to help out over at the paper. Even for a little while. Can't pay you union scale like you're used to, but I can do some better than minimum wage."

"I appreciate the offer, Ivy. But looking after Momma is a full-time job right now." There was no way she was setting foot into the *Independent* office.

Ivy dismissed this concern with a wave of her hand. "That's only a temporary occupation. In a week or two, she won't need you like you think she does. Come to work at the *Independent*! We'll have ourselves a fine old time!" Ivy continued. "Think it over. But just promise me one thing, will you?"

"What's that?"

"That you'll come by and see the paper and let me show you my set-up." Ivy cocked her head. "Will you do that for your old teacher?"

"I'll try. But I'm pretty busy right now, like I said."

"Come by any time. Any time at all. I may not be at my best on deadline day, but you can be sure I'll be happy to see you whenever."

"Thanks, Ivy," Maggie said.

"My pleasure, darlin'," she said. She dug into her eggs. "Seen Roger yet?"

"I've been over to the hardware store." Maggie returned Ivy's level gaze, meeting that famous x-ray vision that had been able to spot anyone who dared to cheat on a spelling test. "Momma's got a long list of repairs I need to make."

"Guess you saw Roger then." Ivy spread a thick layer of butter on her toast, then topped it with a healthy amount of orange marmalade.

Maggie took a bite of handmade hot tortilla. "Guess I did."

"He's had a hard time of it."

"Sounds like." Maggie's voice sounded overly nonchalant, even to herself.

"Bad enough he lost his boy. Between Roger and Tommie, you can imagine, he was some good-looking kid. And smart, too. Talk about pride and joy. No man ever loved a son more."

Maggie sat forward. "Ivy, what happened?"

"You don't know?"

Maggie shook her head. "Not that much."

"The poor boy had a wreck out on Highway 41."

"That's a bad stretch of road. They were supposed to fix it way back when. Was he driving by himself?"

Ivy nodded. "Big rig slammed into him."

"Did they find any alcohol?"

"Only on that Texas truck driver. Doesn't seem fair, does it."

"It's not."

"But then Tommie. She about lost her mind. Weeks would go by and she'd never leave the house. Up all night, the lights always on. Refused to see people who came to call on her until they finally gave up. Poor woman just couldn't handle living in Monte Alto any more. And Roger, he couldn't leave, not with the store and all. Plus, he'd just gotten reelected mayor." Ivy paused for breath. "This town couldn't do without him. Not that Roger and me always see eye-to-eye. But you ought to see some of the things he's done. Cleaned up the parks, raised the money for a new senior center, and now, a new clinic is going up, thanks to him."

"You'd think he and Tommie would have found a way to stay together," Maggie said.

"Jesse's going tore them apart. Saddest thing to see. Poor Roger, he was just lost."

"He seemed okay when I saw him last week."

"Oh, he's turned it around some. And it's been three years now. He's not one to feel sorry for himself. But that man's heart is carrying a heavy load of sorrow, I can tell you. He sure had us worried. Church ladies put out on the prayer chain that he'd find the Lord."

With her napkin, Maggie wiped red chile from her chin. "And has he?"

"Don't know about that. But lately he's taken on some new projects for Monte Alto. We've all got our fingers crossed he'll stick with it. 'Course several young ladies in the neighborhood have come around trying to see what they can do to ease his suffering. Nothing more romantic than a handsome man's suffering. Think of Mr. Rochester." Ivy grinned. "But time heals all, am I right?"

"That's right, Ivy," Maggie said. "At least, that's what they say."

Ivy stood. "Time to get back to work. I hear my deadlines calling." She zipped her red coat and attempted to stuff her silver hair into the hood. Then she coiled the purple scarf around her neck. "How long you planning to stay in town, Maggie?"

"I'll stick around long enough to help Momma get things straightened out. However long that takes." Maggie wondered just what she was getting herself into.

"We'll see, Maggie." Ivy pushed her fists into hand-knit rainbow mittens several sizes too large for her. "We'll see about that. This place has a way of getting its claws into you. You have to hang on for all you're worth or the cold wind will blow you straight to Amarillo. Sure gives you something to fight. It wakes you up. You feel alive. Even when the snow's piled three feet deep and you've got to go break ice and you're wondering when the county blade will ever get here and clear the road."

"If it wakes you up, why do so many people go to sleep here?" Maggie wanted to know. "They just want everything to stay the same, they don't trust new ideas. They figure any new idea, however promising, has sprung from the mind of some subversive outsider. And if they fail to numb themselves out with work and television, there's always booze and drugs."

Ivy patted her on the shoulder. "Honey, you're just off the boat. Wait 'til the place has had a chance to grow on you a while. I think you know what I mean—you've just forgotten 'cause you've been away so long. Monte Alto may not look like much more than a dusty spot in the road, but it has what everybody in this whole dang country is running around looking for." She waved a mittened hand. "Your Momma knows all about that. She'll hold onto her ranch tooth and toenail."

Ivy had read not only her mind, but her confused heart as well. There was no point trying to keep a secret from this woman.

SIX

GRABBING A CUP OF COFFEE AT FIRST LIGHT, Maggie climbed in the banged-up warrior of a pickup and cranked it. She pumped and tried again, until the engine labored and finally turned over. The orange flare of sunrise blazed, then died, as she bumped over rock-strewn, overgrown cow paths that passed for ranch roads. Lucy and Elias had raised Brangus beef, a breed with the ability to tolerate desert conditions and a willingness to travel to find food, but they'd sold their small herd when the drought dried up the land so they had to feed both summer and winter. Until then, they'd been barely holding their own, but their little operation couldn't sustain the triple whammy of feeding, falling cattle prices, and the aches and pains of their aging selves.

A patchwork of abandoned homesteads, the pastures still carried the names of settlers—McAllister, Porter, Morrow—who'd come here a hundred years ago with their hopes and dreams and left with little to show for years of hard work. The remains of an occasional collapsed dugout or rock foundation spoke to the futility of their efforts.

What made the Chilton ranch special, however, were its two blessed water sources. The house stood near a good shallow well that miraculously held up even in the driest of times. And over here, on the north side of the ranch, a sweet sparkling spring insured the land's ability to support the clan. In good years, when afternoon thunderstorms of July and August materialized, little pools of water formed where the spring gurgled out of the rocky sandstone outcropping. Then their sixty-acre meadow thrived on the sub-irrigation, producing a crop of lush green grass, grass that became the hay to feed the stock through the winter months. After they sold their cattle, Lucy would sometimes lease the meadow, and another rancher would fatten his herd here. But other years, if she figured she could get by, she rested it. She loved to watch that tall grass just ripple in the wind during the good years.

Studying the land as she rumbled along, Maggie thought about her mother. All her life she had wished for a warm, kind maternal presence instead of the mother she'd been dealt, but now she recognized it was that very homesteader toughness, that refusal to quit and the will to endure Lucy had shown her that had saved her daughter's skin and sanity many a time. Refusing to be daunted by the impossible, otherwise known as just plain stubborn, was part of her genetic makeup. Maggie paid tribute to those qualities when she named her daughter Hannah, after her own homesteading grandmother who wasn't afraid of anything and knew how to survive.

Maggie checked out the fencing, noting where she'd have to make repairs and calculating the tools and materials she'd need to get the hard, slow job done. Once she got started, she'd have to stay and see the project through. With or without cows, they couldn't afford loosened and downed barbed wire and wobbly fenceposts. They needed clearly defined boundaries first of all. Strong fences were more than a physical detail on the landscape. They declared an identity the rest of the world was bound to respect.

As if it knew the way—which by now it surely must—the truck bumped along to the corrals where they'd done their branding. As a kid, she'd jumped in and helped separate the mamas from the babies after they'd been rounded up the June morning of branding day. Elias pushed the babies through the chute, one by one down the narrow railed passageway, supporting his weight on his arms as he moved them along with his legs,. Once the calf was locked into the headgate and secured, it was turned on its side for its first big surprise.

Lucy stood to the calf's right where a wood fire blazed. Pulling the red-hot iron from the fire, she raised the iron and firmly applied her LC bar brand on the calf's ribs. The unmistakable smell of singed hair released into the corral while black bubbles simmered on the hide where the branding iron had made its mark. Her mother remained absolutely calm despite the noise and commotion. She worked with a sense of pride, knowing she was as good at this as any man, and, as she pressed her brand into the animal's flesh, knowing that each creature in the herd belonged to her.

Meanwhile, on the left side of the prone calf, one of the hands, a neighbor they'd helped out the week before, injected a dose of vaccine. Working swiftly, he gotten the castration going, expertly cutting the testicles. Finally, he snipped off a triangular section of an ear to make their "earmark," a job that would come to Maggie when she got a little bigger. She remembered how carefully she placed those triangles of hairy sinew in the pocket of her apron to tally. Any missing cattle had to be rounded up, and finding those few strays and bringing them in could take as much time as moving the entire herd.

A crank and a rusty squawk of the equipment, and the calf was turned upright and quickly released. He bounded off to join the others as if nothing had happened, demonstrating a rapid recovery that always astounded her.

They worked hard all morning through the rising heat, then, just when they were about to starve to death, the dinner bell rang, and they all gathered around in the wide shade of the sycamore beside the barn and ate a big lunch of grilled steak, beans, fresh coleslaw, and cobbler. Each diner received a flyswatter to go with lunch. After a delicious nap in the deep shade, they returned to work and finished up at dark. Maggie's mouth watered just thinking about that home-grown food—the steak and sweet corn and thick-sliced red ripe tomatoes and juicy dill pickles. She wished Hannah could get a taste of that wholesome fare, that delicious eating that gave a body such strength and contentment.

Maggie wondered if even now, with that spring trickling through the rock, she herself might get a couple of milk cows and some chickens. She could almost imagine Hannah learning to milk and gather eggs; and, she could even see the two of them laughing together as they made their own butter and ice cream.

In good times, when there was plenty of moisture to support a larger herd and abundant grass, when they didn't eat up their profits buying feed, they would get up the next morning and go through it all over again. The work was hot, demanding and dirty, yet neither she nor anyone else who'd ever done it would have given up a minute of it. She still didn't understand the power of it, though she suspected it lay somewhere in the ancient, primal relationship between man and animal and earth. Even now, her hands almost twitched with the desire to be back there, sharp pocket knife in hand, earmarking each one, making it theirs, before it passed through the gate. She wished she could be part of it still. She lingered a good while at the spot, unable to comprehend that a place so recently full of life and raw energy had become so deserted as to seem haunted. In less than a generation, the Old West had become the New West, ranches had become "ranchettes," and SUVs the mud never dried on were the vehicle of choice for people called "amenity migrants."

Maggie turned from the empty corrals, sensing she was not alone. She looked east and watched someone approach on horseback. She got back in the pickup and drove back toward the meadow. When she got in shouting distance, she climbed out of the truck and stood in his path, as deliberately as if she'd held a shotgun in one hand. She called, "You lost, amigo?" the way she'd heard Elias inquire of any stranger who had no business on their land.

The fellow dismounted about twenty feet away, tied his horse, and walked toward her. "Good morning, ma'am," he said as he approached and offered his hand to shake. She checked him out before returning the offer. A slight young man about 5'8", he wore a clean plaid flannel shirt under a tan shearling jacket, with jeans and boots that looked too new to belong to anybody from around here. His hat topped a mass of honey-brown curls, and he sent her a lopsided smile as he introduced himself. Altogether, he looked like he might have a bit too much country music playing in his head. "The name's Randy Bradford," he said with a distinct Texas drawl and no apology that he'd been caught trespassing.

After a moment's hesitation, she returned the handshake. His baby face was set off by a dimpled chin, and Maggie couldn't quite place his age. He appeared as clean-cut as a frat boy out to make an impression on a new professor.

Maggie set about knocking the grin off his face. "What brings you out here on my property this morning?" she asked, looking him in the eye easily, as they were the same height.

"Your property?" he responded. "Why ma'am, I didn't see any posted signs. I was just out riding. I am sorry for the intrusion, miss..."

"Chilton. Maggie Chilton," she said. "You obviously aren't from around here. This property is well known as our family's place."

He shrugged. "Guess I just took a wrong turn a few miles back up the road. I apologize, Miss Chilton. It won't happen again."

"It better not." She'd have to get these fences fixed, and soon. She'd see about the lack of posted signs, but it was hard to believe they were all gone. Still, he should have known better.

"So this is your ranch?" he asked, sweeping his arm in a wide arc across the landscape. The spring trickling through the rocky outcropping on the edge of the meadow held his attention.

She observed the movement of his eyes, as well as his slender fingers and slim wrists as she thought a moment. "Yes," she said, forced to acknowledge that fact for the first time. "It's my family's home." Despite how annoying she found this Randy, there was also something about him that made her curious. His innocence was a cover, she decided, and charm was something he turned off and on as suited his need. Not only was he pretending ignorance about his knowledge of property boundaries, she recognized something else. In her experience, such people put everything they had into getting exactly what they wanted, be it a fancy new toy or a partner for the evening. Rarely were they denied, and when they didn't get their way, they could become nasty.

"And where are you from?" she asked him.

He turned the full power of his smile on her. "My family's from Houston," he said. "But I grew up on my granddaddy's ranch near Lubbock before I got shipped off to school."

She'd bet money it was to a fancy prep school in the East he'd been sent to, followed up with an Ivy League degree or two. "What brings you out this way, Randy?" she asked, shifting her weight. She didn't expect a straight answer, but she was pretty fair at reading between the lines.

"I'm looking around for a place of my own to settle down, ma'am," he replied, meeting her eyes. "I'm visiting, trying to find out how well Monte Alto and I agree with each other."

"And how well do you?" she asked.

"Haven't been here long enough to answer your question. Only landed a couple of weeks ago. But I really like the place, and the people are friendly enough."

Of course they seemed friendly. Like her, they wanted to know what he might be up to. A handsome, well-off young newcomer was a rare enough sight as to arouse suspicion. "If you're intending to make ranching your business, there are easier places to make a living," she told him.

He laughed. "Well, now, Miss Chilton, most occupations are easier to make a living at than ranching, wouldn't you agree?"

"Some people might wonder why a Texas rancher in possession of good grass and water would cross state lines to investigate poor droughty Blue Grama County." She smiled, mostly to herself, at how easily she slipped into the old-timers' lingo and outlook.

"A fella's got to make his own way in this world, Miss Chilton," he replied. "Can't just sit back and brag about what Granddad did in his day. That Texas ranch was sold long ago. But I've got so much ranching in my blood that I want to get back to it."

"I wish you luck, amigo," she told him. He had a real nice story worked out.

He nodded in the direction of the spring. "That's a fine water source over yonder," he said. "Too bad it's not doing anything for you. Could be putting it to good use."

"It's done a lot of good in its time," she answered. "And it will again."

"I'm sure it has," he said, turning toward her. "Wonder if you might consider having dinner with me some time, Maggie. Maybe you wouldn't mind sharing a little of what you know about Monte Alto. I sure could use some pointers," he said, with a warm smile. "Can I call you?"

"To tell you the truth, Randy," she said, "I've just come home after being away a long time, so I'm not sure how helpful I can be."

"Well, okay. I'm just a lonely guy out here on my own, and I'd sure enjoy the company of a beautiful woman," he said.

Don't even try to blow smoke up my skirt, she wanted to tell him. "Sure," she said. No telling what she might learn—like what he was doing snooping around out here. "Wouldn't want you to think we were any less neighborly than folks back in Texas," she told him.

She watched as he rode off. Still and all, the man knew how to sit in a saddle.

SEVEN

"Which one will it be, Momma?" On Wednesday morning, Maggie opened the oak chifforobe that served as her mother's closet. The scent of mothballs and Evening in Paris cologne was suffocating. In fifty years, Lucy hadn't given away a thing. She could have opened a thrift shop with all the period clothing stuffed in there. Lucy didn't believe in waste, and if parting with a still-serviceable garment wasn't wasteful, what was? To Maggie, her mother's holding on amounted to a kind of greed, made worse by the pride Lucy took in her stinginess. The woman had a complete lack of appreciation for beauty.

Lucy pushed herself up in bed. "That navy is fine," she said. Painfully, she raised her arms, no more than two arthritic spindles encased in loose, splotchy skin. Maggie maneuvered the garment over her head as if dressing a fragile porcelain doll. "That looks nice on you. Now come over here and let me fix your hair." She patted Grandma's needlepoint vanity seat.

"Don't you be messing with my do, Maggie. I might not recognize myself in the mirror."

She picked up the alabaster brush. When she was a child, in secret moments she had sat here and run her finger over the birds, vines, and cherubs carved on the back of that brush. She had tried on the dime-store costume jewelry stacked in gold paper boxes in the top drawer, the glittering rhinestones, the fake pearls, the cheap red, yellow, and green strands of beads. She held up the hand mirror and examined her profile from different angles, pushed up her hair and wondered if she was pretty. No one ever told her she was, so all she could do was wonder.

She had sat in this room before bedtime, fresh from her bath in her flannel nightie, as Lucy brushed her ten-year-old's raven hair, talking of cattle and horses and the price of feed and the lack of rain. Lucy never wanted an answer, but she expected Maggie to listen to every word. Continuing the one-way conversation, she turned to the mirror and set to work on her own hair, hanging straight down to the middle of her back. These bristles had untangled that hair as it turned from black to steel and kept turning.

"Your hair is so soft. Let me part it on the side and give you some curl on top. If you don't like it, you can comb it right out and I won't say a word." Somewhere she'd read that people in nursing homes responded well to having their hair groomed.

"I'm warning you. I know what suits me." The set of Lucy's mouth was poised for a negative comment.

"I hear you, Momma. But it doesn't hurt to try something new once in a while." Under her fingers, the bones of her mother's skull protruded. Maggie had seen her mother naked only once, in the early morning, stepping out of the shower. She had awakened early, so eager to go to the bathroom she hadn't bothered to see if it was occupied. A body enormous as a statue emerged from a cloud of steam, the white breasts and tan, freckled arms. It was as if two people inhabited the same body: the worker and the woman. Lucy had grabbed a towel, covered herself, and scolded her back to bed before she slammed the bathroom door.

This glimpse of raw pink scalp beneath thinning hair was another revelation, another sight that both fascinated and repelled her. She hesitated before she pushed her fingers through her mother's hair and rubbed gently on the tight, thin skin. What did it feel like to be old and in pain night and day?

"What in the world are you doing?" Lucy groused.

"Giving you a little massage."

Lucy turned her head away. "Did I ask you for that?"

"I just thought it might help you relax. You know. Feel good."

"I feel just fine, thank you. Can we get this hair fixed so I won't be late for my game?"

Maggie gathered the thinning hair and wound it into a knot. Lucy's oak vanity, a shrine of womanhood, held a porcelain shepherdess standing watch over silver trays of bobby pins, flowered hankies, and hatpins. On the lace-edged table scarf lay the alabaster hand mirror, the witness of Lucy's face as it changed from an unmarked young woman's to an old lady's. Each day she'd applied Elizabeth Arden face powder with a pink puff; at night, she'd performed the cleansing ritual of Pond's cold cream and tissue. No matter. Now her mother's face was engraved by wind and years, dust and coping.

"Too bad you never played bridge, Maggie." Lucy applied some Avon lipstick, Midnight Red, the same shade she'd worn for thirty years. "You'd have made a fine player."

"I never could play bridge with you, Momma. It's a miracle I sat still long enough for you to teach me the game." That was an understatement. Maggie never did get what the fixation on bridge was all about. It seemed like an excuse to get together with your friends and gossip. She'd rather tackle a bushel of algebra equations than remember all those cards.

"Your mind will never go bad on you if you play bridge, Maggie."

"That so?" Maggie combed her mother's hair back into a twist and fastened it with bobby pins.

"It surely is. Look at that Ruby Redfearn. She remembers her cards for two weeks."

"How old is she now?" And how old would her mother live to be? How many more times would they be together? She put her hands on Lucy's shoulders and felt the wasted muscle that encased her bones. Once those arms had been strong enough to pull nails and take down an abandoned homesteader's house, to lift rocks and build a bridge across a flooded arroyo so the cattle could cross over.

"Be ninety-six come July. And still taking home her share of the winnings. Says she doesn't know what she'd do if she didn't play bridge. Her eyes can't see to read anymore. Can't even see the mountains."

Bridge was much more than a game here. It was a measure of your womanhood, as important to your reputation as keeping a clean house or producing well-behaved children. The qualities required to be a decent bridge player—memory, judgment, risk taking, respect for the rules—were what your survival depended on.

"Close your eyes, Momma. I don't want you peeking until I'm done." Maggie teased the top of her mother's hair, formed a spitcurl on her forehead, and sprayed it into place. "All right, you can look now."

Lucy relaxed her expression of displeasure. She patted her hair, adjusting the French twist slightly.

"So? Like it?"

Maggie watched her mother's eyes, and the set of her mouth,

in the beveled vanity mirror. Lucy nodded. "Thank you, Maggie. You got a good do on it. I do believe this is the first new hairstyle I've had since Eisenhower. They'll all be asking where I got my hair done. And wondering what's come over me."

"You are surely welcome." The patient tick of the grandmother clock on the mantle reminded Maggie they'd be late if she didn't get her mother moving.

"You know, Maggie, if you'd been a bridge player, I doubt you'd have left home. If you'd loved the game, you'd have found plenty of company right here."

"I didn't go away because I didn't like bridge." Maggie locked eyes with her mother's in the mirror. Her tone took on a note of self-defense.

"You're not still hurting over all that business, are you?" Lucy asked.

"I couldn't very well stick around here after what happened." It was always a mistake to reveal anything personal to her mother. Like her clothes, she'd save the information and use it someday.

"Sure your pride took a beating when Roger and Tommie took up together. But you'd have gotten over it. You'd have made your own way. You'd have found somebody else."

"Must we go into this?" Maggie picked up the dust cloth she kept in the corner and began polishing the chifforobe.

"They just gave you the excuse you needed to toss your cape over your shoulder and head on down the road." Lucy raised her voice. "That's what you wanted, wasn't it? You got to go out there and see the big world. So no need for you to be carrying grudges."

"Who said I was?" She worked, and failed, at keeping her voice light. Maggie shielded her mother's eyes with one hand. She pressed the button and hissed a halo around Lucy's coif. "I'm really not in the mood to dig all this up now, Momma,"

Maggie turned and walked to the bureau. Her eyes went to the black-and-white photo: two scruffy nine-year-olds, she and Tommie, astride a beautiful palomino. She picked the silver frame up from the lace runner and held it to the light. They looked like sisters. Didn't people always say so? Didn't they like to pretend they were? They wore the same size jeans, same size boots. They put on each other's clothes and went everywhere together.

They belonged together. Maggie's father was gone, while Tommie lived with her grandparents, Tomás and Jesusita. A midwife and herb woman, Jesusita brought Maggie into the world. When Maggie got flu, she brought over her pouches of herbs and brewed *yerba buena* tea. For stomachaches, she had Maggie chew osha root and salt. Jesusita massaged her back, humming, until Maggie dozed off. Through her fever dreams, she heard the two women in the kitchen, talking and laughing. When she woke up, she'd pad into the kitchen, hungry, her fever broken. Then Momma would sit her at the kitchen table and put a steaming bowl of potato soup in front of her, with a plate of saltines.

She'd never had a friend as close as Tommie, never laughed as hard, acted as wild or felt as free. After that betrayal, she'd locked her girlishness in a trunk along with her ice skates and charm bracelets. Because she hurt so bad, she had never even known Tommie's son. And now it was too late. She put the photo back in its place on the bureau then sat on the bed, her back to her mother, and bowed her head. "And Jesse?" she asked in a low voice. She turned away and fiddled with a loose string on the lace dresser scarf.

"Truck hit him one night out on that rough patch of Highway 41. Drunk driver, don't you know. Came at him in the wrong lane. They all said they'd never seen such a wreck. Don't you know that driver, he's out on probation now. He just floorboarded it back to Texas." Lucy sighed. "So it's just us old folks left around here. Nobody to carry on."

"People leave because there's nothing for them to do around here."

"Nothing to do! Somebody who can't find work around here can't find his backside with both hands and a mirror. There's too much to do! Same as there was the day your grandpa arrived. He set to work and built something. Same as we all tried to do." With a pink puff, Lucy applied a mask of powder.

"Somebody who goes out and gets an education is going to want the chance to use it."

"You've got a fine education, Maggie. You've used it. And now you can start to see."

"See what?"

"I've been thinking. You could do something here. You could put your education to a better use than you ever dreamed."

"Do you really see me setting out to change a whole town? More than a town—a whole chunk of country! How am I supposed to do that?"

"You know this place. Out there, you can never be more than one in a crowd. Here you can make a difference."

Maggie shook her head. "I don't know how."

"You're a smart girl. Figure it out! And don't think you have to worry about me. I won't be any burden on you. I can take care of myself just fine." Lucy slapped the top of the dresser to emphasize her words.

"Sure you can, Momma," Maggie assented peaceably.

"At least you could say that like you meant it."

"Yes ma'am. You've certainly changed your mind about my future plans." At least somebody believed she had a future.

"I have, Maggie. Having you here has made me see some

things. Like how we have to look to the future. The town needs you, and, believe it or not, you need Monte Alto. This is your place."

"Maybe it's not so bad having me around." Maggie smiled at her mother in the mirror.

"Never said it was. I just didn't want you to throw away all you'd worked so hard for. But this place suits you. And it ought to. It's your home."

"I'll have to give it a lot of thought, Momma."

"I see." Now Lucy caught her eyes in the mirror. "Maggie, when is Hannah coming to visit?"

"Funny you should ask. I just got a letter from Paul about Hannah."

"And?" her mother wanted to know.

"There's good news and there's bad news," Maggie said.

"I want to see my only grandchild. What did he say?" Lucy had never really approved of her marriage, so she never really took to Paul.

"First of all, Hannah can come to visit. Paul is more than giving her permission to get out of the house. Hannah got thrown out of school—suspended."

"Not for cheating or using drugs, I hope." Lucy said.

"Her grades have dropped, it's true." No sense trying to fake this one. "And she got caught using marijuana."

"That's terrible!" Lucy exclaimed. "I want to know when she's getting here. We're just what that girl needs. We'll straighten her out."

"I know Hannah needs a change. Smoking pot isn't the worst thing in the world, but we want to stop it before the problem goes any further. I'm doing my best. I told you, I'm working on it."

"You never liked it very much when *I* used those words."

"You're right, Momma. I always thought you could do better

when it came to making me happy. Do you want me to apologize for ever having been a child?"

"When have I ever asked you for anything?" Lucy's combination of petulance and aggression drove Maggie crazy.

"You never had to ask. You had all kinds of ways of letting me know what was expected of me. Your looks, your silences, your judgments, your rightness. You had me exactly where you wanted me."

"I raised you right. Yes I did. Don't you dare go blaming me if things didn't turn out exactly the way you wanted."

"Let's not fight, Momma. I told you Hannah will be here, and she will, if I have to fly to Washington and get her myself."

"Thank you." Lucy put her lipstick, compact, and hanky in her handbag. turned away. "Here's your coat, Momma." Maggie held out the sleeve of the indestructible black wool.

Hotel Manzano, the Victorian-style railroad hotel, was the town's sole attempt at grandeur. It was the tallest building in town, three stories high, with a balcony on the third floor. Once there had even been a rooftop garden. Forty years ago, it had stood in the midst of barbershops and grocery stores and clothing emporiums that bustled on Saturdays when everyone came to town. Back then, it had been the place for Sunday dinner, where people celebrated their anniversaries and birthdays. Every politician from here to Santa Fe had his favorite table, where he sat and held court. People always knew where to find the county commissioner or the congressman, even the governor. Now it stood surrounded by empty storefronts, the Golden Eagle and the White House, secured behind locked iron gates, stores that looked like museums advertising outdated shoes and garments at absurdly low prices.

With carved granite façade, leaded-glass windows, and

gargoyles frolicking along its pediments, the hotel had been an establishment imposing enough for the town's founders to entertain their associates from Denver, El Paso, Tucson, and Santa Fe. The lobby still had a sense of former glory, with its flocked red wallpaper and wainscoting, its cushioned sofas upholstered in ruby, emerald, and peacock-blue velvet. But now the velvets were shabby and musty and frayed. Under these crystal chandeliers, big as wedding cakes, honors were conferred, toasts raised, and once, a famous Russian violinist performed.

A painting on the lobby wall told what the place had been like in the old days. In past decades, light glowed behind fringed lampshades in the oak-paneled dining room as gentlemen on cushioned banquettes cut into thick prime rib, sipped French wine, and planned for the future as the passing train outside sounded its whistle. Their companions, perfumed ladies in garnets and silks, sipped champagne and nibbled lobster salad.

There had always been rumors of a bordello upstairs, and it was well known that a twenty-four-hour poker game stayed in progress in the back room. During Prohibition, "white lightning" was available there as well, if you were known to the bartender. Even in Maggie's time, the hotel proprietor, Mr. Laurent Bergere, a dapper little man who smelled of hair tonic and wore a monogrammed handkerchief in his pocket, had been known as a ladies' man.

The Wednesday Club had been playing bridge at "its" corner table in the dining room since the doors opened in 1911. There was only one excuse for missing a meeting: you had to be dead. If you missed because you were sick, you'd get an African violet delivered to your door—a quiet message that you'd let your friends down.

Invitations to join the Wednesday Club were issued only when a member passed on. Membership went from mother to daughter, from aunt to niece.

Maggie held the hotel door open for her mother.

"Won't you come in and say hello, Maggie?"

"I will when I come back to pick you up, Momma. I've got errands to run." She needed a little break from her mother. She put her arm around Lucy and kissed her goodbye on the cheek.

From the door, Maggie watched Lucy greet her friends. She recognized a few of them. These were rancher women who could spend a day in a pickup sliding around in caliche mud looking for a lost cow—or branding half a herd in the morning—yet when they went out to socialize they looked good and they smelled good. The seams on their stockings stood ruler-straight. Their high heels matched their handbags and changed color with the season. They wore white gloves immaculate over manicured nails. And their hairdos were preserved, for all eternity, with Aquanet.

"See you by five," Maggie called. But Lucy didn't hear her.

―――――◆―――――

At the card table where her three friends waited Lucy sat in the fourth chair. The table, covered in a pink linen, was arrayed with china dishes of sugar-coated almonds and bridge mix, score pads, pencils, and a pitcher of iced tea. It had been set exactly the same way every Wednesday since 1943, and maybe even before that.

"Guess we can shuffle the cards now," Elvira Orme said. "What are you waiting for?"

"Do you want it done or do you want it done right?" Opal Munroe shuffled the cards and slid the deck over to Lucy, who cut the deck into three stacks. Elvira said, "Get those almonds away from me. You know they're poison on my teeth."

"If I tried you'd get the right swoop on my hand and it'd come up missing," Lola Adkins replied.

"Your bid," said Elvira. "Put those candies my way. I need my chocolate fix. I can't open. Lucy?"

"One diamond."

"So Maggie's in town for a visit?" Elvira said.

"That's right."

"Too bad about her divorce."

"Everybody's divorcing these days," said Lola. "They don't know how to see it through."

"We didn't think of divorce. You made your bed and you laid in it. Simple as that," said Elvira. "They think it's supposed to be easy."

"What'd that lady journalist say? 'There's so little difference between husbands, one might as well keep the first,'" said Lola. "One heart."

"That's what you get for being town librarian. A wheelbarrow full of famous sayings," Elvira said.

"We all know good and well what men are like," Opal said. The other three ladies chorused agreement.

"Men are very good for certain things," Lucy said.

"It's good to have one when you need him," said Elvira.

"But how often do you need him?" The ladies laughed together.

"Two spades," Lucy said. "Maggie will be fine."

"What brings her to town?" asked Elvira.

"Since when can't a child come visit her mother?" Lucy said.

"Four no trump," said Lola. "Her and Roger making eyes at each other again."

"One kisses, the other turns the cheek," Opal murmured. "Pass."

"Don't be ridiculous," Lucy said. "Five clubs. That's ancient history."

"Seven no trump," Lola said. "Heard it myself from Lorraine when I was over at the Crowning Glory."

"You must think you have a slam," Elvira said. "Pass."

"Lorraine. Now there's a reliable source. The woman could get herself hired by the FBI," Lucy said. "Pass."

"Roger's a good man," said Opal. "I haven't been feeling a hundred percent lately. Wonder if I should get my blood pressure medication checked."

"Roger's been down to his last biscuit and his last stick of dynamite. What man could stand up to losing a wife and a son in the same year?" Lola said.

"He's carrying on. He's his daddy through and through. The apple doesn't fall far from the tree," said Opal. "Maybe the Lord sent Maggie back to help out with the ranch. To take over for Elias."

"You must miss Elias something awful, Lucy," said Lola.

Lucy laid her cards on the table. "Is this what we need for a grand slam?" She smiled. "Did you bring that coconut cake to eat or to look at?"

They all looked at Lucy. She knew it, but smiled at her cards, knowing she had the winning hand no matter how they stared at her.

Maggie walked in the winter afternoon. She turned toward the mountains, heaped with snow and plenty more on the way. Monte Alto had the dark look of a coming storm. They could use the moisture, but if that snow melted too fast come spring, there'd be floods. Drought had baked the land so dry it wouldn't be able to absorb the moisture when it finally did come.

Low gray clouds gathered as she walked down Main Street. When she got to Dawson's, she tapped on the front window. In a minute, Roger came out from behind the paint display. She waved, and he opened the door.

"Come on in," he said. "It's freezing out here."

"I feel like a walk. Want to come?"

He appraised her, taking in the beat-up leather jacket she'd found in the front closet, the ski sweater that had been a long-ago Christmas present, the faded jeans that she'd pulled out of the bottom dresser drawer, her boots with plenty of miles on them, her windblown hair and windburnt face. She folded her arms and leaned against the storefront window. She caught the moment in his eyes when his "no" changed to "yes."

"So?" she tilted her head. "How does some fresh air sound to you?"

"All right," he said. "It's close enough to quitting time." He went back to his office and returned in a sheepskin jacket. His black Stetson cast a shadow over his face. She still liked the way he moved, calmly and deliberately, with a grace as distinct as a signature. He bolted the door. "If you want to freeze, you won't get to do it alone."

"Slow day?" she asked.

"Slow day, slow week, slow month. I might as well be running an amusement park at Christmastime." His voice held no bitterness. "Don't know what else I'd do though. It's the only real job I've ever had."

"Let's go past the café. Give Lorraine a thrill."

"Sure, something spicy to serve up with the morning coffee."

"You don't give the woman enough credit. She'll have this sighting on the wire before nightfall." Her stride matched his.

He studied the threatening sky. "Storm coming from the east."

"When, in the wintertime, isn't there a storm coming in from the east? Just as one's blowing out, the next one's coming in." She thrust her hands in her pockets and faced straight into the cold wind. "At least I won't be chopping ice out of the tanks tomorrow morning, with the temperature five below and the wind blowing out of the east. No more cattle left to tend."

"Do I hear a little bit of regret there?"

"Would you believe me if I said no way?"

As if they had agreed beforehand, they walked down Main Street to the railroad station. Stepping over a downed barbed-wire fence, their shoulders touched. Neither broke the contact. They walked like that, connected by accident, into the deserted rail yard overgrown with greasewood, salt cedar, and Russian olive. He reached inside her pocket and took hold of her hand. The warmth surprised her.

"Your hands are cold," he said.

"Yours aren't." She turned to him. Shadows lay under his eyes, now flares of indeterminate darkness, and in the hollows of his cheeks. He stood close enough to embrace, close enough to kiss. "Guess I forgot my gloves." In the warm pocket of her coat, she twined her fingers around his.

Alongside the tracks stood the faded red storage elevator, a tower two stories high, where beans used to be loaded into the waiting railroad cars. Maggie could still make out faint square black letters painted on the elevator: The Pinto Bean Capital of the World Welcomes You.

They stood beside tracks that stretched out long empty miles in both directions. She tightened her clasp on his hand as a light beamed from the south. Soon a yellow, orange, and black Santa Fe Burlington Northern Railroad locomotive whistled through without stopping, pulling a dozen boxcars.

"Not too many of them stop here anymore." He kicked a stone out of their path.

"Always something a little dangerous about this place," she said. "Never knew what might jump at you out of those bushes."

"Just a dusty, empty old lot. Something else somebody could do great things with. Pull the weeds. Open a café for tourists, a trinket shop, an art gallery, in that fine old Mission-style stationhouse. A place for people who'd appreciate some red tile and vintage stucco."

"Sounds like a not-bad idea."

"There's no shortage of ideas." He rubbed the toe of his boot in the dirt, as though he were stubbing out a cigarette.

"Tommie and I loved to come here. Momma would kill us if she ever found out. We'd ride our bikes down and light up Marlboros. We figured we'd hop aboard one of those trains sometime." Her tone became wistful.

"Just you and Tommie?"

"I guess that was the plan. At one time."

Roger smiled and shook his head. "You two were something else."

"Can you do that again?"

"What?"

"You know. Smile."

"For you? Anything. Anytime. You know all you have to do is wave your little finger my way." He squeezed her hand. "How's Lucy doing?"

"She's acting her age."

He nodded. "That can be rough. Where does it put you?"

"Don't know. Thought I could just look after things, get Momma straightened up, see about selling the ranch. But it's taking longer than I thought. Momma won't even discuss selling the place."

"It'll kill your mother if you move her off the ranch."

"You're right." She shook her head. "I can't do it." They stopped beside a ragged grove of desert willows. The alcove of trees screened them from view. "But I'm not prepared to live here."

He laughed. "Who is?" He put his hand on her shoulder. "But some of us can't get away. We're planted here like these scraggly greasewoods. Can't grow anyplace else but in this dried-up worn-out dirt. You'll let me know if I can do anything for her—or for you?"

"This is a new one. I've finally got some political connections. Thank you, Mr. Mayor."

"I hope you'll think of yourself as very well connected."

She put her arms around him and drew him close. He gasped. The contours of his body fit hers. She shut her eyes and leaned into his shoulder. He buried his face in her hair. "Oh Maggie. It's so good to see you. Never thought I'd see you again."

She stood absolutely still. "Just tell me one thing. I never understood. Why did you leave?"

"You're the one who left, Maggie," he said.

"Is that what you think?"

He stepped back. "Of course. Isn't that what happened?"

"Not the way I remember it."

A cold edge came into his voice. "And just how do you remember it?"

"You left me. When I went to school in August, everything was fine between us. We wrote, we talked on the phone, we made plans. By the time I got back at Thanksgiving, you were gone. You dumped me for my best friend, and you never even bothered to say goodbye." Her voice dropped as she fought back tears. "You'd been seeing Tommie behind my back. I never even knew. I had to come home and hear all about it." Darkness fell fast around them.

"That's not the way it happened, Maggie," he said.

"What are you saying?"

"I'm telling you things weren't all the way they looked. You need to have Tommie tell you about it."

"I don't think so." She turned away.

He gazed at the horizon. "You're the one who left town, Maggie. You did what you had to do. You left. That said it all." His voice was so low she could barely make out his words.

"That's it? That's all the explanation you have?" His dismissal astonished her.

He buttoned his coat. "Let's head back, baby. It's getting late."

When Maggie rushed into the Hotel Manzano, the clock read 5:20. She spotted her mother's displeasure immediately. "I'm sorry I'm late, Momma."

Lucy perched on an overstuffed velvet sofa, her black coat draped around her shoulders, pretending to read a magazine. "Where were you?"

"Just had a few errands to take care of." She lifted her palms in explanation. "You know how it gets."

"You just missed 'em. Everybody already went home."

"I can visit with the ladies next time." Maggie avoided her mother's eyes. "How'd you do, Momma?"

"I'd like to have shook my own hand." Lucy moved slowly toward the car.

"You tired?" Maggie asked.

"I guess so."

"We'll take you home and fix you supper. I picked up some groceries."

"Well good." Lucy sniffed. "What's that I smell?"

"What do you mean?" Maggie asked.

"Is that man I smell?"

"What do you think? I come to town and start running around?" What right did Lucy have to supervise her?

"You didn't answer my question."

Take it easy, she told herself. She smiled at her mother. "Why don't we just keep this my little secret?"

"You're a big girl. And you'll do as you please, regardless."

"Thank you, Momma."

They drove in silence. Maggie turned on the radio and found the news. "Maybe next time," Lucy said.

"Next time what?" Maggie wondered.

"Maybe next time you'll come and stay a while. Play a few hands."

"Don't scare me like that. I could never play with the Wednesday Club."

"Oh, you're good enough," Lucy replied with conviction.

"Well, you'd better start coaching me, if you expect me to play with those ladies," Maggie retorted.

"I heard today that Lola Adkins is selling her place. Artists from Santa Fe coming in. People with money. Not gonna subdivide. So they say."

"I know you want to stay on the ranch, Momma. I'm not going to fight you."

"Thank you, Maggie." She took out a hanky and blew her nose. "You know it's all yours, anyway. Paid for. If you'd hold onto it, Hannah would always have a home, come what may."

Maggie could not imagine her punky roller-blading daughter living out on the ranch.

"I know you. You'll do what you think is the right thing when the place is yours," Lucy sighed. "I hope it'll be the best thing. Your grandfather used to say: 'This land can promise you more and give you less—or promise you less and give you more—than any country you've ever seen.'"

EIGHT

On a cold, sunny Saturday morning, Maggie pulled into the last parking space at the Old School House. Built of red brick from Gallup, it stood empty most of the time, too expensive to heat or keep up now that there weren't enough children to justify keeping it open. When she attended this grade school, the place had been alive with rowdy kids from town and nearby ranches. But if they didn't get to work on it soon, another historic building would be lost to time and the wind, and another set of memories would be erased.

The Opal Munroe auction was set for eleven a.m., but the crowd had been gathering for the preview since eight. Maggie spotted Ivy and made her way down the hall past knots of folks sipping coffee and munching donuts. She caught bits of their conversations. "Such a shame!" "I just saw Opal buying groceries!" "Well, I saw her at the Rexall, getting new blood pressure medication." "Do you know it was two days before anybody found her?" "A stroke like that isn't such a bad way to go."

Here the ritual of death included a dispersal of whatever

possessions relatives didn't claim. Friends wanted some little piece of memory, a white china horse for the knickknack shelf, a crystal candy dish, a lace table scarf—something to add to their own bundle of accumulation. The clap of the auctioneer's gavel scattered the artifacts of a lifetime to the community.

After the burial came the auction. First, a stranger turned your dresser drawers upside down and your closets and kitchen cabinets inside out. Then, posters went up all over town. On Saturday afternoon, your secrets were set out with your chipped china. The Old School House was crammed with the treasures and necessities of a lady's long life, plus all the odd, broken, and separated items she couldn't bear to part with or was saving because they might come in handy some day. Now they were all available to the highest bidder. A box of Mason canning jars and lids. A pile of cross-stitched linen pillowcases and napkins. Old 78s. Sheet music. Posters and souvenirs. Teapots and toasters, pressure cookers and Christmas cookie cutters, rhinestones, arrowheads, Singer sewing machines, Depression glass, Fiestaware, kerosene lamps, harmonicas, Navajo rugs.

Ivy took a bite of her Optimist Club hot dog. "Opal's kids don't want her quilts. Can you imagine? They've already sold the outfit to Texas developers." She shook her head. "And as hard as she worked to keep that place up. Did you know Opal Munroe?"

Maggie's hand lingered on a log-cabin quilt of denim strips. She remembered a delicate-looking white-haired woman with a face like a pressed flower. She heard Opal's singsong voice speak to her.

Wiley's parents were health-seekers. They sold everything they owned, outfitted a wagon, and came out here for his mother's tuberculosis. After she died, his father went back to Indiana. But Wiley, he didn't want to give up that homestead.

One of our neighbors said to him: "I think you need a wife. I'll have my wife cook Sunday dinner, and we'll invite the Staffords and some of the neighbors and you come along." Well, he'd already seen me. And so he came and we met him. And we got ready to go home, and Wiley had a Model-T pickup. Just had one door.

So he was underfoot from the last of January to October, when we got married. He was underfoot all the time.

Then we got married and I moved over the hill. 1927. Been here ever since. About every third woman in this community that had a baby died. When I got pregnant, I was pretty scared. So Wiley took me to Albuquerque, where all my children were born.

Anybody else would have thought it was pretty hard on the ranch, but we didn't know the difference. So we just did it. One year we had $600 for the whole year. Sheepherders, we paid 'em $15 a month. So I cooked for the sheep camp. You could buy flour for 98 cents a sack. And for a year, I baked a sack of flour every week. It was eight loaves every other day. On a wood stove, with mutton tallow for shortening. It made the best crust. Those sheepherders loved it. And you could go pick up split beans from the elevator floor for nothing. It was half a bean and maybe two rocks. And I'd cook it.

You know the salt lakes east of town? Las Salinas, the Spanish call 'em. Juan de Oñate said they were one of our four treasures. Makes you wonder what he thought the other three were. And way before the Spanish got here, the Indians were trading that salt. There's a crust on 'em about that much. Well it don't cost you a thing. You go down there with a scoop shovel and scoop that up. Salt for the cows. So one day we went down real early. We took twenty-five to thirty tow sacks. And we pulled off our boots and rolled up our britches.

And we started out. And that crust would scrape your legs and the salt would get in 'em. We scooped up about two tons of salt that day.

Didn't hurt a bit to be poor. Everybody else was, too. I'd can everything I could get my hands on. Pressured your corn and your beans and your meat. Grew everything, except what Wiley swapped for. We had lots to eat, but it wasn't always what you wanted. I didn't have any running water, unless I ran and got it. You didn't see any dirty dishes in my house. I made all our clothes. We each had one good outfit for church.

I spoiled my husband. We'd been riding all day, and he said: "I sure would like an apple pie." Made thousands of apple pies.

Oh honey. I bet I've ridden a million miles. Lots of cow work to do. I sure was glad when we sold those sheep. I could spend all day and part of the night telling you the deficiencies of a sheep. I did all the branding. Takes calm. I've branded thousands of calves. Pulled the windmills. Thank the good Lord we lived in shallow water country.

Wiley was a good swapper. That was his joy in life. One day he swapped a little old heifer for a whole bobtail truck of apricots and plums. I canned two hundred quarts that one day. He taught me the hang of swapping. That's how I got these Navajo rugs. Traded skins for 'em. Wore out the blade on my skinning knife.

You see some hard hard things. You want to throw up your hands and quit, but you don't. That road over there isn't going to be any easier than the one you're on.

I like to feed people. Steak and roast, chicken and dumplings in the summertime. From millionaires to tramps, they'd all end up at my kitchen table. I guess they knew they'd be fed.

Wiley knew everybody. He got a letter once marked: Wiley Munroe, New Mexico.

———◆———

Maggie pulled a green and purple patchwork from a pile of museum-quality pieces.

"It's not the prettiest of the bunch." Ivy rubbed a corner between her fingers. "Nor the best made. These were the colors we had to work with during the war. Dull."

"It's lovely." Maggie unfolded the soft purple and green patchwork. "A friendship quilt." On each square, a woman had chain-stitched her signature. Opal Munroe. Ida Belle Myers. Bessie Eldridge. Lucy Chilton. "Here's Momma's square."

"Be careful how you nod your head once the selling starts." Ivy patted Maggie's arm. "This could cost you."

They sat through the auctioning of the dining room furniture, the rugs and lamps and mirrors. A murmur went through the crowd when the quilts were brought out. "Here's what they've been waiting for," said Ivy. Maggie picked up her bid card. She watched as the exquisite quilts—precise appliqué, delicately stitched white-on-white, crazy quilts of silk and velvet—were bid up and sold. Finally, the two young women assisting the auctioneer held the friendship quilt up for display.

"What am I bid for this masterpiece of fine stitchery?" the auctioneer called. "Do I hear a hundred dollars? A hundred dollars to the cowboy in back! A hundred ten? Who'll give a hundred ten for these precious memories? Surely these memories are worth more."

Maggie raised her bid card. "A hundred twenty to the dark-haired lady on the right."

"Looks like you've got some competition here," Ivy said, nodding her head in the direction of the last bidder.

Maggie looked over her shoulder and saw the bidder was

Randy Bradford, who flashed her his lazy, lopsided smile. She was determined to bring this quilt home to Lucy. The bidding rose as Randy, competing with her for the prize, matched her dollar for dollar. When the auctioneer asked $300, her arm shot up. "Sold! Sold to the young lady in row five." A buzz went up from the crowd as one of the associates folded the quilt and brought it to Maggie.

"I know. Don't tell me. I paid way too much," she told Ivy.

"That's a lot of money around here. But I'd say you did fine."

Maggie hugged the quilt as she carried it out to put in the car. She put her face to the folds of soft fabric and inhaled the faint lavender scent. Finally, she had found a present that would please Lucy. Her mother never wanted anything for herself; she was impossible to buy gifts for. She always said, "That's very nice, dear. Thank you," in the same dismissive way, no matter what Maggie gave her. This time would be different.

Randy, dressed in black western shirt and black jeans, with a turquoise bolo around his neck, waited for her in the doorway as she returned to the auction. "Looks like you got the best deal today, Miss Chilton."

"That quilt has quite a bit of personal meaning for my mother," she told him. "There's plenty of others to bid on."

He folded his arms. She tried to go around him and get back inside. "I hope you're still of a mind to have dinner with me sometime, Maggie," he said. "I've got a few ideas I'd like to run past you."

She stopped and faced him. "Such as?"

He reached over and gave her shoulder a squeeze. "You'll just have to share a bottle of wine with me to find out. I promise you won't regret it."

She shook her head and walked off. She couldn't figure out what his game was.

"I'll call you, Maggie," she heard him say as she walked away.

During the break, Maggie and Ivy sat on the back schoolhouse steps. Mauve and rose clouds sailed toward Monte Alto. The dust of dry grasses floated in the golden four-o'clock light.

"Do you know anything about that cowboy who was bidding against me?" Maggie asked Ivy. "You're up on everyone in town."

"You've come to the right place," Ivy said. "That young fella been sniffin' around here represents his family business, Western Century. Big Texas real estate developers. He's been out here making offers on a few of the old places. So far he hasn't had much luck, though. He thinks by playing cowboy folks will trust him, but that game isn't working so well for him. I'm just putting the finishing touches on a big exposé about him and his Western Century. But enough about him. What about Roger?" Ivy asked, handing Maggie a lemon square.

"What about him?"

"Aren't you all big-eyed and innocent!" Ivy flung one end of her long woolen rainbow scarf over her shoulder.

"Aren't you stepping a little bit out of line, Mrs. McGrath?"

Ivy rubbed her nose thoughtfully. "I think you still like him."

"I'm polite to him." Maggie didn't want to be rude, but she wished Ivy would back off. The woman needed to mind her own business. She really wasn't interested in getting anything going with Roger, but if she protested too much, she'd only incriminate herself.

"Good girl. Manners is the first language."

Ivy would never get over being a schoolmarm, free to lecture whenever the mood struck her. Maggie examined her work boots and tied a lace, wondering how to deflect Ivy's so-called good intentions. "A new relationship is the last thing I need right now."

"Famous last words. You might as well sit up and beg Cupid to shoot you," Ivy said with a knowing grin.

"Besides, I'd never take up with somebody who did me like he did."

"You were only kids, Maggie."

"Right." She turned toward the darkening mountains. "That's a real nice excuse."

"You were crazy about him. And there's always two sides to a story."

"He left me for my best friend. What was I supposed to do? Come back and enjoy the spectacle?"

"A lot of us missed you. A lot of folks didn't want to see you go." Ivy pulled at the knotted fringe on her scarf. "Other women seem to have figured out that he's single."

Curious, Maggie swiveled to face her. "What do you mean?"

"Oh, it's probably nothing. That sweet little blond schoolteacher from Sherlock just likes to do her paint shopping at Roger's store. I suppose that's the only place she can find the right shade of blue for her bedroom. And that lawyer from Albuquerque. Suit and briefcase and high heels and a fancy car. Little Jaguar, wasn't it? But that was probably just business."

"Thanks, Ivy. You've made your point. There's plenty of women on the prowl, even in Monte Alto. Both me and Roger are as tangled up in our own business as the threads in the bottom of your sewing box."

"Sometimes people can help each other get untangled. Besides, it's better not to be alone, better for two people to be happy together. Every pot has its lid." Ivy folded her arms.

"If you think you're going to see me and Roger back together, you can wait for a herd of buffalo to stampede down Main Street. Just because we went together in high school doesn't mean we have any business together now." Maggie shook her head. "You can deal me out of any hand you're shuffling, Ivy."

"Just promise me one thing, Maggie."

"Not 'til I hear what you've got in mind."

"Give Roger some waggin' room. Don't give up on him before you know what you're throwing away."

"He gave up on me a long time ago." She got up to open the gym door and looped her arm through Ivy's. "The auctioneer is starting up. Are you coming in?"

Maggie got home just before dark. As she pulled up the gravel driveway, she noticed that somehow the house looked different than when she left that morning. Nothing had changed, no repairs had been made, but the old adobe seemed more properly settled. She opened the front door. "Hi, Momma! I'm back."

Lucy sat in her rocker, wrapped in an afghan like a wizened baby, her face suffused in blue television light. She seemed to shrink as days passed. A buzzer sounded; an audience applauded.

She couldn't wait. "Momma, I found you something."

"*Jeopardy* is on," she said, without turning her head from the TV. "My favorite show."

Maggie thrust the quilt at her mother.

"What's this?"

"Take a look." Maggie unfolded her find.

"No." Lucy traced the embroidered names with her fingertips as though they were stitched in Braille. "My friendship quilt. "

"Yes it is."

Lucy put her hands to her face in astonishment. "I don't believe it. Where in the world did you get this?"

"From the Opal Munroe auction."

"Poor Opal."

"Guess you've beat her at bridge for the last time."

"Look at this. All those ladies who worked on it. All gone now. Except me and Ida Belle. I remember when we made this. Opal was the only one with a radio. We'd gather at her house and listen to the war news. The men were gone. We waited to hear. Opal's husband was a Flying Tiger. We never knew who would be shot next, or when we would see our husbands again. Or if we ever would.

"All the cowboys had gone to the war, so we had to run the places by ourselves. Those suppers at Opal's were the best times we had. Maybe the only times we laughed in those days." She put her arms around Maggie's shoulders. "Bless you, child. You'll never know what this means." Her voice broke. "I thank the Lord for sending you home to me."

Never before had Maggie seen her mother cry. As gently as she could, she put her hand to her mother's cheek and wiped the tears. As Lucy wept, Maggie took her fragile form in her arms and kissed her lined forehead. She smoothed her mother's hair until she quieted.

Lucy had kept the same friends all her life. Look at all they had been through together. They really had something. What was Maggie's dearest friend, Tommie, doing now? Was there any laughter left in her dark eyes? She wished she and Tommie were sitting at the kitchen table again, listening to the radio. Every once in a while, when a good song came on, one of them would get up and dance, just like they used to.

NINE

The ringing phone woke Maggie early. She pushed her way out of sleep until she broke the surface of Monday morning. "Hello?"

An unsteady voice came on the line. "Maggie, can you get over here?"

She squinted at the light of day. "Ivy? What is it? Are you all right?"

"There's been trouble, Maggie."

She sat up, immediately awake. "Where are you?"

"At the office. Looks like hell to breakfast over here." Ivy's voice wavered. "Somebody broke in."

With the phone tucked between her head and shoulder, Maggie flung off quilts and started to dress.

"My filing cabinets look like they were attacked by a pack of angry bobcats. Do you know what that feels like? To see your work so torn and scattered it makes no sense? I'll never be able to get this straightened out."

"Sit tight. I'll be right there."

A police car was parked in front of the *Independent*'s storefront window, now shattered into a jagged spider web of cracked glass. The door stood open. The turn-of-the-century brick building, with its twenty-foot-high ceilings and solid oak floors, provided a spacious home for the newspaper's computer, light board, and copier. Flyers announcing community events papered the walls: meetings of the CowBelles; of cowboy poetry gatherings; of ranchers impacted by White Sands Missile Range; of those wishing to join a prayer chain at the First Baptist Church. In the back, the old Chandler-Price letter press with its drawers of type fonts stood undisturbed.

Inside, Officer Alvin Shaw, a twenty-something fellow with a premature paunch and acne-scarred baby face, his dirty-blond hair carefully combed in well-oiled stripes, scribbled in pencil on a notepad as Ivy pointed around the room.

"Find out who did this!" Ivy demanded.

"Yes ma'am," he said. "We'll do our best." He took a tour of the mess, looked in the corners, knelt down to inspect the upended furniture. After his review of the premises, he nodded at Maggie and left.

Disoriented, Ivy paced among scattered papers and file folders. She shook her head and muttered to herself like the survivor of a disaster, a fire or flood.

"What will I do?" Ivy sighed, lost in the midst of her familiar surroundings. She looked up at the pressed-tin ceiling, hoping for some answer. "Whatever will I do?"

"Just let me take care of this. It's not as bad as it looks," Maggie lied.

"I'll lose my press time," Ivy whined. With this violation, her years had finally caught up with her.

"When's your deadline?" Maggie's hands kept working, taping cardboard over the shattered window.

"We have to be to the printer by Wednesday, four P.M. sharp."

"No problem. As soon as we sweep up, I'll help you with the stories. You just fill me in. We'll get it all done."

"Thank you, Maggie." Ivy wiped her eyes.

"Tell you what," Maggie said. "After we get this place straightened out, I'll buy you lunch at the Seven Cities. Do we have a deal?"

Maggie sat before the computer and for the first time since Ramona's death, felt as if she could think and write. Even her stomach sickness was gone. An hour later, with enough order restored to begin, Maggie turned on the computer. For the first story, she began: "On Monday night, February 24, 2000, an intruder broke into the office of the *Monte Alto Independent* at 455 Main Street..."

When she finished the story, she printed out a copy and handed her draft to Ivy.

"This'll do," Ivy nodded. "This'll do just fine."

―――――

The first thing Maggie noticed when they walked into the bar, dark even at one in the afternoon, was the giant plastic ice cube inscribed with the Coors logo glowing over the pool table. Tarnished brass statues of conquistadors stood guard at either end of the bar. Owner Lukie Swanson took a lot of pride in his collection of four hundred hats. His prize was the gray Stetson hanging over the bar: John Wayne's hat. Lukie claimed the Duke had worn it in *Way Out West*. He liked to tell how the Duke left it behind when he stopped by for a beer on his way over to Monument Valley.

Lukie came over to take their order. His smile revealed a mouthful of broken teeth. "What can I bring you ladies?"

"Two green chile cheeseburgers with fries and two Cokes," said Maggie.

He scribbled their order. "How do you want that?" he asked.

"Take the bawl out of it," Ivy replied.

He took the order to the kitchen.

"When's the last time he went to the dentist?" Maggie said.

"Lukie doesn't believe in spending his money there. When he's got a toothache, he goes across the street to the barbershop. Roscoe pulls it, then he epoxies the tooth back in."

"Very few have that kind of talent with epoxy," Maggie said. "You know, maybe it was just some crank who broke in."

"Use your head for something besides a hat rack." Ivy rapped her knuckles on her creased temple. "Cranks write letters to the editor."

"What about the police? Can they handle it?"

"The police in this town can't catch a cold." Ivy drained her Coke glass. "Besides, you never know who they're working for." She stared at the back of the bar. "What do you know. There's Roger Dawson in the back booth. What's he doing with that Texan?"

Maggie swiveled her head. Roger's lunch partner happened to be Randy Bradford. "Why don't you go investigate?"

"Why don't you, Maggie?"

"All right. I will." She slid out of the booth and walked to the back of the saloon. The eyes of the men at the bar followed her. She didn't appreciate all the attention. Hadn't they ever seen a woman in jeans that fit?

Roger was drawing a long sip of Coors as he listened to the young Texan. As she approached their booth, Randy stopped talking and they both looked up at her. "Hi, Roger." She felt a tug as she looked into his face, as familiar as her own reflection. Yet this man was a stranger hunkered over a bottle in a bar that smelled of stale beer, cigarette smoke, and overheated frying grease. She acknowledged his partner. "How are you."

"Hi, Maggie," he replied. "What's going on?"

"Stopped by with Ivy to grab a bite." She made no move to leave.

"Maggie, this is Randy Bradford, from Houston. Randy, Maggie Chilton."

"I've already had the pleasure," she said. She extended her hand in Randy's direction. In this setting, he no longer looked so young or so green. In Old West terms, he looked more like the out-of-town stranger who'd ridden in for the big backroom poker game.

"Good to see you again, Maggie." He gave her one of his lop-sided smiles. "Roger and I were just talking a little bidness. Care to join us?"

She indicated her booth with Ivy. "'Fraid not. I already have a date. Roger, can I talk to you for a minute?"

The two men exchanged a look. "Sure, Maggie." He got up. "Excuse me Randy. I'll be right back." As Willie Nelson sang, he followed her down the hallway to the corner illuminated by a low-wattage light bulb over the pay phone.

"What is it, Maggie?" As the kitchen door swung open, he stepped toward her, closer than he needed to avoid getting hit. She felt his heat, or maybe it was her own temperature rising. The clatter of dishes and background chatter dimmed. Meanwhile, the words of a bittersweet love song they both knew well floated between them.

"You Were Always on My Mind" was playing on the radio back when she'd had such a terrible crush on Roger, even before they started going together. Listening to it then had made her lonelier for him. She placed her palm against the rough cement block wall and took a deep breath. "Did you hear about the break-in at the *Independent* office?"

"I didn't know. Been in a meeting all morning." He shook his head. "That's awful. A break-in right on Main Street. We can't be allowing that. Ivy didn't get hurt, did she?"

"She's pretty shaken up. Roger, somebody trashed the place."

He placed a hand on her arm and held it there. "I promise you we'll get right on it. We'll find out what's going on. We'll take care of it." He gave her arm a squeeze. He didn't move his eyes from hers.

She lowered her gaze to the stained gray-brown carpet and spoke too fast. "I hope you'll keep on it. I don't want anything else to happen to the paper. Or to Ivy."

"Want to dance?" he said.

"I thought you were in the middle of a business meeting."

"I was until you showed up."

"What's Bradford doing in town?"

"Thought you'd know by now. The man's got deep pockets. Wants to spread some money around here," he said.

"Why?" she asked.

Roger shrugged. "Guess he thinks he'll make some more. He's representing his family's company, based in Houston. Western Century. Ever hear of them?"

"I know the name. Big-time real estate developers." She glanced away. "I better get back to Ivy."

He stepped in her path. "You're not turning me down, are you Maggie?"

She remembered that lazy smile of his. She returned it with one of her own. "What are you asking for?"

She turned from him before he could answer. "Nice seeing you, Randy," she said as she passed by the booth. "Be careful of that chile. It's a lot hotter than you're used to."

Ivy munched the last of her fries. "That looked pretty cozy. What'd you find out?"

"Nothing much."

"Nothing you're willing to say?"

"Come on, Ivy. You know a lot more about Bradford than I do," Maggie said.

"I know his company hired Floyd Burch as a consultant."

"Didn't Floyd graduate about three years ahead of me?"

"Maybe so. But now he's county commissioner." Ivy seemed to be recovering from the morning's debacle.

"Have you run any stories yet about Mr. Burch's new job?" Maggie asked.

"Only what his wife Darla told Esperanza at the Crowning Glory when she was getting her hair done for a trip to California."

"Did you attribute your source?" Maggie wanted to know.

"What do you think this is, the *New York Times*? I have to live in this town," Ivy exclaimed.

A voice interrupted them. "Hello, ladies. Mind if I join you? My lunch buddy had another appointment."

"Why, hello Roger. Certainly. Please do." Ivy brightened immediately. She slid over to make room. "Sit yourself down."

He removed his hat. "Thank you, ma'am." He displayed the manners of a perfect schoolboy, while under the table the toe of his boot found Maggie's. "I'm sorry to hear you've had some trouble, Ivy. I hope you'll feel free to call on me any time at all."

"That's very kind of you, Roger." Ivy beamed. "We're so fortunate to have you as our mayor. Isn't that so, Maggie?"

"Absolutely," she said. "Really." She gave his boot a light tap. "I mean it."

———

Back at the *Independent* office, Maggie proofread the paper, then handed the pages to Ivy. While Ivy proofed the layouts, Maggie picked up some back issues. She settled down on the sofa. Practically every issue had a story about the municipal improvements sponsored by Mayor Roger Dawson: new streetlights, new trees, a new soccer field.

A loud knock startled her. She looked up and saw Randy Bradford at the front door. She walked over and opened it. "Can I help you?" she asked.

"Mind if I come in for a moment, Maggie?"

"Please do." Her initial gut impression of Randy seemed to be proving out by the moment.

He stepped inside. "Looks like you've had trouble this morning," he said, surveying the disarrayed office.

Maggie stood facing him. "What can I do for you, Randy?"

Ivy walked over and Maggie introduced her. He turned to Ivy. "I was sorry to hear about all this," he said, nodding toward the room. "Mrs. McGrath, my family would be more than pleased to do whatever we can to help. We know how important the *Independent* is to the folks in this community." He reached inside his jacket and withdrew a checkbook. His official gestures clashed with his folksy demeanor.

"We do appreciate the offer, Mr. Bradford," Ivy replied. "You're more than kind. But Maggie's already come to the rescue, and with her help, we can get along quite nicely, thank you."

Randy turned toward Maggie, seeking a second opin-ion. "She's the boss," Maggie said. "Thanks, but we've got it covered."

He shrugged. "Very good, ladies. But here's my card, just in case you change your mind." He handed the card to Maggie. She tucked it in the back pocket of her jeans and walked Randy to the door.

"You know," he said, "there would be opportunities for you with our company, Maggie. And we are interested in your ranch. When can we talk?"

"Must be my lucky day. I'm getting more job offers than I know what to do with today."

"You're obviously a person with a lot of talents, Maggie." He boldly looked her up and down.

"We know all about Texas gentlemen over here, Randy." She folded her arms. "If you'll excuse me, we're pretty busy today."

"Maggie, just hear me out before you toss me out into the cold," he said. "Change is coming, whether you and Ivy like it or not. We want to do what's best for Monte Alto, and that's going to require some acceptance of change. You know the town. You would make an excellent interpreter, explaining things in a way people could understand."

"Thanks for the offer, Randy. But the answer is no." She closed the door and watched him climb into a Range Rover.

Ivy waited for her. "Well, that was interesting," she sniffed. "Thanks for taking charge, my dear."

"You took care of him just fine," Maggie said. "Are you done with that layout?"

"Sure am. And I'm serious about that job offer. How does managing editor sound?"

"I'll think about it. Money's not a problem for the time being. I'm living on savings." Maggie stretched. "We got this place cleaned up all right."

"Can you give me a ride home? On top of everything else, my truck died this morning. I need a new battery."

"Hop in."

Ivy gave Maggie directions to her house on the western edge of town.

"I moved off the ranch when I took over the paper," she said. "Here we are. Come on in for a minute, Maggie. Something I want to give you." Pots of scarlet geraniums crowded the front porch windows of the snug tin-roofed adobe.

Annabelle, Ivy's border collie, her belly distended toward the ground, ran up and barked a greeting. Ivy petted her and tossed her a biscuit. "She'll be having her pups soon," Ivy said.

She bustled about her kitchen, queen of her domain. She put some kindling in the cast-iron Home Comfort and blew on the embers. Warmth, along with the sweet fragrance of piñon, penetrated the chilly kitchen. Maggie heard the clink of glass as her old teacher rummaged in the pantry. She came out holding a Mason jar of white beans the size of shirt buttons. Ivy rattled the jar. The beans glowed like fantastic pearls.

Maggie couldn't take her eyes off the jar. She'd never seen beans so large or lustrous.

"These are my Quarai beans."

"Have you invented a new strain?"

"No dear. I've recovered a very old strain. During the Depression, George had a WPA job excavating that ruin at Quarai. He dug up these beans, and just for fun, he tried to grow them. We've planted them more than fifty seasons now. The same beans the Old Ones grew here five hundred years ago."

"Why are you giving them to me?"

"February's the time to sprout your seeds."

"I can't do planting."

"Why not? If they're tough enough to survive five centuries in a tomb, you're not gonna hurt 'em. They're tasty, hardy. Easiest thing to grow at this altitude."

"Who says I'll be around long enough to grow them?"

"Who says you won't? I say you'll be happy to have a pot of these beans simmering on your stove next winter."

"You know that's not my plan."

Ivy raised her eyebrows. "I didn't know you had a plan."

TEN

Maggie left Ivy and drove into the early dark brought on by the approaching storm. The heater in her pickup rumbled like an old tomcat not at all pleased about being disturbed. By the time she passed the blinking yellow light on Main Street, the road was pasted with snow. Her aged defroster was almost useless. She rolled the window down, but the windshield fogged up anyway. With her sleeve, she swiped the inside of the windshield, only to watch it fog over again. This is just a little squall, she thought. It would stop soon.

But then a cloud ripped open. Snowflakes so large she could see their crystal structure swirled down at her. She'd been taught every snowflake was different, a poetic idea, but one she'd doubted until now. It was wet snow, the kind that made good snowballs, that piled up fast then melted just as fast, the kind that signaled spring was on its way.

She seemed to be heading into the worst of it. No other vehicles were on the road. Whiteout erased familiar landmarks. The drive home from Ivy's was only ten miles. She'd take it at a crawl. It had been a long time since she'd driven in weather like this. It wouldn't take much to veer off the road into a bar ditch.

The storm worsened faster than she would have believed possible. Visibility diminished by the minute. As she downshifted to second, the wheels slipped. She worried that her wipers would freeze, that she didn't have enough weight in the bed.

She thought about getting off the road until the worst had passed. But there was no telling when that would be. Besides, where would she stop? She could turn around and head back to town, but going back was as difficult as keeping on. There was no way she'd chance turning around here, anyway. That's when a sixteen-wheeler would come charging down the road. She just had to keep her foot on the pedal and pay attention.

So she'd managed to get caught in a blizzard. Lucy would be plenty worried by now. Maggie dreaded what her mother would say when she finally showed up. Or what she wouldn't say. She'd wear her patented look of contempt, pursed lips and all: "You of all people should have known better." As Maggie drove through even deeper drifts of snow, she held on to that image of her mother, who would insist she drink a lemony hot toddy and wrap a blanket around her shoulders to keep off a chill, when she finally tramped into the well-lit house, warm with wood fire.

Out of nowhere, an obstacle emerged from the blinding snow. It was a truck, stopped on the road. She hit the brakes hard and her pickup did a ninety-degree spin and swerved into the wrong lane. She gripped the wheel, remembering to turn toward the skid, and missed the truck by inches. As soon as she finished cursing, she started to tremble.

Something was very wrong. No one would leave a pickup parked in the middle of the road like that. Somebody out there was hurt or worse. She pulled off the road and grabbed a flashlight from the glove box. Then she reached again into the compartment and took out her .22 High Standard and placed it in her coat pocket. She slammed the door as she got out, knocking a layer of snow off the pickup's roof.

"Hello?" she called. "Anybody out here?"

Silence answered. All sound was submerged by the deepening white blanket.

She approached the truck. Anyone inside would freeze to death out here tonight. The vehicle looked in too good condition to have been abandoned, but you never knew. Somebody could have been hurt, tried to go for help, and not made it.

The wind gusted and ice crystals whipped her face. She cast a look at the sky swirling down on her, then searched up and down the road with her flashlight beam. Fifteen yards ahead, she made out a dim shape crouched behind the white veil of weather. Whether it was a person or a downed animal, she couldn't say. She had no idea what awaited her as she struggled toward it.

She tried to run, but Tony Lama boots weren't made for this weather. Every step required tremendous effort. Her feet went numb, and she was out of breath. She knew she would quickly become exhausted, that it would be easy to lose direction and be unable to find her way back to her truck. She stumbled on the ice beneath the snow and sank to her knees. Gasping, she shoved herself back onto her feet.

As she approached, she saw a man slumped on the highway. A drift was piling up around him. He was beating his fists into the snow and sobbing next to a ghostly white wooden cross, one of the descansos planted on the side of the road.

The stink of alcohol slapped her face. Falling snow had all but buried the empty pint of whiskey lying next to the homemade shrine.

In a flash, she made the awful recognition. "Roger!" she shouted through the dense falling snow.

He looked up at her, bewildered. "Maggie. What're you doing here?"

She grabbed him by the arm. "This is a hell of a place to come across you!"

He would not, or could not, move.

She strained to lift him to his feet. "Let's go for a ride, cowboy. You look like you could use a cup of coffee."

"What are you doing out in this?" he shouted. He waved an unsteady arm at the sky.

"I sure wasn't looking for you!" She lugged him like a sack of feed back to her truck. Fueled by an overload of adrenaline, she managed to get his weight piled into the front seat. "Where are your keys?"

He fumbled in his pocket and handed them to her. She went over to it and moved it off the road. He could come back for it in the morning.

She got behind the wheel of her own pickup and turned her key in the ignition. The engine roared. "Are you okay?" she asked.

He nodded. "I will be," he said.

The wiper blades squeaked over the frozen windshield. She turned the heater on as high as it would go. His entire body was shaking, from what could be hypothermia. It would be quicker to get him back to town than to the ranch.

"Hey," she said. "Got any feeling in your toes?" She reached over and placed her hand on his shoulder. He trembled under his sheepskin jacket, though the temperature inside the truck was already stifling.

"Where am I taking you?"

"Alamosa and Fourth."

"What happened?" she asked.

"I got caught in the storm. Guess I had one too many."

"It came up pretty fast. What were you doing out there, anyway?"

He didn't answer.

"Never mind," she said. "I guess I can figure it out."

They drove in silence for a while. After creeping around a treacherous curve, she glanced at him.

"It's funny what you remember," he said.

"What are you remembering?"

"What keeps coming back to me are Jesse's habits. Just the little things he did. The ordinary things you hardly notice."

"Like what?"

"How he'd use his spoon to spread peanut butter. The way he slept, with his arms tossed up over his head." He paused. "How he was always ready to be happy. I knew there was something he could teach me about that. I always planned to learn it from him."

"Maybe sometime those memories will come back to you as something sweet."

He shook his head. "I don't imagine that day will ever come."

"They say it does."

"I don't know who 'they' are." He stared straight ahead. "He'll haunt me 'til the day I die. And that's a good thing. Because I don't want to forget a bit of him, no matter how bad it hurts."

By the look of his crimson face, his circulation was returning. He turned to her. "Thanks, Maggie."

"Any time." She patted his hand. "With any luck, we'll have you home in a half-hour." The lights of town appeared, small golden pinpricks glimmering through the snow. "Give me directions," she said.

Fifteen minutes later, she pulled up in front of a neat brick ranch house in the new, suburban-looking part of town. The house spoke of security, of belonging, of a certain kind of acceptable, packaged comfort. It was just the kind of house she and Tommie had in mind when they pictured themselves grown up and married.

Roger quickly pulled himself together. He wasn't as inebriated as he had first appeared. She'd seen plenty of worse cases at happy hour in the bar across the street from the paper. He unlocked the front door and flicked a switch. Lights in shiny brass fixtures came on. Maggie and Roger peeled off their sopping coats and boots and left them to dry in the entryway. Every piece of furniture looked brand new. A contemporary dining room set, including a backlit knickknack cabinet and glass-topped table, sat on a beige wall-to-wall carpet. The living room was decorated in generic Southwest style, with large kokopelli lamps atop end tables that bordered two mauve, rose, blue, and tan Indian-rug-patterned sofas. Framed prints of R. C. Gorman's Navajo women and Georgia O'Keeffe's hollyhocks hung on the walls. Not a speck of dust lay anywhere; not a scrap of paper was out of place. The house was frighteningly neat, as though no one lived here. The kitchen was well equipped with microwave oven and dishwasher. Cooking gadgets that looked brand new lined the glossy ceramic tile shelves like a small army of apprentices awaiting orders.

Maggie put the copper kettle on to boil. She spooned instant coffee into two large mugs, one with Van Gogh sunflowers on the side, the other with Degas dancers. She filled them with boiling water. "Here. Drink this." She put the mug down in front of Roger, who sat with his elbows folded on the dining nook table. "It'll thaw you out."

"I'm already thawing. My fingers are coming back to life." He rubbed his hands together. "I owe you one," he said. Returned to his own house, he quickly regained his composure.

"I'm sure I'll get my chance to collect." Maggie gazed into the back yard. "This snow's coming down so hard, I don't know how I'll get home."

"You can stay in the guest room."

She shook her head. "Momma will worry."

He pointed to the telephone. "Call her."

"And tell her I'm spending the night at your place? That's a good one." She inspected the tired, windburned face of the man sitting across from her. "Feeling better?"

He rubbed his eyes. "Not really, but kind of," he replied.

"You'll want some aspirin. And be sure to drink lots of water." Listen to her. Nurse Maggie here.

"If you hadn't come along, I'd still be out there howling at the wind," Roger said.

"You've got reason to howl." She spun the salt shaker shaped like a strawberry. "But if you ever pull a stunt like this again, I swear I may just leave you out there!"

White crystals fell on the table. She threw a pinch of spilled salt over her shoulder. She remembered the shaker from the years it sat on Jesusita's green formica table. She held it in her hand, feeling its familiar curves. The kitchen it came from, where she and Tommie had played Chinese checkers and made pâpier maché masks had always smelled wonderful: warm, appetizing, friendly, ancient. Jesusita's pots and piles of dried herbs were arrayed everywhere.

"Tell me something, Roger."

"Anything." He waved his arms open.

"What are you and Randy cooking up together?"

"Hey, Maggie, I thought he was a friend of yours."

"Don't know where you got that idea." She stood and paced the kitchen. "Why is he so interested in Monte Alto? What do you know about him, really? He comes in here with a big bankroll and right away he's buying up every piece of land he can convince someone to sell him. What's his game?"

"Honey, don't you know progress when you see it? It's the American way. It's what folks call 'doin' bidness.'"

"Don't evade me, darlin'," she drawled. "You know more than you're saying."

"Go easy on me, Maggie." He put his hands out in defense. "I know how tough you can be."

"So why is Randy so interested in our little outpost?"

"Since when are you so interested in local affairs?" he shot back.

"Since I got back and had a chance to look around." She twisted the silver and turquoise bracelet on her wrist.

"That's real nice. And where were you for the past twenty years?"

"You know where I was," she said, straightening her back. "It's no secret."

He stood over her. "You hightailed it out of here faster than a roadrunner. We stuck around. We tried to keep the town breathing. Most of the time we had to give artificial respiration. We're still waiting to see if it's going to live!

"Where were you all those days when the wind tried to blow us to Texas? You had your opportunities. You took 'em. You didn't look back. You didn't spend your time in California worrying about us back here. You went after the big stories. You hung around the important people."

He sat across from her, his fists clenched on the table. "So don't think you can strut back in here and tell us how to run Monte Alto. You haven't paid your dues, Maggie. You may think you're a local, but what you are is a California local."

His voice became calm, but anger sharpened the planes of his face. "Have we become quaint to you? Do you want to preserve us, get us designated a historic landmark, put up plaques on our beautiful empty buildings? I want to keep us from becoming another mystery to keep the archaeologists employed. If Randy Bradford and his Western Century have the dollars to invest, I say fine. And what's more, there's a few people in town who happen to agree with me."

Exhaustion suddenly caught up with him. His words slowed. "You haven't got a clue about what it's like trying to keep a business going in this ghost town. Randy is the best thing that ever happened to this place. His Casas Encantadas is the only development we've had in fifty years, not counting prairie dog villages. I'm happy to work with him any way I can."

"You left out one thing, Roger," she said.

"What's that?"

"Where's the water for your development supposed to come from?"

He exploded. "Don't tell me you've turned out like one of those know-it-all environmentalists who sit in their offices in Santa Fe and Washington, D.C., and tell us how to live!" He slammed his hand on the table. "We've got plenty of water. I can show you the hydrologists' report, if you're interested."

She answered him. "When the Bradfords of the world talk about 'progress,' they mean greed. They take what they want, including their big tax breaks, and then they disappear, leaving their mess behind for other people to deal with." Maggie stood. "The snow ought to be letting up soon. Maybe I can make it home now."

He looked out the window. "It's not letting up. It's getting worse. Every road from here to Tucumcari is ice by now. Stay here tonight. Everything you need is in the guest room. Plenty of blankets, reading lamp, everything. Nobody's going to bother you, if that's what you're thinking."

She hesitated. "I don't think I can stay."

He took her hand. "I'm asking you to do this one thing for me: Don't make me worry about you out on that road alone tonight."

He was right about the road. After her experience this evening, she had no desire to challenge those icy stretches again. Outside, the snow was still falling thick and fast. You couldn't see a pair of taillights if they were under your nose. "I'll call Momma."

He handed her the phone and left the room. She made her call. Roger returned with a pile of fresh towels. "New toothbrush, shampoo, everything is in the bathroom," he said. "Goodnight, Maggie." He kissed her chastely on the forehead. "Sleep well."

She went to the chilly, unused room and closed the door. She was wired; she had no idea how she'd ever get to sleep here. She worried someone would see her truck parked outside. She pulled on a pair of gray sweats and cotton socks she found in the bureau.

She padded to the bookcase and looked over the titles. She found a volume in maroon leatherette that she knew well—*The Bobcat*. She pulled it out now, their old high school yearbook. Sitting on the edge of the bed, she leafed through the pages. She studied the black-and-white photos. Had these children ever been as innocent as they looked? She found what she hadn't realized she was hunting for: the full-page shot of her and Roger holding hands as king and queen of the Pumpkin Festival their senior year. How perfectly matched they appeared, both tall, dark and slender, with shy but proud smiles on their open faces. They had been so young. How could they even have begun to handle the profound emotions they ignited in each other? She fingered the glossy page as if the pictures of who they had been could explain who they had become.

She replaced the yearbook in its slot on the shelf. She pulled the blankets up around her and settled in. She fell asleep immediately.

She woke early, not truly rested but unable to go back to sleep.

Sun streamed out of a dazzling sky onto a frozen white world. Still in her sweats, she went into the kitchen to make coffee. She found the jar of instant crystals, filled the kettle, and turned on the gas. She reached into the cabinet and pulled out two mugs. When the kettle whistled, she heaped a teaspoon of coffee in each mug and poured hot water. She heard footsteps.

As she stirred the coffee, she turned her head. He stood in the doorway, barefoot. He was unshaven, and his eyes shone with the deep blue light of the sky after a storm has passed. He wore his jeans like they'd been invented for him, and his white tee shirt stretched tight over his shoulder muscles.

"Good morning," she chattered, looking away. "How did you sleep? I slept fine. You drink your coffee black?" She dropped a spoon. It clattered to the floor. "Oops," she said.

She picked up the spoon and stirred. Hot coffee splashed onto the counter. "What is wrong with me?" she asked. "Just can't seem to get it right today."

He didn't answer. Rather, he crossed the room and stood directly behind her. He put his hands on her shoulders and turned her toward him. Then he dropped his arms to his sides and studied her, waiting, watching her gravely.

He always made her come to him. He never pushed her, never had to ask. He knew he only had to wait. With patience he aroused in her a longing so deep, so intense that she had to move toward him.

With a cry, she wrapped her arms around him. She clung tightly to him as long-buried memories of the most sensual moments she had ever known surged through her. His touch and his kiss had erased all fear and shame. The purity of their connection, so simply and obviously right, had set her free.

She tilted her face up to his. When she kissed him, his lips remained cool, unmoving. He waited to receive her passion before he began to respond. At first he returned her kiss with a gentle acknowledgement; after a moment, he joined her explorations with his own. In the space of their kiss, a new bloom emerged from her heart. When he slipped his hand under her sweatshirt and slowly caressed her bare back, the contact provided pleasure so fierce it turned to pain before flashing back to pleasure once again.

"Come with me," he said.

She took the hand he offered. He guided her down the hall. They entered his bedroom. He kicked the door shut.

His and Tommie's bedroom.

Orange and brown plaid curtains kept the roost in darkness. The bed faced a TV parked on a utility cart; the remote control sat on his night table. The room felt isolated from the rest of the house, as well as from the rest of the world. Whatever it had been, it was now a distinctly male chamber, with a deer head mounted on the wall. Empty beer cans filled the wastebasket to overflowing. An entire corner was dedicated to his dirty laundry. The room existed to serve a purely utilitarian purpose, not because of any comfort or pleasure spending time there might bring.

The reality of *his bed*, with its tousled blankets and wrinkled sheets, stopped her in her tracks. He felt her tense. "What is it?" he said.

"Nothing." She sat on the edge of the unmade bed.

"Can I get you anything?" he asked.

"No thank you."

He pulled her to her feet. He placed his hands on her shoulders, drew her to him, and kissed her deeply. She responded by wrapping her arms tightly around him.

"Wait here," he said.

He left the room. A drawer closed. A cabinet door slammed. "Goddamn it!" he cursed. He stalked back into the room and rummaged in his top dresser drawer. Not finding what he wanted, he pulled the drawer out and turned it upside down. "Do you have anything with you?" he asked.

She shook her head. "No. I never dreamed I'd need anything."

"Do you take anything? Are you . . . "

"On the pill? No."

"Lord almighty." He looked at her. "Will you wait here while I go out for something?"

She took his arm. "Don't go."

"What are you saying? We have to use something."

She folded her arms across her breasts. "I know."

"Lie down with me, Maggie. Let me touch you."

She remembered their years of touching, of torture. Her obsession with his touch had consumed years of her life. Long after their relationship ended, she remained marked by it, branded by him.

"I don't want it to be that way," she said. She walked into the kitchen, picked up her coat and put it on. "What the hell am I doing here, anyway?"

"Where are you going?" he called.

"I need to get home. This was a big mistake."

He walked out of the bedroom toward her, his face a dark mask. "You're leaving? What kind of a tease are you?"

It occurred to her that he might hit her.

"I'm sorry. I really am. I didn't mean for any of this to happen."

He waved her off. "I don't want to hear any more. Just go if you're going."

He sat at the kitchen table, still and pale as a statue, surrounded by the pristine surfaces of his perfect kitchen and the appliances that looked as though they'd just been taken out of the box. Locked gates covered his dark blue eyes. He had shut her out.

Now she remembered the way he'd withdraw into himself. She had never been able to deal with his sudden coldness, his impenetrable anger. He would retreat to his solitary, unapproachable mountaintop, and he hadn't changed. When he was up there, anything she said sounded ridiculous; he made her feel helpless. Whenever he got that way, she'd felt like the world was coming to an end.

She turned and walked to the door. Her hand gripped the cold brass doorknob. She faced the door. If she walked out now, they might never speak again. Every time they passed on the street, they would wave hello, and that would be that. And every time it would hurt. She whirled around. "No, dammit!" she said. "I'm not walking out of here and leaving you like this."

"Why not, Maggie?" came his cold reply. "It wouldn't be the first time."

"It's not something a friend would do."

"So whose friend are you?" he asked. "Not mine."

"How do you know? You won't even give me a chance."

He laughed bitterly. "A chance to do what? Amuse yourself while you're stuck out in the boondocks? It'd sure make a nice story to laugh about with your San Francisco friends over a glass of good California Chardonnay, wouldn't it?"

She shook her head. "You've got it all wrong."

"I don't think so," he said. "You walked out on Monte Alto, and you walked out on me. You did it then, and you're doing it now."

"How can you say that? You left me for my best friend." Anger edged into her voice. "You showed me how low someone can go."

"And you still think that your going off to Berkeley had nothing to do with that? Everything that happened was because of the choices you made." He thumped the table with his fist.

"It was not! And I didn't notice anybody try to stop me!" Her old, painful anger spilled out. He would never know what their breakup had cost her. No one would.

He folded his arms and leaned back in his chair. "So you would have stayed here? Given up that scholarship and everything that went with it?"

"People do stay faithful through separations, Roger. We had an agreement, remember? When I came home at Thanksgiving, I found out how much our agreement meant to you."

"Sure I was lonely. Who wouldn't be? Anyway, I knew you'd be out the door with the first English major in a tweed jacket who called you for a date. He'd look a lot better to you than I did, Maggie. You'd drop me like a bad habit." He set his hands flat on the table. "And you know what? Nothing's changed."

His age and his disappointments settled over his face. She wanted to look away. The boy she had loved was gone for good.

"I'm still not going anywhere," he said. "And you are." His voice was barely audible. "This is my home. I'm not giving up on it, even if I'm the last one left and I have to turn out the lights and lock the door. This is where my son is buried. And my grandparents."

"So are mine. It's my home too."

He looked up at her. "In your sentimental moments, maybe. When you pick that glass paperweight up off your desk and shake it and watch the snowflakes fall over the little village inside, you can think about how pretty it'd be to live in a small town and wonder what's become of the folks you used to know. Maybe you'd even find time to come back for the high school reunion every ten years."

She looked down at the floor.

"Hey, Maggie. It's okay. It's not your fault. You needed something else. You were, and you are, entirely too bright, too beautiful, too ambitious for this place. You'd have been miserable penned up here."

She bent and kissed the top of his head. "Goodbye, Roger."

He looked as though he'd stay locked up here alone with his demons forever. "'Bye, Maggie. Take care out there."

"You too." She walked to the door and closed it behind her.

ELEVEN

THE ROAD HOME DEMANDED MAGGIE'S complete attention. A layer of ice sheathed the asphalt beneath the hard-packed snow. She gripped the wheel and followed a narrow tunnel plowed through four-foot drifts piled on either side of the highway. The blinding whiteness made a twenty-minute drive an hour long.

She remembered returning home like this years ago, after a night with Roger. She'd supposedly been spending the night at a sleepover party with some girlfriends. The roads weren't quite as bad then, or maybe she just hadn't paid them as much attention. Her mind had been elsewhere. He had told her he loved her. He loved her! She would have gladly done anything he asked. But no. They would wait.

She had no idea how, but her mother had uncovered her alibi." Where have you been?" Lucy wanted to know when she walked in.

She pulled off her boots. "At Brenda's," she said. "You know that."

Lucy stood above her, arms folded. "Don't lie to me," her mother said. "How dare you." Lucy pulled her up by the arms and stood inches away. She slapped Maggie so hard she knocked her to the floor. On the way down, Maggie hit her head on a kitchen chair. "I'm not raising any tramp," Lucy spat. "Don't expect to go out, get yourself pregnant, and leave your troubles on my doorstep. Don't you know by now that men only want one thing? You're not to go anywhere without my permission from now on." Maggie withstood her mother's shaming curses with a stoic expression. She held in her tears, then ran to the bathroom and threw up.

That had been the closest her mother had ever come to explaining what in those days were known as the facts of life. Maggie had been grounded indefinitely, and it was just as well, because she didn't want to have to explain her bruised face. During that time, she spoke to her mother only when absolutely necessary, answering with a "yes ma'am" or "no ma'am," only when she was spoken to. By the time her face healed, the distance between Maggie and her mother had become hard and permanent. She swore she'd never again allow her mother to come near her, and she'd kept her vow all this time.

After inching her way, she finally reached the ranch driveway. She turned in, but the pickup couldn't make it any farther than the cattle guard. She got out and hiked the rest of the way.

Only a curl of smoke from the chimney indicated the isolated house was occupied. Maggie stomped the ice from her boots. Aromas of toast and bacon greeted her. She was hungry after her long cold trek. "Good morning, Momma."

Lucy, a dwarf in a man's plaid robe, turned from the stove. "Well there you are." Her mother's face seemed drawn and pale.

"How'd you sleep, Momma?" Maggie asked as she tugged off her iced-up boots.

Single-handed, Lucy cracked an egg on the side of the pan and dropped it into the sputtering bacon grease. "All right, I guess. Slept better toward morning." The egg sizzled. "How many do you want?"

Maggie took a seat at the kitchen table. "Two, please." She pulled off her damp socks and set them on the cracked linoleum alongside her boots.

Lucy lifted the eggs from the pan with a spatula. "Ivy called. She wanted to see if you'd gotten home all right."

"When did she call?"

"Last night." Walking unsteadily, Lucy set the platter of fried eggs and bacon down on the table. "About an hour before you did." She sat down hard, and the chair received her with a squawk.

Maggie dipped a knife into the jar of gleaming crimson preserves. She changed the subject. "Did you make this?"

"That's my chokecherry jelly," Lucy said. "From the last batch I put up, two summers ago."

"It's delicious. Not too sweet."

"It was always your favorite." Lucy brightened. "That's your grandmother's recipe. Pure chokecherry."

Maggie swallowed her toast. She reached across the table. She clasped Lucy's hand as though it were a folded paper bird. "I didn't want to worry you. You know what it was like out there. Turned out the best thing was to stay in town."

Her mother sighed. "People will talk, Maggie."

"They always did." She took a sip of coffee. "Does it bother you?"

"It's not me I worry about."

"I can take care of myself."

"I hope so." She passed a hand across her pale marble eyes. "Even if I knew what's right for you, I couldn't tell you what to do. Never could. Not gonna start now."

"Thank you, Momma. I love you."

"I love you, Maggie. You're a good girl."

"Thanks for breakfast." She finished her breakfast and stood. "I better get that snow shoveled before it freezes up. The radio said there's another storm coming in."

Outside, Maggie cleared a path around the house. She cleaned off the driveway, working until the muscles of her arms ached and she was soaked under her jacket. She wanted the rhythm of the shovel, the weight of the snow, the blinding sunlight. She wanted to breathe the frigid air and exhale white clouds. She wanted to keep watching the hawk that soared above her in a sky too vividly blue for any photograph or painting to ever capture, too blue for anyone who lived anyplace else to believe. She just didn't want to think about what had happened this morning.

This will all pass, she told herself. Next week, in a few days, even by tomorrow, it won't seem so awful. One thing she knew: she had to stay away from Roger. And if that was impossible in this small town, she'd make sure she was never alone with him. Roger just opened up too many doors she'd rather leave closed.

The path she dug ended at the door of the one building on the ranch she hadn't yet entered—Elias's bunkhouse. She propped the shovel against the side of the low wooden structure. Then she unfastened the padlock. The hinge creaked when she pushed the door open.

She struck a match and lit the kerosene lamp. Everything remained exactly as she remembered. Lamplight flickered over a room as plain and carefully ordered as a monk's cell. For all the years he'd lived out here, Elias hadn't accumulated any more possessions than he could pack in a duffle bag.

All she knew of male kindness, he had taught her. He had always shown her patience, and she had never heard him say a cruel, angry, or harsh word in her presence.

She sat on Elias's narrow bed and rubbed her hands over the rough brown woolen blanket, and it seemed she caught a whiff of his pipe tobacco. When she picked up the worn Bible on the nightstand, yellowed pages of Spanish script came loose from the binding and fluttered to the floor. An ancient carved santo, crude and magnificent, gazed down with eyes of undying faith. Elias's five big Dutch ovens rested on shelves he had built. On hooks made of rusty horseshoes hung his stirring spoons, his *gancho*, the running branding iron he used to lift the lids, his singed potholders. Out of the flickering shadows came the accents of his voice.

When I come home after the war, nobody was left over at Abo sheep camp. All I had was my bedroll and my father's Dutch ovens. He used to cook for the sheep camps, so that's how I learned.

Sure, I got hurt pretty bad over there at Bataan. Lotta guys from New Mexico, you know, all over, Deming, Santa Fe, they never come back. They say half of us never came back. After they took us on that death march, I couldn't work all day like I used to. But I could still break a horse and train him. And I could still cook. Your grandfather, he found me a place on this outfit.

Maggie ran her hand over a cast-iron kettle, a polished onyx mirror of the past. She saw Elias, a compact man, his face full of weather, buttoned up in his plaid jacket. Again she heard the gravel rolling in his voice. She listened hard and picked up his words blowing in the winter wind.

Watch now, mi'jita. This is how you build the fire. First, you take your cedar. Cedar is good, it burns hot and clean.
You put it on the ground here. Your pieces of tin, they go on the sides, so you keep your fire where it belongs. You got to know fire. You got to be able to make a fire anywhere. You wait for your coals, then you put your grill over them. You get the coffee going first. Then you put your beans on. Your chile goes in the next pot. Then your rice goes in over here. You make sure the lid is on tight over your biscuits, then you shovel your coals on top to bake. You can cook anything like this.

You know how to fix arroz con pollo? First you brown the rice with a little oil, then you add your chopped garlic and onions. When that's all browned, you put in your chicken, add a can of tomato juice, with a can of water; half a cup of chopped green chile, two spoons of red chile, a spoon of comino. Then you simmer it 'til it's done. When the rice is all cooked, you move it to the edge of the fire to keep it warm. Food stays hot a long time in these Dutch ovens. Those cowboys, they always say everything tastes better with a little wood smoke.

See those cowboys over in the corral? They've finished up branding now. They smell that coffee. In a minute they'll ride in, and we'll be all ready for them with dinner.

Had she ever known a more satisfying moment than helping him feed those cowboys dinner right off the fire, listening to the melodies of their laughter and their jingling spurs? When they had eaten their fill, after piling their plates high two and three times, they'd lean up against the truck, to roll their cigarettes and smoke out of the wind. Then, as they poked fun at each other and recounted the hard and good times of the morning, Elias sent her around with the big pot to pour a little more coffee into their blue speckleware mugs.

As much as she yearned to bring back that time, they were all gone now. The corral was as deserted and silent as Elias's bunkhouse. Only her memories lived. They were like bright cholla blossoms that occasionally surprised the dry, prickly plant that bore them.

Do you remember, Margarita, how I'd come for you mornings and put you up in the saddle with me? I thought I'd teach you to ride, but it's like you already knew. Nothing scared you. You understood a horse better than anybody, man or woman. I never worried about you, because anybody could see. When you walked into the corral, those horses, they had respect. You had that from the time you could pull on your own boots.

Just remember, 'jita, the first thing you gotta do is keep those horses alive. They're depending on you.

As the santo watched, Maggie bowed her head. Elias. Forgive me. I didn't mean to forget.

Exhausted, she lay back on the narrow bed and drew the brown woolen blanket around herself. When she opened her eyes, Maggie didn't know how long she had slept. Late afternoon shadows darkened the bunkhouse. She stretched and stood, then picked up the fallen pages of the Bible from the floor. An envelope had slipped out, too, the ink faded to light blue. She recognized her mother's handwriting, the flowing script of precisely taught penmanship. She slipped thin sheets out of the envelope. Unfolding them, she smoothed the creases and held the pages to the light of the lamp:

April 23, 1956
Dear Elias,
I was so surprised by what happened last night. I too care

for you. You are such a fine man. In all this time, I have come to see that more and more. I can never thank you enough for all you have done for me and Maggie. But what happened last night can never happen again. I am not sorry it happened. I guess it had to.

I won't blame you if you have to go. I don't know how we will manage if you do. I hope you'll stay and we can go on as we were. We don't need to mention this ever again.

Lucy

Maggie sat down hard on the bed. Her heart beat rapidly as she struggled to understand. Questions zigzagged through her mind. Her mother and Elias? She thought she knew them, but she didn't have a clue. Elias had loved her mother. But why had she turned him down? Was Lucy afraid what people would say about a woman who took up with the hired hand, worried how they might treat the daughter of such a family? What was the truth here? What had actually gone on between them, what secret gazes, whispers, smiles had they exchanged, in the barn at dawn, in the kitchen, over her head, invisible to a child?

Maggie refolded the letter. How sad that those two, such good partners, lived their lives separately when they could have chosen to be together. She ran her fingers over the edges of the fragile envelope. She wondered how many times it had been opened and reread, then folded up again and put away. Lucy had set the rules, and Elias had followed them, however much he might have wanted to try again. He knew Lucy would banish him from the ranch in a minute no matter how much she needed his help if he did.

Carefully, she placed the envelope back in the Bible. She would never ask, and her mother would never tell her any more than Maggie knew at this moment, but she would wish to know with all her being, for she loved them both. She wished they could have done the same for each other. It just seemed fair, the right thing. She blew out the lamp then latched the bunkhouse door. Time to get back to the house and get supper going.

TWELVE ~

A BRIGHT THREE-QUARTER MOON lit Maggie's way. As the evening star shimmered in the below-zero stillness, the pure cold cast a radiance over the whitened landscape. At this hour, the land was a contrast of shadow and revelation. The cold sharpened her senses to a fine edge, amplifying sound and scent. Up ahead, the house was dark. A thin plume of smoke curled from the chimney.

Although she felt alone, Maggie was not the only creature about. Diminutive tracks of raccoon crossed her path. The bark of a coyote triggered the pack's yipping chorus. The hair on the back of her neck shot up in response to the piercing voices ascending the scale of wildness. Owl and coyote, night hunters, populated the darkness; meanwhile, their prey, nimble mice and rabbit, fled to the shadows. Life-and-death, hunt-or-be-hunted drama played out in the tangles of fallen limbs, behind the pillars of tree stumps and beneath rocks.

How quickly the clamor of the city faded. Images of Ramona, of their time together in the shelter and that final scene in the ambulance no longer obsessed her waking hours. Maggie had pretty much given up thinking she could have done it any other way. She believed in the story and she told it as truly as she could. She mourned the loss of her friend and always would, but she didn't blame herself quite as harshly for Ramona's murder.

Empty quiet spaces had replaced constant noise and rushing crowds, as the expanses of sky and land meshed with the contours of her heart. The raw beauty of the land living for its own purpose seemed, at this moment, sufficient. She stood still and allowed herself the solace of this place.

She sensed the flutter of wings and whirled. What, or who, was out there? *Daddy?* If he *had* been there, he was gone now. She saw only her own footprints disappearing into the darkness. Suddenly tired, she returned slowly to the house.

Back in the kitchen, Maggie threw a log in the woodstove and blew on the smoking embers until they burst into flame. "Momma?" she called. "What do you feel like for supper? How about spaghetti and meatballs?"

When she got no answer, she walked down the quiet hall toward her mother's bedroom. She knocked. "Momma? Are you asleep?" She opened the door. Lucy lay in bed slumped on her side, her arm flung over the side of the bed at a peculiar angle. Maggie's heartbeat thumped, and she froze in her tracks.

"My God!" she cried. Adrenaline—liquid fear—shot through her veins. She bent over her mother. "Momma! What is it? What's happened?" she shouted.

Her mother's body was limp. Maggie took her hand. Still warm. She held her wrist and checked for a pulse. Lucy's heart was still beating. She was sure of it. She ran to the phone. Her hands shook as she dialed 911.

While waiting for the emergency crew to arrive, Maggie covered her mother with a faded quilt from the pile on the bed. She had no idea how long she sat on the floor with her mother's head cradled in her lap, incoherent prayers tumbling from her lips. *I'm sorry... please... forgive me... come back... get well.* When she heard a distant siren, she got up and threw a jumble of Lucy's things with her own into an overnight bag.

Finally, the ambulance turned into the driveway. Two broad-shouldered young fellows, wearing only tee shirts and jeans on this freezing night, and who didn't look old enough to have their drivers' licenses, lifted Lucy onto a stretcher.

Maggie turned out the lights and locked the door. She climbed into the pickup and floorboarded it, passing other cars recklessly as she followed the flashing red lights down the road through town and to the interstate. She took the sixty miles up I-25 to Albuquerque as fast as the old beater would go. At St. Joseph's Hospital, she found a parking space at the far end of the crowded lot. The stars had vanished. Halos of street lights shone into the smoky city night. She ran for the emergency room entrance.

A square-shouldered nurse, an African-American woman in a green jumpsuit and tinted glasses, sat behind the reception desk. "May I help you?" she asked Maggie.

"I'm trying to locate Mrs. Lucy Chilton. My mother."

The nurse, according to her name tag, was Coralee Davis, R.N. She rustled through several clipboards. "Oh yes. She's being examined now. Her condition is stable."

"May I see her?" Maggie hated the impatience in her voice, but she couldn't stop herself from showing a nervous, overbearing attitude.

"Not just yet. We'll let you know when they finish admitting her. Please have a seat in the waiting area." The nurse gave Maggie a hard stare. Her severe tone of voice forbade argument or hysteria.

Maggie backed away. The one thing she couldn't tolerate was

sitting still. She paced, and time lost its familiar movement. The longer she waited, the angrier she became. She wanted to explode at someone, or at least kick the wall.

When daylight brightened the windows, she had no additional information on Lucy's condition. Whenever she'd approached Coralee Davis, R.N., she'd been put back in her place: "We'll let you know as soon as we find out. We're doing everything we can for your mother. We need you to sign these papers."

Tattered magazines, Styrofoam cups, crumpled candy wrappers—the ruins of the night littered the lounge. Sprawled on leatherette sofas, the exhausted relatives of other patients snapped to attention each time a doctor or nurse walked through the swinging doors of the ICU.

At last Maggie dozed, to be startled almost immediately awake when a doctor in surgical green called her name. "Your mother has had a stroke," Andrew Zelnick, M.D., told her. "Her right side is paralyzed. We're trying to reverse it."

Lucy, paralyzed? He had no idea what he was saying.

"Is my mother dying?" she wanted to know.

The neurologist seemed not to hear her question, but continued his explanation, which sounded rehearsed. "The first forty-eight hours are most critical. That's when we watch for a re-bleed. The more quickly we can get her responding, the better her chances at recovery."

Dizziness overcame her. Dr. Zelnick grabbed a hard plastic chair and placed it behind her to catch her before she fell. "Lean over and put your head between your knees," he said. "You'll be all right in a minute."

She did as he said. She closed her eyes. Tiny blue stars orbited the darkness. The dizziness passed, and she sat up. Fluorescent light burned her eyes. She had to get out.

The lobby now buzzed with activity. Visitors entered the

doors carrying bouquets. She pushed open the front door. Cold air slapped her awake. She pulled out of the parking lot and drove through the downtown Albuquerque neighborhood. Street people pushed shopping carts loaded with their possessions. Above, lights from old Albuquerque High, long a deserted hiding place for vandals, beamed with newfound prosperity. The building had been renovated and turned into a chic place to live, offering loft spaces and apartments.

A few small businesses—a dry cleaner, a bakery—had opened their doors. The neighborhood had hopes for a revival, but it had a long way to go. She turned the corner and drove past UNM on Central Avenue and past run-down motels with their neon cacti and lariats left over from Route 66 days. Finally she found a somewhat decent-looking motel. Best Western, she figured, would be a good bet.

Maggie checked in. She ran the shower until the bathroom steamed. Then she stripped off her clothes and got in. She stood under the hot spray until her muscles began to revive. A good hot shower, she believed, could almost substitute for a night's sleep. She rubbed herself down with the skimpy towels. Then she took the luxury of smoothing aloe lotion over her dry skin. Clean clothes did wonders, as did a little bit of makeup, mascara and plum lipstick. She called the hospital to see if there had been any change in Lucy's condition. There hadn't. At the Village Inn on Central, she ate breakfast and ran her eyes over the paper, then returned to the hospital to wait some more.

At 10:30 A.M. they finally came for her. She heard her name and went limp with relief: now at least she would know *something*. She followed a pink-shirted nurse down the hall into the ICU. The nurse left her at the door. The stroke had transformed her mother into a mummy attached to the twenty-first century by slender plastic tubes.

Electric red lines monitored her heartbeat and a respirator amplified the strain of her breathing.

She leaned close to her mother's face and whispered, "I want you and me and Hannah to be together again. Come home." The nurse touched Maggie's shoulder and led her out the door of the ICU. Maggie returned to the waiting room. She lay down on the green couch, curled up, and fell asleep.

At 1:30, Coralee Davis stepped through the doors. Didn't the woman ever go home? "Maggie Chilton?"

"Yes."

"The doctor would like to speak with you."

"Dr. Zelnick?

"I believe so."

"What is it?" Maggie bit off her words and spat them out.

"If you will just be patient. The doctor will be here in a moment. He's very busy."

Maggie could have punched the woman. "Why can't I get some straight answers around here?"

Just then another nurse wearing surgical greens marched through the swinging doors toward them. Her energy immediately brought everyone to attention.

"What's going on here?" she asked. Her voice, though calm, demanded an answer.

As she approached, the tag above her uniform pocket became a legible name: Tomasita Herrera, R.N.

Maggie froze. "Tommie?" She took in the dark wavy hair, the rose-olive skin, the sensitive line of her mouth. With time, Tommie had become more boldly and more vividly herself.

"Yes, Maggie," Tommie said. "This is where you find me." Her body seemed animated even when still. She radiated heat; her presence was the most solid and alive element in the room. Breathless, Maggie reached for the arm she extended. "My mother. Tell me."

"When I saw Lucy's name on the admitting list this morning, I came over as soon as I could. She's holding steady. Her heart is strong; her breathing regular."

"And?"

"With therapy, she could recover some function. Maybe most. But a lot of her recovery will depend on how hard she wants to work at it." She delivered the news in her well-trained, deepened, professional voice. "For now, most of the use of her right side is gone. The part of her brain that controls it has been knocked out."

"So she's going to make it."

Tommie hesitated. Again she studied the chart on her clipboard.

Maggie grabbed Tommie's wrist. "Please."

"She's going to make it, Maggie. The doctor says she can go home by the end of the week."

Maggie covered her eyes with her hand. "Thank you," she whispered. "I don't know what to do."

Tommie took Maggie's arm and led her to one of the orange vinyl chairs. "Don't expect miracles, 'jita," Tommie said. "When you bring her home, she may not be the same."

"I understand," Maggie said. "And that's all right. So long as she comes home with me."

"It won't be easy, Maggie. You have no idea what you're in for. You may not be able to do much more than watch her go downhill," Tommie spoke softly. "Why don't you sit here and wait to talk to the doctor? He'll be able to answer your questions on exactly the kind of care your mother will be needing."

Maggie sat as she was told. She would wait as long as necessary.

THIRTEEN

EVERY TABLE IN THE DINING ROOM of the Hotel Manzano was draped in white linen cloth. The room was empty except for the Wednesday Club women at a table near the windows.

"I see you brought your Waldorf salad, Elvira," said Ruby Redfearn. She removed the film of plastic wrap from the gilt-edged china dish and gave her salad a stir with an ornate silver serving spoon. The lights in the dining room chandelier flickered as a gust of March wind huffed at the old hotel. It had been more than thirty years since anyone had stayed in the rooms upstairs. Even this dining room, once so grand, was closed now, except for their weekly card games and a few other meetings. The wiry ninety-six-year-old woman sat in a single rigid motion and straightened her bony back, then drew her crocheted yellow shawl around her shoulders.

"And I see you brought your French silk pie," Elvira Orme

replied. She patted her waves of silver hair into their proper place. "That was always the big hit at the CowBelle potlucks." Her friends had always tolerated her vanity. They exchanged looks she pretended not to see whenever she touched up her lipstick at the dining room table the way she did, peering into the knife blade. At ninety-two, her vanity had become an asset.

"We know you gotta get your chocolate fix," Ruby said. "I wish you'd bring your turtle cheesecake, Mercedes." She addressed the woman with a neat brown pageboy making her way toward the table in a walker. With effort, she pulled out a chair and sat.

The three ladies of the Wednesday Club gazed out the windows at Main Street. They appeared to be waiting for guests to arrive at a party, but the guests were long overdue. Maybe they weren't coming.

"I'll give you the recipe," Mercedes Torres said. "But that cheesecake is too much work for me anymore," she rasped. "It's an all-day deal."

Elvira fingered her strand of good pearls. "I don't know, Mercedes. I never was the cook you are. You can boil water and make it taste good."

"Since when do you give away your recipes?" Ruby wanted to know. A grade school teacher who'd never married, Ruby had the kind of voice that still made her former students perk up their ears and sit up straight. "I've been trying to pry that cas-sou-let recipe out of you since 1958."

"I told you, it's not written down," Mercedes spoke with effort. "It's a little this and a little that. You have to come watch and write it yourself." Her eyes, sunken dark stars, still saw everything, even if she wasn't able to do much anymore. She had kept riding well into her seventies, and it seemed a shame she couldn't even get up on a horse anymore.

Now she watched her friends make silent note of the deepening creases that ran from her mouth to her chin, the lines around her eyes. What could they say? Her face was a map to the place they were all going.

Ruby removed Mercedes's casserole cover for her, releasing a burst of fragrant steam. "Oven-fried chicken, mashed potatoes and gravy."

"There's chile colorado on the side," Mercedes smiled. "I made enough for you to take some home. Those are the chiles my son in Peña Blanca grew."

"No siree," Elvira said. "The Wednesday Club's not gonna starve to death." Each cold March gust stirred the floor-length dusty rose velvet drapes and rattled the windows, as sun and clouds debated whether it was yet time to let go of winter and allow spring to begin.

Mercedes took aim with her fork.

"Got that drumstick dead center," Ruby said. "You always were a good shot." She filled a plate for herself. "Watch your fingers, Elvira," She said. "That casserole is hotter than a two-dollar pistol at a police auction."

"Either of you been to see Lucy?" Mercedes asked. She toyed with her fork. Food remained untouched on her plate.

"Yesterday. Brought over that broccoli casserole she likes," Elvira said.

"How'd she look?"

"Like she'd been drug through a knothole backwards. Her color was pretty good, considering. You know staying in the hospital turns you gray." Elvira cut her food into tiny pieces.

"How long has she been home now? Just over a week? Is she able to move?" asked Ruby.

"She's paralyzed on her right side." She shook her head. "Hard to think of Lucy sick in bed. She never was ill a day in her life!"

Elvira looked down the vacant length of the dining room. "Do you remember how she'd march in here every Wednesday? 'Let's get down to business, ladies,' she'd say. 'What are we waiting for?'" Elvira sighed.

"Maggie fits in so well," Ruby said. "It's like she never left."

"She was giving the kitchen a new coat of yellow paint," said Elvira. "Fixing it up for when her daughter back east comes to visit, she said.

"Then she showed me these plants of hers she's got going on the windowsill," Elvira said. "You should see 'em. Like a jungle already, twining up the strings she's set for 'em. 'Oh Elvira,' she said. 'Those are beans I started from some old seeds Ivy gave me. I'm just waiting for it to get a little warmer before I transplant 'em.'"

"If she likes old seeds, I've got plenty she can have," Mercedes said. "Bolita beans and calabacitas squash from my grandmother's garden."

"And I've got some blue corn from Isleta, and some of that Mrs. Burns lemon basil I grow," said Ruby. "Came from Oklahoma Territory. It's plenty tough."

"I'll get her some of my hollyhocks that came from Mabel's house in Taos," Elvira said. "Once they get going, she better watch out. Nothing can kill them."

"Well, good," said Ruby. "Maggie won't leave as long as she's got a garden going."

"She's not going to leave as long as she's got her mother to take care of," Mercedes said. She laid her fork down.

"What's the matter?" Ruby asked.

"I don't know. I'm just not very hungry today," Mercedes replied. Her soft brown pageboy swayed as she shook her head. Just then, she could have cried.

"Poor Lucy. And we just lost Opal, too," Ruby said. "We don't even have four to play today."

"That's what I want to talk about," said Elvira. "We do need another hand at the table."

The other ladies nodded.

"So I propose we ask Maggie to join us."

"Elvira, in the entire history of the Wednesday Club, we've never broken our rules," Ruby said.

"How do you know?"

"I've got the rule book right here."

"I'm from Missouri," Elvira said. "Show me that rule."

"Well, here it is." She thumbed through a small black leather-bound book.

"Where is it then?"

"Do you want it done or do you want it done right? It says so here in black and white: 'The only time a new member shall be considered for membership is on the demise of a regular member.' That's the way the founders set it up. You want to go and break that rule now?"

"That rule was written eighty years ago!" Mercedes said.

"That goes to show what a good rule it is," said Ruby.

"As I see it, here's the choice: we either change our rule, or we disband." Elvira stood. Her high heels wobbled on the threadbare Persian carpet. "Just today I called three ladies who've belonged to the club as long as we have. The only ones left won't go out of the house. They can't see to drive or their arthritis is too much for 'em. There's no one left who isn't gone or homebound."

"What kind of a player is Maggie?" Ruby asked.

"I guess we'll have to deal her in to find out," Elvira said.

"It wouldn't hurt her to get out some," Mercedes commented. "But let's ask her to play before we invite her to join."

"I saw Roger at the grocery store yesterday," said Elvira.

The ladies turned to her. "And?" Ruby said.

"Now that you ask, I believe he's looking more fit. We had quite a conversation," Elvira said. "Bless his heart."

"Could be he has the inspiration he needs to straighten up," Ruby said.

"No doubt about it," said Elvira. "He's a man, isn't he?"

The ladies laughed together. "No disagreement there," Ruby said. "If I was only forty years younger, I'd give Maggie a run for her money."

Elvira raised her eyebrows. "Forty years younger?"

"So what was your conversation with the mayor all about?" Ruby asked.

"Oh, he thinks we're in for better times with this young Texas developer coming in," Elvira said. "'We've got plans you'll be glad to hear about,' he told me."

"Do you believe that?" Mercedes asked. "New Mexico is crawling with developers. Is anybody better off? I'm still happy to have wood for my stove and beans for my table. Go take a look at Santa Fe before you open your arms to those developers."

"I haven't been to Santa Fe in years," Elvira said. "I used to love to eat at the La Fonda."

"You wouldn't recognize it," said Mercedes. "My son took me to the Pink Adobe for my birthday. You wouldn't believe the traffic. He couldn't find a place to park."

"I think we could give Roger a chance," said Ruby. "And that young Texan, he seems like a nice enough fellow. He stopped by and made me an offer on my place last week."

"Like we gave that Farley Goodnight a chance? That's who the man from Texas reminds me of," said Mercedes. "He's a real smooth talker, if you ask me."

"Who's that?" Ruby asked.

"Don't you remember? When the drought hit in the fifties we hired a rainmaker. Farley Goodnight. With the long white hair.

He sat on the mountain all summer, pounding on his drum, and we paid him $2,000 whether it rained or not."

"Did it rain?"

"I don't remember," Mercedes said. "The drought ended eventually. It was like winning $2.20 on a two-dollar bet."

"Did you see my Jell-O chiffon mold?" Ruby scooped a spoon of pink fluff studded with maraschino cherries on her plate. "Will you please go to nibbling on it."

"I'm fixin' to help myself," Elvira said.

"This is good," Mercedes assented, "but I like your lime better."

"With the pineapple? I'll bring it next time," said Ruby. "So how do we want to help Maggie out?" she asked.

"With looking after Lucy?" Mercedes said.

"That's right. Cowboy up."

Ruby said, "Maggie must have a jillion things for us to do."

"We know how to make ourselves useful," said Mercedes, patting her mouth with the corner of her napkin. "Elvira, you must know something about it. Didn't Theo have a stroke?"

"I know all about it. I looked after him night and day two years before he went. That was only two months before our golden wedding anniversary. A blessing in disguise."

"We've had our share of those," said Mercedes. "That's about the only kind of blessings we get around here."

"Truly. Theo hated big parties. Hated parties altogether. Rather be out in the barn talking to the horses. But I was determined to have me one heck of a bash to celebrate fifty years of living with that man. Some men mellow with age. Not Theo. Just as hard-headed at the end as the day I met him. At least his going saved us a fight over the invitation list."

"But it seemed like Lucy was pretty much out of it when I went over," Ruby said.

"Don't fool yourself. She can hear everything you say. And knowing Lucy, she probably knows what you're thinking, too," said Elvira.

"Can she get well?" Mercedes asked, fanning herself with a dog-eared menu.

"She can do a lot, if she wants to," Elvira replied. "She's got that sweet physical therapist coming to the house." She began clearing the dishes. "That was real good, ladies. Coffee?"

"Sure," said Ruby. "Since we can't play bridge, how about a few hands of five-card draw?"

"Fine with me," said Mercedes. "I'll bring Maggie some red enchiladas tomorrow."

"A nickel for the pot?" Elvira asked. "Just to make it interesting."

"I'm in." Ruby opened her purse and spilled a pile of pennies on the table. "You deal," she said. "I'll cut the cards."

FOURTEEN

MAGGIE CARRIED A PLATE OF MERCEDES'S enchiladas into Lucy's sickroom. "Momma, your friends brought dinner by. Would you like some?"

No answer. Why did she expect any? Every day Lucy seemed to be mysteriously evaporating, becoming a fainter presence. Maggie lifted her mother's head and fluffed her pillow. She straightened the bedclothes and tucked in the sheets. The sight of her mother's feet was the hardest to take. Mottled brown and purple bruises stained the flesh above her arthritic, swollen ankles. Maggie was afraid to touch the skin, even to wash it. The affliction covered her legs and arms. But it was only age, the marks life inevitably branded you with. Maggie squeezed her own strong, solid calf, unable to believe this degeneration would ever come her way, or that her own slim, well-muscled legs would ever succumb to this humiliation. She believed she'd rather die first.

Lucy groaned. Maggie took a pulse and temperature, then

recorded the results for the visiting nurse who would look in tomorrow. The moment Maggie sat on the bed, Lucy's eyes flew open. "Hi, Momma," she said, in the low, monotonous voice she reverted to when speaking to her mother. "Feeling any better? Anything I can do for you? Your Wednesday Club friends all say hello. You should see what all they brought by. Can't fit another covered dish into the refrigerator. Those ladies sure know how to cook. Look at all the get-well cards they've sent. Over here on top of the TV. They expect to have you back in the game real soon." She dug a forkful of food from the plate and offered it.

Lucy went for the food like a greedy bird, as though eating was all that mattered or would ever matter. Maggie thought she made out two words pronounced from the mobile left side of her mother's mouth—"Thank you"—but she might only have wished them. The job of taking care of her mother bore no resemblance to what she'd hoped for. Finding healing between the rounds of changing sheets and bedpans was like hunting for gold in a played-out mine. You had to really love someone to take care of her and feel gratified, and so far Maggie was performing out of duty, not love. Her mother was a hard woman. She'd had to be. And now there was no way Maggie would ever find the connection she'd hoped for.

This enforced closeness was more than she'd had, but far from sufficient. Certainly, she felt no closer, no warmer, no more connection than she ever had with her mother. Back in San Francisco, when she rode the bus or went shopping, she had a habit of observing interactions between mothers and daughters, looking for clues about how such a relationship ought to work. Were they happy or simply bound together? she wondered. She really didn't know. Before it was too late, Maggie wanted her mother to know her, the whole of who she was, not just the pieces Lucy needed to see and now depended on.

"Momma, would you like to try to write what you want to say?"

Straining, Lucy shook her head twice. Anger gathered in her eyes. Out of the broken sounds, Maggie made out the words "hate this."

"Hate what, Momma? I'm sorry I can't understand you very well. I'm trying. I hope I get it soon. Do you want me to tell the Wednesday Club something?" Since her stroke, Lucy was no longer predictable. Intense, unprovoked emotional outbursts came frequently. A lifetime's withheld emotions had finally found an outlet. The stroke had destroyed the practiced control mechanisms that Lucy had relied on to regulate her life. She ranted and cried while Maggie stood by. She tried at first to listen and respond, but the only way she could tolerate her mother's condition was to tune down her engagement with Lucy's spells.

Lucy raised her hand slightly. Maggie picked the word "sorry" out of the next garbled speech, a phrase Lucy repeated over and over. She straightened the blankets, smoothed the sheets. "No need to apologize, Momma."

Lucy moaned.

She stroked Lucy's drooping cheek. She wanted to cry, seeing her mother helpless and dependent, and sometimes, a few hot tears spilled out. The energy Maggie had spent on deadlines, stories, interviews, friends, her entire complicated San Francisco life, she now lavished on one individual. "Are you warm enough? Too warm? Would you like me to open the window? Read to you?" Maggie prattled on. "I'll just get that mystery you were into." She squeezed her mother's hand. We'll read another chapter. How's that?"

She retrieved the paperback and continued what amounted to a one-way conversation. "Guess what, Momma? Hannah's coming tomorrow. That's right. I'll pick her up at the airport in

Albuquerque tomorrow afternoon," she announced. Lucy blinked her eyes and responded by squeezing Maggie's fingers.

After reading a little while until her yawns made it uncomfortable to continue, Maggie collapsed into the armchair beside Lucy's bed. She wrapped herself in an afghan and zapped the channels until she found a nature documentary on the public TV station, a program about the life of the hummingbird. She closed her eyes, just to rest them for a little while, and in moments, she was asleep.

In her dream, Maggie and Hannah were riding through an open field covered with potsherds left by the people who had lived here and vanished: Mogollon brownware, Chupadero black-on-white, Tabira kachina-figured black-on-white, red-glazed Kotyiti, broken wings of Anasazi thunderbirds—countless fragments of an impossible puzzle scattered on the ground. The prayers of all the potters and all the people who had used those pots to carry water and store corn rose hummed on the wind. Ahead loomed the three-story red sandstone wall of the Abo mission ruin, its empty windows eyes staring at approaching storm clouds.

Her horse stepped along a narrow ledge of red sandstone beside the wall. The wall, in her dream, was inscribed with petroglyphs, a gallery of signs. Spirals told of migrations; thunderbirds lifted wings in prayers for rain; bear claws indicated places of healing; Kokopelli, the hump-backed flute player, brought fertility to the land and the people; a horned mask marked the presence of the shaman.

She looked around for Hannah. The girl had vanished. She called her daughter's name. "Where are you?" she shouted. The wind swallowed her voice. In despair, she rode outward from the wall in widening circles as the storm came closer. When she looked back at the petroglyphs, she saw Hannah astride her horse. She waved, beckoning, then watched Hannah come toward her.

The wind shook the cottonwood leaves and lightning flashed. "Let's tie the horses and get inside," she told Hannah. They dismounted and ran into the old church as heavy raindrops began to fall. But the roof was missing, and only the vigas, beams of splintered tree trunks, remained while the soaking rain poured down.

Holding Hannah's hand, Maggie stumbled. She knelt to examine what had caught her foot and found a tightly-woven oval basket. Cautiously, she lifted it to reveal a female mummy covered with a turkey-feather blanket decorated with mandalas of bluebird feathers and under that, a yellow blanket of canary feathers. The mummy's face was painted red, her body was painted yellow, and her long hair was neatly combed. Around her neck and wrists were bands of shell, coral, and turquoise. She looked as though she was sleeping.

"I can't believe she's dead," Hannah said.

"Watch where you walk," Maggie said, taking Hannah's hand. She saw the black diamond-shaped head of the snake coiled in the dark corner at the same instant she heard him. His buzzing set her heart pounding. Again he rattled, louder.

Maggie woke to the blue-light buzz of the TV. Almost five A.M. She immediately checked on her mother, who slept, breathing regularly.

Maggie went downstairs to make coffee. She wanted it strong enough to float a pistol. She had a lot to do today, including drive to Albuquerque.

By 11, she'd finished getting the house ready for Hannah. Since it was too early for wildflowers, she'd cut a small bunch of each variety of dry grass she could find on the place. She tied a purple ribbon around the bundle of grasses and set it in a vase on Hannah's night table. She'd hung old photos and prints in the room and put the prettiest quilt on Hannah's bed. She'd polished and dusted and scrubbed the house so it was spotless. The old adobe was a far cry from Hannah's posh quarters in Washington, but she wanted her daughter to know how much her visit meant and how welcome she was, especially now. She didn't want to lash out at Hannah because of her past mistakes. She wanted to give her daughter a fresh start, and she'd decided to start out by trusting the girl.

At the bottom of the dirt road, she found a big manila envelope stuck in the mailbox. It was stuffed with a dozen white envelopes, each neatly folded and wrapped with a blue rubber band. First she opened the one labeled "Manzano Yellow." Inside she found corn seeds, hard golden kernels of the kind grown for generations in these mountains. Other envelopes held seeds of Acoma blue corn and Isleta white, cultivated for centuries in this high dry country by people who watched over them and prayed over them, people who believed dances were prayers you made with your feet. She liked their belief that if they touched the earth at the proper time, in the proper way, they'd keep the planet spinning and the rain falling.

She found Mrs. Burns Famous lemon basil, Magdalena Big Cheese squash, brick-colored Santa Fe Red sorghum seeds, Ghost Ranch calabacitas, hollyhocks from Mabel Dodge Luhan's house in Taos, bachelors buttons from Adolph Bandelier's garden on Canyon Road in Santa Fe, Ocate bolita beans, Chimayo chile, Dixon garlic. From the envelope marked Santo Domingo, she unraveled a note on a scrap of paper: "These melons grow by the river. You never know what you'll get." The envelope contained hybrid seeds from which all shapes and sizes of melon would come, in variable hues of yellow, green and orange.

Getting the old garden going would be a project that she hoped might interest Hannah, a project they could do together.

Accompanying the melon seeds was a formal invitation, penned in a flowing hand in blue fountain-pen ink on fine linen stationery. Maggie was invited to play bridge with the Wednesday Club—not an invitation easily refused. But she would have to turn it down, and the ladies would have to understand. She wasn't going to become a stand-in for her mother at the bridge table.

When Maggie reached the Kowboy Kafe for her lunch date with Ivy, the place was packed with men in caps and coveralls and ladies in starched white blouses and high heels. Lorraine's curls quivered from her race to keep up with the lunch-hour crowd. Winded, red in the face, she stood at Maggie's booth, order pad in hand. "What are you all in the mood for today?" She wore crimson stretch pants and a tee shirt printed with a large winking chile pepper and the words "Hot Stuff" spanning her bosom.

"How's the chicken fried steak?" Ivy asked.

"Real good," said Lorraine. "You can have it on the special. Comes with mashed potatoes, green beans, roll, and salad. $3.95.

"Remember, Lorraine, I like plenty of gravy." Ivy folded her menu and stuck it back in the chrome cowboy-hat holder. "Make those potatoes swim."

"I know what you like," she said, as she penciled the order.

"But put the thousand island on the side, will you?"

She put her hands on her square hips. Her plastic chile-ristra earrings jiggled. "I know. Now quit."

Maggie studied the menu. "I'll have the cabbage soup." Then she scanned the dessert selections on the board beside the counter. "And a piece of cherry pie. And hot tea, please."

"Friend of yours—Roger—came in just a while ago. Ordered him up a big stack of pancakes and bacon and eggs. Ate every last bit." Lorraine beamed at Maggie. "Bless his heart."

It didn't matter how Maggie replied. Word went around. The grapevine would have its way with her. She returned the smile. "Nobody fixes a finer breakfast than you, Lorraine."

"Likes his bacon extra crispy, dontcha know." The waitress toddled toward the kitchen.

"I came across some interesting papers at the state engineer's office in Santa Fe last week," Ivy said. She pulled a fat file folder from her purse. "Just nosin' around."

She slid the folder across the table toward Maggie. "You like a good mystery? This one will keep you up all night." She thrust her hands in the pockets of her stretched-out brown sweater. "I promise."

Lorraine delivered their lunch. "Our mayor's been looking well these days, hasn't he?" she beamed as she set dishes on the table.

Ivy compressed her lips and shot her the annoyed schoolmarm look. Lorraine clapped her hand across her mouth and retreated.

Maggie peppered her soup. "Now I remember why I left this place. They know what you did before you do it."

"Now, Maggie. They don't mean any harm." She took a knife and fork to her chicken fried steak, popped a piece in her mouth, and started chewing. "Tough as a boot."

"They don't mean any good, either." Maggie picked up the folder and leafed through the documents. "Did you come by these honestly?"

Ivy rolled her eyes toward the ceiling. "The catchin' comes before the hangin'."

"That's what I thought." Maggie sipped her tea. "Nobody saw you copy them?"

"Do I look like a danger to the great state of New Mexico?"

Maggie sighed. "All right. I'll give it a look-see. Any word on your office break-in?"

"The police have come up with the brilliant theory that it was just some kids looking for trouble. That's as far as it'll go."

"Maybe they're right."

"Maybe they are." Ivy chewed. "And maybe they're not."

"As long as you're safe now."

"I'm carrying on and the paper's getting out on time."

"You're going to tell me not to worry about you?"

"Don't worry about me. I'm so tough the coyotes wouldn't have me." She waved toward the register. "There's the man himself. Getting a coffee to go."

Maggie wondered how Ivy could be anti-development and pro-Roger at the same time, but she didn't want to go into it then and there.

Roger crossed the café floor toward their table. "Good afternoon, ladies." He was clean-shaven and his shirt crisply laundered. His sharp edges seemed to barely contain a male energy that wanted to burst out of his seams.

"I was just leaving." Maggie stood. "I've got to get to Albuquerque to meet a plane."

"Company coming?" he asked, ever sociable.

"My daughter, Hannah." The way her voice broke when she said the name surprised her.

"I'll walk you out," he said, taking her elbow.

Maggie was conscious that the eyes of everyone in the café were on them as they made their exit. Did he want the whole town to think they were an item? He held the door for her and didn't speak until they were outside in the bright sunlight. Cold wind blew a dust devil down Main Street. Billy the Kid weather, she'd always called this wild, uncertain time of year. Just when you thought warm weather had arrived to stay, the wind kicked up again. A day could start out calm, and by afternoon serious winter had returned. You couldn't trust it.

"What was that all about?" she asked. "Feeding time for the town gossips?"

"Sorry 'bout that, Maggie." He removed his hat and held it to his chest. "Didn't realize being seen with me was a problem for you." He gave her a smile that probably got him through 99 percent of life's little difficulties.

"Listen, Maggie," he said. "I've thought about it. I want to apologize for what happened that morning." He dropped his arms to his side.

She looked at him standing tall as the wind skimmed down Main Street. The truth was, she still liked everything about him, including things she probably shouldn't. Right now, she especially liked the look on his face, the tenderness and concern behind an amused smile, the eyes that could go from serious to playful in an instant. If she was but a smidgen less wise, she'd hop in his truck and go anywhere he might suggest.

"Apology accepted. You were telling the truth. And I wasn't exactly an innocent bystander." She opened the door to her truck.

He pushed the door closed and waited until she rolled down the window. "No. Please. Listen. I don't want things wrong between us. That was a rough night. You got me at a time I wasn't fit company for anybody. I said some things I probably shouldn't have. You can understand that, can't you?"

"I understand perfectly," she said. "Nothing's wrong."

He placed a hand on her arm. "Wait, Maggie. I know you're concerned about Monte Alto, and I appreciate what you're saying about the water situation. I don't want you thinking we're handing the place over to developers. You have my word we won't go ahead with any new projects unless they're in balance with our resources.

"There's so few of us who care about what happens to this old place. We were friends once. We ought to be friends again.

Monte Alto needs every ally she can get." He paused for her reaction.

"All right Roger. You can think of me as your pal."

"Things must be tough with Lucy just out of the hospital. I'd like to help out."

"You're welcome to come by whenever you find the time." She cranked the truck and pulled away from the curb. She watched him in the rearview mirror until there was nothing left to see.

———•◉•———

Nothing to do but wait. The flight from Washington had been due in at the Albuquerque airport at 5:17, and here it was after 6:00. Maggie gave up trying to read the new Tony Hillerman mystery she'd picked up at the newsstand. She couldn't bear just sitting still. She went to the window and scanned the sky. As the sun neared the horizon, its last light hit Sandia Crest, traveling clear across the solar system to cast hot pink flame over its jagged western side. In school she'd studied the Sandias and learned they contained five of the earth's seven life zones. But now the gray wolf was gone from the country, the few survivors of the species penned in at the Rio Grande Zoo while ranchers and environmentalists fought bitterly over his right to roam free. The last bighorn sheep had disappeared thirty years ago, and now drought threatened the black bear population.

Lavender and gold lingered in the sky. Then as indigo twilight settled over the desert, somebody turned on the lights of the city, tiny beacons shining from an ancient sea floor.

Maggie reached into the pocket of her denim jacket for the note Paul had handwritten on his fancy letterhead.

Dear Maggie: You ought to know Hannah has been having some problems lately. Her grades are down, and we aren't really happy with her friends. She's been cutting classes with them and worse, as you know. You'd think an expensive private school like the one we send her to could think of a better way to deal with her than suspending her, but they didn't. She's angry at me and angry at Robin, who's at the end of her rope. Maybe you can get through to your daughter...

She paced the waiting area. Still no daughter. Maybe Hannah was marooned in St. Louis or there'd been a hijacking. Maybe she'd been kidnapped. These things happened. The plane was so late, maybe there'd been a wreck, and they just weren't saying.

She marched up to the desk. A young, blonde attendant stared at her with a bored expression. "And how can I help you, ma'am?" she drawled. Maggie forced calm into her voice. "Excuse me. Flight 617 from Washington is more than an hour late. Is there anything you can tell me?"

The attendant chewed her gum thoughtfully before she answered. This girl got her kicks from toying with people's anxieties. She answered in a whiny drawl. "I'm sorry, we have no new information. That flight is delayed. We'll be announcing the new arrival time soon." The girl turned away to pick up a ringing phone.

Maggie walked to the observation windows. She leaned her forehead against the cold plate glass and closed her eyes. *Please God, can you just do me one little favor this time? Please just get Hannah here safe. Do this for me, God, and if I can't be good, at least I'll be better. Honest.*

People walked through the arrival gate. A plump woman in a hot-pink jumpsuit handed her crying baby to the man who waited for her with flowers. A Navajo woman in a colorful broomstick skirt and velvet blouse, wearing armloads of turquoise, hugged a teenage boy wearing a black leather jacket.

Men from Washington with briefcases marched off, bound for Los Alamos, each brisk step loaded with efficiency and self-importance.

Then she saw Hannah. At first she wondered: who is that? The girl looked like a refugee—thin, pale, disoriented. Gone were her waves of dark hair. Instead, her unevenly chopped locks were streaked with neon green. She wore a dozen tiny gold hoops pierced into the curve of her left earlobe. Love Animals Don't Eat Them, her tee shirt proclaimed. Her bare midriff revealed her pierced navel. She walked listlessly in clunky, thick-soled shoes, a battle-weary soldier engaged in her personal war. She hesitated, glanced through the crowd, and rebalanced her backpack. Her eyes found Maggie's wave, and she bobbed toward her mother, the line of her mouth unwilling to bend into a smile.

Hannah held herself apart from Maggie in a stiff embrace. Maggie slammed the brakes on her emotions. She hugged her daughter gently, as much as Hannah would allow, though she longed to hold her close, to touch her face, to smooth the rough ends of her hair. She thought she caught a whiff of marijuana, but she may have been imagining it. *Thank you, God. I owe you one. I swear I won't say a word about that tattoo. And if her tongue is pierced, protect me from the knowledge. Just wait 'til they get a load of this at the Kowboy Kafe.*

An hour later, a band of deep rose streaked across the canvas of slowly darkening sky as they coasted along the twists of Highway 17. Maggie took the turns slowly, on the lookout for deer leaping across their path. The soft spring evening air smelled faintly of earth and pine. "You must be tired from your trip. Been on that plane all day."

Huddled in the corner, Hannah sounded far away. "I guess."

"What's that you're carrying in your backpack? It looks heavy."

"Just my books," she answered, only slightly exasperated by the question.

"We have a library here. We can get you a card tomorrow."

Hannah brushed off her mother's suggestion with disdain. "That's okay."

"What are you reading?" Maggie asked. She knew all about that aloofness routine. She was not giving up.

Hannah answered in a bored monotone. "Nothing special."

"Are you hungry?"

"A little. They gave us a snack on the airplane but I couldn't eat mine. It was only mystery meat on a bun."

"Airplane food. You wonder where they get it from. We'll have supper as soon as we get home. How's your dad? And Robin and Emily?"

Hannah looked out the window. "They went to the beach. Delaware."

"You didn't want to go?"

Her silence told Maggie everything. She reached out and gave Hannah's shoulder a squeeze. "I'm so glad you're here. And Grandma will be so happy to see you."

"Is she going to die?" She asked almost eagerly, as though the question interested her the way a science class experiment might.

Maggie looked at her daughter's delicate profile in the darkness. "She's very weak. She's partially paralyzed. But she can get much better."

"What's wrong with her?" Curiosity cracked through Hannah's deadpan delivery.

"She's had a stroke. She's worked hard all her life, and she's just worn out. Your being here is the best possible thing for her." Maggie gripped Hannah's arm and felt the precious bones under the purple sweatshirt. The girl's stillness sent the message: You won't get a thing from me.

Maggie spoke. "This is a great place. I'm excited about sharing it with you."

"What's so great about it? Where are we, anyway? The middle of nowhere?" Impatience and implied criticism underlined her questions.

"I could tell you what I like about it, but I want you to have a chance to discover it on your own. Make your own decision. It's a big place and it looks empty to some, but the closer you look, the more you see." What is this? Maggie wondered. The chamber of commerce? "You like animals?"

"Of course. Animals are better than people. I thought you knew that."

"I know what you mean. I can show you deer and elk and wild turkey and eagles. And antelope. Would you like that? You're just in time for wildflower season. We can hunt for wild iris. We can drive to Bosque del Apache, the bird refuge south of here, with lots of blue herons, cranes, Canada geese. Wait 'til you see them all fly in at sundown."

Hannah nodded. The brights of an oncoming truck momentarily blurred Maggie's sight. She gripped the wheel and focused on the broken white line that marked the road ahead. She glanced at her daughter. Hannah's head relaxed against the neck rest as though she was dozing. Maggie let her sleep.

A half-hour later they passed through the ranch gate. Hannah stared straight ahead as they rumbled down the washboard dirt road to the house. "Why don't you just go on in and make yourself comfortable? I'll grab the rest of your things."

Without reply, Hannah walked into the house. She set her duffle bag down in the hallway. Using some compass of her own, she walked down the hall to Lucy's room.

Maggie lit the woodstove and put the kettle on, along with a Dutch oven of vegetable soup. She understood Hannah needed her tattoos and dyed hair. Didn't they all do that now? It didn't mean she was a bad kid. At least she hadn't put a ring through her nose. Yet.

She hoped her daughter's hostility would soon evaporate. After all, she has good reason to be angry at me, Maggie thought as she stirred the soup with a long wooden spoon. She blames me for the divorce, and she blames me for her unhappiness. But now I have the chance to show her another side. Patience, honesty, and love can do wonders, Maggie told herself.

The door to Lucy's room was slightly ajar. Maggie knocked, then pushed it open. Lucy sat propped against a mound of pillows. Hannah sat on the edge of her grandmother's bed. Her animated silhouette played on the wall across the room in the golden lamplight. She gestured as she told Lucy about the flight out. A corner of Lucy's mouth lifted in a crooked smile. In reply to Hannah's words, Lucy let out a clamor of groans, and Maggie was amazed to see her daughter reply clearly to the incoherent sounds. Hannah continued describing her classes.

"You can understand what she says," Maggie said.

Hannah turned to her. "Of course. Can't you?"

Maggie shook her head. "To be honest, no. I can barely figure out what she's saying. How do you do it?"

Hannah's eyebrows, wings of surprise, lifted. "You listen, Mother." She resumed her conversation with her grandmother, emphasizing her words with her gestures. The two of them had instantly developed a private sign language. All Maggie could do was stand by and watch.

"Look, Mom. It's easy. Don't shut down just because you don't like how she sounds. Everything she says makes sense," Hannah explained. "All you have to do is listen to her."

Lucy's groans grew louder. "What is she saying now?" Maggie asked Hannah.

Her daughter's eyes were bright. "She's saying she's happy you brought me here. Can't you tell?"

"No. I really can't." She had no idea what Lucy's happiness sounded like.

Maybe Hannah could give her a clue.

FIFTEEN

MAGGIE DUG HER SPADE INTO THE hard red earth, locked tight as a rusty trunk. A dust devil, a fast-moving swirl of grit powered by cold spring wind, swirled around her, and she squeezed her eyes shut against the torrent of stinging sand and tasted grit between her teeth. A clamor sounded in the distance. She opened her eyes and scanned the sky. To the south, she spotted a V formation of Canada geese. The flock stretched into a wavy line across the sky, then compressed back into a V again, continually forming and re-forming its order as it flew. She admired them for their powerful ability find their way home. They knew exactly where that place was, and nobody was going to get in their way of it.

Again she tore at the ground with her spade. It had been years since this field next to the house had been planted and years since she'd grown anything more ambitious than a potted ficus. Now she wanted flowers, she craved color: bright red and orange zinnias along the fence; hot-pink four-o'clocks in front for the hummingbirds; marigolds between the tomatoes to keep the cutworms away, and she'd tuck in some gopher purge while she was at it. She'd plant osha to keep snakes away.

She gripped the splintery handle, placed her foot on top of the blade, and pushed. Her unexercised calf muscles burned. She pushed harder, sending her energy down into the land. The earth loosened. Using all her strength, she thrust the spade two inches deep into the dry crust.

Where was Hannah? She'd come out earlier to help and stayed ten minutes. Then she'd wandered off into the house. "I can't stand this wind," she'd said. "I know," Maggie told her. "The wind always makes me jumpy, too." Hannah would rather sit in her room with her earphones on than stay out here and get sandblasted. But if they waited for the wind to stop, the garden would never get planted.

Was Lucy awake? She seemed to be improving, and was sitting up now. What a relief to have Hannah answering some of her demands. Maggie was beginning to catch some of what her mother was saying. Was that because Lucy's speech was becoming more articulate, or was Maggie learning to understand her mother's language?

Maggie pulled a crumpled red bandanna from her pocket. She mopped the sweat and sand from her face. She looked up and noticed the unmistakable green-gold aura on the front-yard globe willow. Always the first tree to push its leaves out, it was bolder than the cottonwood out back. Those natives knew enough to wait until the danger of a late freeze had passed before they revealed themselves. Maybe that's why they lived so long.

"What can I get you, honey?" Lorraine stood ready to take the order of the girl seated at the counter.

"Do you have any veggieburgers?" Hannah asked.

"'Fraid not. Just good old-fashioned hamburgers is all we serve."

"I really wanted a veggieburger and fries."

"Meat's got excellent nutrients, dear." She squinted through her glasses. Then she raised her eyebrows. "Looks like a hamburger wouldn't hurt you any. Give you some color."

"Oh, I never eat meat," Hannah sniffed.

"That's too bad, honey." She patted the girl's hand. "Folks around here count themselves fortunate to have meat on their table. But I can bring you a grilled cheese sandwich. Think that'd do?"

"Okay, I guess. With fries, please. And a coke."

"Take a side of green chile on that?"

"No thank you."

"That's okay, honey. Have it your way." Lorraine ambled over to the kitchen to place the order.

While she waited, Hannah investigated the Kowboy Kafe. She wandered over to the jukebox and studied the song titles. She wondered who Hank Williams was, there were so many songs by him. She placed a couple of quarters in the Wurlitzer, pressed the buttons for "Your Cheatin' Heart." She tapped her foot and looked around. The only other place she'd ever seen a snake skin was in a natural history museum. She examined the pencil sketches of cowboys framed on the wall. Cowboys sitting on fences. Cowboys roping. Cowboys hanging onto bucking broncos. What was with all these cowboys? She meandered over to the photo display above the booths. The picture of a dark-haired girl in a blue-spangled outfit on horseback caught her eye.

"Wasn't she something pretty to see?" asked a shaky voice. An elderly lady with a perfect crown of wavy silver-white hair stood beside Hannah.

"Who is she?" Hannah asked.

"Why, that's our Maggie." The old lady seemed surprised at the question.

"You're kidding." Hannah's eyes opened wide with amazement.

"No, honey, I'm not. That's Lucy's girl, all right."

"I can't believe it." Hannah took a step back, then forward. She scrutinized the photo.

"It's the truth, child," the old lady smiled. "That there's Maggie Chilton, none other."

"But that's *my mom*."

Elvira beamed. Her smile wrinkled soft, rouged cheeks. "So you are Lucy's granddaughter."

Another frail pink-cheeked lady glided toward them. Both were the same size and had the same mechanical way of moving. Even their high-pitched voices sounded alike. "Elvira, have you been leisuring this morning?"

"I've been busy straightening out my kitchen cupboards, if you must know." Elvira put her glasses on. She peered at Hannah. "Ruby, look who's here. Lucy's granddaughter!"

"You don't say!" Ruby studied Hannah. "She's her grandma all over again," she said. "And cute as a bug." She reached over and touched Hannah on the head. "But honey, who's been doing your hair?"

"I have!" she said. Hannah stared at the ladies in their dark dresses sparked with costume jewelry as though they had waltzed out of the past. "You know my grandma?"

"No better friend in this world," Elvira said. "How is she feeling today?"

"I think she's about the same," Hannah said. "Nothing's really changed."

The ladies' heads bobbed up and down in unison. "The

prayer chain's been praying hard for her recovery," Elvira said. "We all sure do miss her."

"I'll tell her you said hello," Hannah said.

"Tell me something, honey," Elvira said, looking Hannah up and down. "Do you by any chance play bridge?"

"I don't know how," Hannah said.

"Do you think you might like to learn some time?" Elvira said.

Ruby elbowed Elvira in the ribs. She whispered, "What about our rule?"

Elvira turned to her friend. "Do you want to play or don't you?" she hissed.

"I see your point," Ruby said.

"That's sure a nice shirt you have on," Elvira told the girl, continuing her inspection. "All those pretty little animals. Very colorful."

Hannah looked down. "Thank you."

"What is that, a Noah's Ark?"

"Extinction is Forever." Hannah proclaimed the words printed across her tee shirt.

"Isn't that the God's truth," Elvira said. "But there's none of us going to live forever." She shook her head. "Just not in the plan. What is your name, honey?"

"Hannah. I was named for my great-grandmother."

"It's very nice to meet you, Hannah."

"I'm very pleased to meet you." She extended her hand and clasped each of theirs in turn.

Elvira turned to Ruby. "Isn't she the sweetest thing you ever saw?"

"Well, of course she is," Ruby replied. "What do you expect?" She reached over and patted Hannah's cheek.

"Thank you," Hannah said. "Nice meeting you."

"You too, Hannah," Ruby said. "And honey, if you want to do something with that hair, we've got an excellent hairdresser right here in town. Esperanza over at the Crowning Glory would find the perfect do for you."

"Order up!" Lorraine called.

Hannah returned to her place at the counter as Lorraine set the platter down. "You have a picture of my Mom over there."

Lorraine smiled. "So you're Maggie's girl." She took a good look. "Sure you are. I see it now. Sure do. What's your name?"

"Hannah."

"Well, Miss Hannah, we're mighty happy to have you here. Tell you what. I'll just order some of those, whatchamacallits, veggieburgers, and keep 'em in the freezer for you. Next time you come in, you just ask." Lorraine leaned forward to offer a conspiracy. "Do you like pie?"

"It's okay."

"Tell me, what looks good to you?" She waved toward the glass case that displayed the pies.

Hannah pointed to a creamy white mound that towered six inches above the plate.

"Good choice. How about a slice of that coconut cream for dessert? On the house. Real whipped cream, you know, none of that stuff out of a can. You take a bite and let me know what you think, will you?"

"Sure. What did you say your name was?"

"I'm Lorraine." The fringe of her aqua satin blouse shimmied as she extended her hand.

"Thanks, Lorraine."

"My pleasure, darlin'. Any time."

Hannah drenched her fries with ketchup. She reached into her backpack and pulled out a zine to read. Half an hour later, she looked up. The café was filling with a lunchtime crowd.

Lorraine buzzed past like a plump bee. "How're you doing darlin'? Can I bring you anything else? Guess you liked that pie all right." She looked at the crumbs on the plate. "Would you like another? Sure won't hurt you none to have another slice."

"No thanks. Do you know where I can catch a bus?"

"No buses in this town, honey. We're lucky we've got a few trucks that still run, though how they do is a matter of faith and duct tape."

"What's duct tape?"

"You are new around here, aren't you! Why, it's that silver stuff that keeps everything going. Cars, machines, when they break, you just tape 'em up. It's one of the greatest inventions of all time."

Hannah scratched her elbow. "Really."

"Well, how'd you get here?"

"Walked." Hannah looked down.

"That's a mighty long walk from your place. Guess you don't feel like making that trip again today."

Hannah shook her head. "I can, but I don't want to."

"Want to call your Mom to come and get you?"

Hannah shook her head again. "Can you call me a cab instead?"

"The only taxi driver we've got is old Harmon Medders, and you put your life at risk when you get in his cab. Besides, he doesn't stir his bones before two P.M." Lorraine viewed the crowd. "Let's see what we can do," she said. "Be right back," she winked.

In a minute, she returned with a tall, lanky man at her side. "Got someone here for you to meet. Hannah, this is our mayor, Roger Dawson."

He held out his hand. "Pleased to meet you, Hannah."

She scanned his cowboy hat, boots, starched white shirt, denim jacket, and long hair tied back. She shook the offered hand. "Are you really the mayor?"

"That's what they call me," he smiled.

"Where's your badge?"

"Didn't say I was the sheriff. That's the fellow wearing a badge. They wouldn't trust me with one of those. But I understand you could use a ride. I'd be pleased to take you home."

Hannah gave Lorraine a skeptical look. "It's okay, honey," the waitress said. "Honest. He'll get you home safe."

Roger reached over and picked up Hannah's check. The register chimed his payment.

"You don't have to do that, Mr. Dawson. I have my own money."

"Guess you never heard of the code of the west. We don't let ladies pay around here." He grinned at her. "Call me Roger. And you're welcome." Once they were seated in his truck, he asked her, "What brings you to Monte Alto?"

"Just visiting my Mom." She looked out the window at the wide-open landscape.

"You don't sound too happy about it."

"It's boring here." She fiddled with the ends of her hair. "Nothing to do."

"What would you do if you were home?" he asked.

"Listen to music. Hang out."

"You sound a tad homesick." He turned to her. "Do you like to ride?"

"You mean, like on a horse?"

"That's what I mean," he said.

"It's okay." She fiddled with the radio dial and found too much static. Annoyed, she snapped it off.

"Only okay?"

"That's what I said I wanted to do when I came out here. But there's no horses on the ranch."

"How's that?" he asked.

"She says she's not ready for one. And she's too busy taking care of my grandma to find us one." She hunted in her backpack for something.

"What a shame."

"I guess." She turned to him. "Do you know my mom? Everybody else around here does."

"Everybody knows each other in a town this small, Hannah. And yes, I do know your mom." The wheel turned slightly under his two hands.

She curled up against the door like a cat. She eyed him from her nook. "Did you know her when they took that picture of her in the café?"

He watched the curving road ahead. "Sure did."

"That was a long time ago."

"You're right about that." He smiled at her again. "Your mom and I went to school together. Graduated together."

"Hmm," she said. She looked out the window again. After a long pause, she asked, "What was she like then?"

"Beautiful. And serious. She liked to win. But nobody was more fun than she was. She loved to take chances." He paused. "I can tell you this, Hannah. She had the freest spirit you ever saw."

"Doesn't sound much like my mom," she said.

"Plenty of times she rode circles around me. Made my head spin."

"Like when?"

"Like when we'd go up and race across Heartbreak Mesa. She usually managed to beat me," he said.

"Where is Heartbreak Mesa?" she asked.

He tilted his head over his left shoulder. "See that big flat mountain back over there to the east?"

She turned to look. "Why do they call it that?"

"Lots of stories about that name. Some say it's because some miners lost everything trying to find gold. Others will tell you it's a place where a young man got his heart broken by a young lady."

"What happened to him?"

"Nobody knows for sure. But people say he's up there still. They swear some nights you can see lights flickering from the cave he lives in up top."

"Which story do you believe?" she asked.

He paused. "Personally, I think it's a place that's beautiful enough to break your heart, and that's how it got the name."

She turned again to study the distant mesa. "Honestly, I don't think it's so pretty. It looks kind of dry and bare."

"Maybe it takes a while to know how beautiful it is. Maybe you have to go up there and see for yourself," he said. "Hannah, does your mom know where you are?"

"I don't think so."

"Why not? Didn't you tell her where you were going? Don't you think she might be worried about you?"

Hannah shrugged.

"How'd you get into town, anyway?"

She kept her face turned away from him. "Walked."

"Really? All that way?"

She mumbled.

"What time did you leave? Had to be before sun-up to make it into town by 10:30."

She didn't answer. She got busy digging in her backpack.

"You don't need me to give you a lecture on how dangerous it is to hitchhike, do you?"

She straightened up in her seat. "The guy who picked me up was really nice. He just gave me a ride and let me out in the middle of town."

"You were lucky, that's all. We've found girls who weren't so lucky. Left in ditches. Or we never found them. They just disappeared. Is that what you're aiming for?"

She shook her head.

"Then don't try it again. I'm sure your mother will drive you wherever you need to go. And if she can't, call me. Here's my numbers. Home and work." He reached in his pocket and handed her his card.

She tucked it in the pocket of her jeans. "Thanks Roger."

"No problem."

Hannah sighed. "It's still boring here."

"My granddad always said if you're bored you're either lazy or not paying attention."

Hannah waved his words away.

"Don't want to hear that, do you? I'm sure there's plenty for you to do around the house. Your mom has her hands full, and she can use your help right now. Isn't that right?"

"Yes," Hannah answered in a low voice. She played with the silver ring on her middle finger.

"You like animals?"

"Sure. Better than people."

"Tell you what."

"What?" Her eyes widened a bit.

"We'll see what we can do to make it a little more interesting for you while you're here."

She brightened. "How?"

"Just be patient for a day or two. I have something in mind. Something I'm sure you'll like."

"Okay."

They drove up the gravel driveway. Maggie ran out of the house as though it were on fire. "Where have you been?" she demanded.

Hannah didn't respond.

"She showed up at the café. Lorraine asked me to run her home," Roger replied.

Maggie grabbed Hannah and held her. "Now I have to worry about you running away?" she asked. After an attempt to wriggle out of the cage of Maggie's arms, Hannah stood still. She grimaced.

"I don't think you'll have to worry about that anymore," Roger said.

"Would you like a cup of coffee?" She wiped her hands on her jeans. She wasn't in the mood to deal with the emotions the sight of him stirred up. She wanted to find out what was going on with Hannah.

"I need to get back," he said. "Thanks anyway." He didn't turn to leave, however.

"Thanks for returning my daughter," Maggie said.

"Any time." He folded his arms and leaned his weight to one side. He seemed to plant himself into the ground.

Was he staying or going? "Sure you can't use some coffee?" she asked.

He shook his head, watching them together. "Hannah told me she's hoping to do some riding while she's here," he said.

"We're going to work on getting that going," Maggie said. She gestured toward the house. "But it's been kind of crazy out here. We've been on the ropes."

"Listen, Maggie," he began.

"I'm listening," she said. "What's on your mind?"

He looked over the house and yard. "Nothing. Never mind."

"Well, then," she said. She followed his glance toward the garden. She couldn't stand out here all day playing guessing games with him. If he had something to say, let him come out with it. She'd had enough worry for one morning.

He placed the tip of his boot under a broken fencepost. "Looks like you've got some fences need fixing around here."

"That's only the beginning of it. I've got a list from here to Las Cruces."

He knelt to examine the damage. "Not too big a job. I could give you a hand with this sometime if you'd like."

"You could never stand to see a thing broken without taking a hammer to it."

"Well, sure," he said. "A guy's got to be good for something."

"You must be busy." What would she do with him underfoot all day?

"Not too. We can get some things crossed off your list."

"We can sure use the help," she said. "But we don't want to be a bother."

"No bother at all. You've got some valuable property here, Maggie." He glanced up at the old windmill. "Especially with that good well and your springs. Sure it's run down. But it wouldn't take much to bring it back. I'll come by and we'll get this job taken care of," he promised.

"Thank you. That'd be great." What a relief. He appeared to be leaving, finally.

"See you, Maggie."

He waved from the truck. "See you Hannah."

"Bye, Roger," Hannah called to the swirl of dust his truck made as he drove away.

Maggie took Hannah by the hand. "Are you all right?"

"Sure," she said. "I'm fine."

Maggie noticed a new tattoo on her daughter's wrist, a filigree of blue roses. So those tattoos of hers were only paste-ons! "What happened to you this morning?"

"Nothing."

Maggie took Hannah's shoulders in her hands. "When you take off like that without letting me know where you are, I worry about you. Do you understand?"

Hannah nodded her head rapidly up and down. "I understand."

"We can't have that. If we're all going to get along out here, we need to cooperate. I don't want to ground you, but I'll have to if you keep this up. And if you don't believe what I'm saying, just try me." She took a deep breath. "Want to help me in the garden?"

"Okay. Whatever."

Maggie handed her a hoe and pointed out the section that needed attention.

They worked together, with only the sounds of the spade and the hoe for conversation.

SIXTEEN

THE NEXT MORNING, MAGGIE WAS PLEASED to see Hannah go to work in the garden without prompting. She wore earphones as she moved to a rhythm only she could hear. She didn't greet her mother or say anything for a long while. Finally, she stopped to catch her breath. She looked around, calculated how much she'd done and how far she had to go, then she sniffed. "It's nice out here," Hannah said. "Do you think Grandma would like to sit in the sun?"

Together, they hoisted Lucy into her wheelchair, arranged her limbs, and brought her to the porch. Wrapped in an old Pendleton blanket like a mummy, she watched as Maggie and Hannah continued preparing the depleted soil. How many of her female ancestors, Maggie wondered, had dug in this garden just this way, growing calluses on their hands while they imagined the bounty they would coax out of this blank earth.

Maggie didn't mention the cigarette butts she'd found when she took the trash out earlier that morning. And she'd again caught that whiff of marijuana creeping out from behind Hannah's closed door last night. If confronted, Hannah would deny they were hers and accuse Maggie of getting on her case. At least, that's what Maggie would have done if she had been in Hannah's position.

Maggie looked on as Hannah placed a few dandelions on Lucy's lap. She'd found the first greens. Hannah knelt beside Lucy, telling her something. Lucy groaned in response to the girl's words. Hannah continued talking and gesturing, taking Lucy's response as encouragement to continue.

Maggie felt a chill, as though the temperature had dropped suddenly. "The wind's coming up," she said. "Let's get Grandma inside."

After Lucy was safely back in bed, they returned to work outside. Hannah put on her earphones, making talk impossible.

An engine hummed up the road. Maggie leaned on her shovel as the white Ford pickup hitched to a horse trailer turned in the gate and drove up the gravel path. Roger stepped out. She heard his boots crunch the gravel. He eyed the old adobe crumbling at the corners, in need of replastering, the faded red barn, the corral fence in need of mending. She saw him assess what it would take to put it all right again.

How happy she'd once felt to see him walk up that driveway. When she lost him, she had lost the ability to feel that pure senseless joy. She'd never found it again.

Now she didn't know what to do with him. She didn't know what he wanted. What's more, she didn't know what she wanted.

"Hi, Maggie. What're you doing out here in the wind?" he asked. He squinted against the dust and shaded his eyes with his palm.

She shook her head. "Got to keep going on this garden, or it'll never get planted in time," she said.

"You out to build the world in two days? You'll turn this place into another Garden of Eden by the Fourth of July," he said.

"Just so long as there's no snakes in my garden," she said, sliding her dirty hands down the sides of her jeans.

"Snakes have their place," he said. His eyes locked with hers.

"I agree with you. But their place is not in my flower beds." She turned another spadeful of earth. She tilted her head toward his truck. "What's in the trailer?" she asked.

"I thought Hannah might like to ride Jesse's horse while she's here. Zia needs to be ridden. And she needs the company. She's lonesome. Way too lonesome."

"I've got a girl here who's lonesome, too. And who's got too much time on her hands for her own good." A gust of wind threw dust at them. "But I don't know if we're ready for this."

Hannah dropped her hoe and started ambling their way. "Hi, Roger," she said. She'd removed the earphones.

"Hi, there Hannah. How're you getting along?"

"Fine," she smiled. She moved away from her mother and closer to him.

Maggie flinched. Hannah had that habit of going to her father, deliberately making an alliance that excluded her. Hannah knew how to play "Daddy's little girl" very well; how to get what she wanted even though Mom had said no.

"Brought something to show you," he said.

Hannah followed him over to the trailer. He unlatched the rig and the door clanged open. He led a beautiful little palomino down the ramp.

Hannah whooped, "She's incredible!" At the sight of the animal, her slight body straightened like a wilted plant after a good rain.

"Wait 'til you ride her. She's gentle as can be."

Roger brought tack out of the truck. He placed the bridle over her head and slipped the bit in her mouth, then placed a saddle on the horse. He adjusted and fastened the girth. He offered Hannah a hand up, but she ignored it. She put one foot in the stirrup and mounted on her own, while Zia waited, patient and attentive. Maggie marveled once more at her daughter's refusal to be intimidated.

Roger led Zia to the corral and opened the gate. Hannah appeared small and fragile astride Zia's strong back. She took the horse on a walk around the corral. Roger's eyes didn't move from the horse and rider. Hannah urged Zia into a trot. The hoofbeats raised small clouds of red dust. Hannah's look of intense concentration changed to one of exhilaration.

The horse responded beautifully to the girl's quiet commands. Maggie had no idea her daughter showed such grace in the saddle. "Hi, Mom!" Hannah called. It was the first time since she'd arrived that Maggie had heard joy in her voice. Color brightened her daughter's face; at this moment, she was completely alive.

After taking Zia on several lopes around the corral, Hannah returned to the gate. Roger helped her dismount. "Wow!" Hannah said. "Awesome!"

"Who taught you to ride? Not too bad for a city girl," Roger said.

"I took lessons in Rock Creek Park."

"You don't get on a horse the first time and ride the way you did just from lessons. You've got horses in your blood, Hannah," Roger said. "Did you know your mother was state champion barrel racer?"

"Oh, sure. She's done lots of things. So she's a rodeo queen or something."

"Anything she sets her mind to, she's the best."

Hannah rolled her eyes.

"Roger is being very kind," Maggie said.

"Are you really going to leave Zia here?" Hannah wanted to know.

"She belonged to my son."

"Doesn't he want her anymore?"

Roger stroked the animal's withers. Zia was certainly well cared for. Maggie imagined Roger groomed and fed her with devotion. As his last link to his son, he probably talked to her a lot. Maybe he cried over her, too. And now he was going to part with her.

"We lost Jesse three years ago, Hannah." He turned to lift the saddle over the fence. His hat shadowed his face.

"I'm so sorry!" Hannah said. Instinctively, she put her arms around him. "Thank you so much." Tears filled her eyes.

Hannah's spontaneous compassion filled Maggie's heart. Hannah's adolescent hijinks might cause a few jitters, but, she told herself, the girl was turning out A-okay. After all, she herself was no angel at that age. Maybe she just worried too much.

"Jesse worked at the Bluebird stable over in Sherlock where he found her. Zia had been abandoned by her owners. She'd been hit by a pickup and lost some vision in one eye. They thought she was finished, good for nothing anymore. So they quit feeding her. She was real sick. He took care of her, brought her food and medicine. By the time she got well, they were inseparable." He placed his hand on her cropped head. "I'm sure he would be happy to know you're looking after her."

"I'll take good care of her, I promise. Mom, can we clean out that stall in the barn for her?"

Maggie nodded. "Are you willing to take care of her?"

"Of course I am!" Hannah said, exasperated and impatient. She led Zia toward the barn.

"Would you like a cup of coffee? I can make some fresh."

"Sure. If it's no trouble." He followed her up the porch steps into the house. She filled the battered coffee pot and set it on the stove. "Have a seat," she waved him toward a chair.

"Thanks, Maggie," he said. He removed his hat and looked around the room. She watched him inventory the familiar objects: the knotty-pine State of New Mexico clock, the ceramic hen cookie jar with chipped beak, the blackened cast-iron skillets hanging from pegs above the stove, the heavy crockery bowls for mixing bread, the antique Mixmaster. "Hasn't changed much," he said.

"Hasn't changed at all, I don't think," she said. "Care for a piece of spice cake? How about some peach cobbler? Red velvet cake? Apple pie? There's enough here for a Wednesday Club bake sale."

"A slice of that red velvet will do. Didn't we used to have that for Valentine's Day?"

"Always. In the shape of a perfect heart." Once a year, they'd gorge themselves on the rich, moist cinnamon red chocolate cake with fudge frosting.

"The ladies keeping you well stocked?"

"You bet. If you can live on green-bean casserole and stuffed cabbage, it's not bad."

"Sounds pretty good." He leaned back in the chair, stretched his long legs, and crossed his dusty boots. The gesture, his relaxed male presence in her kitchen, were utterly familiar and somehow comforting. They might have sat together this way, pie and coffee set out on the yellow oilcloth, all their lives.

What if they had been together all these years? Night after night, listening to what happened in the store, dishing out solace with supper, would she still feel like his presence brought her to life? Would she have remained eager to be the focus of his gaze? Would she have continued to enjoy the nuances of mood that flickered across his features?

"What's this?" he asked, reaching for the overstuffed file folder on the table. He pulled it toward him.

She reached over and slid the file back "Just some papers Ivy wanted me to look over. From Santa Fe."

"Did you look at them?"

"I glanced through," she said, taking a bite of cake. She had no intention of sharing her information with him.

"What'd you find out?" he wanted to know.

His prying annoyed her. "Why're you asking?"

"Just curious," he said. "Wondered what she was up to. If there's anything new."

"Guess you'll just have to read about it in the paper like everyone else." She picked up the file and shut it in the cabinet.

"In an article you're writing?"

She held out her stained hands. "I'm doing more digging than writing these days. Any calluses I get are from a shovel, not a keyboard."

He pushed his chair back from the table. "Listen, Maggie. We're very close to signing a deal with Bradford. A development deal even you would approve. Twenty new houses, solar, energy-efficient, well-priced. Believe me, it's going to be a beautiful development."

"Where's it going to be?"

"On the west end of town, right side of the road before you go over Abo Pass. Some good views over there."

"Wasn't that your Uncle Albert's old place?" she asked.

"That's right."

She stood in front of him, hands on her hips, and smiled. "So the raw land is yours?"

He smiled. "You got it."

"That's right next to the old pueblo. No telling what you'll turn up there once you start to excavate," she said.

"We'll leave that to the archaeologists. If they're not worried, no reason for us to be."

She placed the dishes in the sink.

"Hey, Maggie," he said. "It's not going to hurt a thing. It'll only bring in some new life. Would you rather see this place go on and become a ghost town? Personally, I'd prefer to see some new people paying taxes for decent roads and schools around here."

"You know what my mother always said about politicians."

"What's that?" he asked.

"Anybody elected in New Mexico, if he's served more than two terms and he's not a rich man, he can't be much of a politician."

"I'm only in my second term. Give me a break."

"Are you planning to run for reelection?

"Do I have your vote?"

"Depends on your agenda," she countered.

"Maybe I ought to poll the constituency."

"It's interesting to watch who you'll get in bed with, Mr. Mayor."

"I know for damn sure who I'm not in bed with." He shot her a look.

Where was this going? "You said you wanted to be friends," she said.

"Look at me." He spoke each word slowly. He clasped her arm and pulled her toward him. "Do you really think I would do anything to harm this place? Do you honestly think I'd allow outsiders to help themselves to our water for a golf course?" He relaxed his grip and pushed her arm away. "You act like I don't have the brains God gave a screwdriver."

"I don't know what you would or would not do," Maggie answered. "You talk about the general good, but you've got plenty of your own reasons for letting the developers have their way."

"The right kind of development is not harmful," he said.

"It can be done without drawing down the water table any further. And if it can't, it won't happen. But I don't want one of Ivy's half-baked stories to jinx the deal."

"Where in New Mexico do you see the 'right kind' of development? Albuquerque? Santa Fe? Taos?" she asked. "Doesn't seem like there is any 'right kind.' But people have to live somewhere. And when they come in, you can say goodbye to everything that matters to those who already call the place home. Well, you're right. Monte Alto could use some new faces with new dollars in their pockets."

He smiled bitterly. "So now you're carrying on about the loss of 'our way of life.' You may not like to hear it, Maggie, but you sound just like a newcomer. You're the last one in, and now you want to shut the gate." He sighed then pointed a finger at her. "Are you even going to stick around?"

She spread her arms as if to embrace the room, the land. "Maybe. I'm still here!"

"So get involved. Get out there and work for historic preservation, write a grant, raise some money to save the old schoolhouse. If you really care about the old homestead, for God's sake, quit griping and go do something!"

"I have my hands full," she said.

"That's exactly why developers get their way. People are too busy, they keep to themselves until it's too late. Besides, if you got involved, that'd be a commitment to sticking around, wouldn't it? And you're not ready to sign on the dotted line, lady."

"I wish you'd asked me first about Zia," she said, changing the subject.

"Would you have said yes?"

"Probably not."

"Then you'd have missed the chance to see Hannah so happy." He stirred the black coffee she'd poured in a thick white mug. "You have a beautiful daughter, Maggie. But she's on the way to becoming another runaway, lost or worse."

"How do you know that?" She put her hands on her hips. "Hannah's just fine! Kids her age all have their struggles."

"I talked to her yesterday. Do you think she's the first kid I've had to round up and bring home? You have to give her something more, Maggie, if you want her to be okay here."

"I think I know what my daughter needs," she answered.

"Hey, I was just trying to help you out. And . . . " he paused. "I was trying to help myself. I had to get away from that horse."

"I can understand that. But who are you to give me advice on how to raise my child? If I need help, I'll ask for it. Zia is a whole lot of complication for us."

"I thought Hannah would be better off. And so would you. You must have changed more than I realize, Maggie. When did you ever think about saying no to a new horse on your place?" He stood and reached for his hat. "Thanks for the coffee," he said. "I'll be on my way."

Maggie let him walk out without a goodbye. She turned her back to the door. The whine of the engine faded as he drove away. And then she heard the silence.

"Who are you to give me advice on how to raise my child?" *Why had she said such a terrible thing to him?* He was only trying to be kind. She'd thanked him for his generosity by stabbing him in the heart.

Later, Hannah wandered into the kitchen as Maggie was getting supper. "Is Roger your boyfriend?" she asked, propping her cherry-Jell-O-colored head against her open palm. She wore a row of tiny silver hoops in each ear. An aquamarine twinkled from one lobe. She was dressed entirely in black, in a tee-shirt that said, "Mean People Suck."

Maggie opened the refrigerator door, but her mind went blank.

She couldn't remember what she was looking for. "No, he is not," she replied. She grabbed a bunch of parsley, carrots, celery, a hunk of cheese. She kicked the door shut. "We went to school together."

"But he *was* your boyfriend, right?" Hannah swung around on the kitchen stool.

"Who told you that?"

Hannah persisted. "So what happened? How come you broke up with him?"

"Where do you think you would be if we'd stayed together?"

"How come, Mom?" she insisted.

"We were too young." She knew how inane the answer sounded.

"So, how old were you, anyway?"

"Oh, sixteen or seventeen. And things were different then. We listened to Elvis and the Beatles, not rap and hip-hop, for starters. We knew we'd better listen to our parents or else. That was the dark ages, Hannah, before they started passing out condoms in schools." Maggie stopped herself mid-rant and walked over and put her arm around her daughter.

Hannah counted on her fingers. "I'll be sixteen pretty soon."

"And I hope you'll be smart about making your decisions then."

"How come you and Dad didn't stay together either?"

"I thought you understood about that."

"I know that Daddy wanted to be with somebody else. Daddy says you're just hiding out here. He says you can't face the real world anymore." Hannah bit into an apple.

"Your Daddy has his own way of seeing things. Looking after your grandmother is my priority right now." She sighed. "Then you do understand about the divorce?"

"I suppose." Hannah wasn't finished yet. "How come you don't ever stay together with anybody?"

Maggie gripped the edge of the sink with both hands. *Thou shalt not smack thy daughter's face.*

"I can only do my best. And I'm staying with you."

"How do *I* know?" Tears burned in her voice. "You haven't exactly stuck around so far."

"Try me." Hannah may have gone with her father, but she still wished Maggie had fought harder to keep her. She put both arms around her daughter, then dared a kiss on her cheek. "I love you," she told her.

"I know," Hannah sniffed.

"Maybe sometime you'll be able to forgive me for not staying with your dad. I just want us to go on and be a family to each other, even if it's not the perfect family you wanted."

"Sure, Maggie." Hannah nodded. "Know what?"

"What?" She smiled. "I think your old boyfriend still likes you."

"What makes you say that?" Maggie felt a blush coming on.

"*Please*, Mom. Isn't it *obvious?*" Hannah sniffed.

Maggie dumped the load of vegetables in the sink. "Not to me." She turned on the cold water and began scrubbing them. "I'll help you clean out the barn for Zia," she said. "We'll make a comfy place for her."

Hannah ambled into the living room. Suddenly, she sprang a cartwheel across the carpet. A minor collision with the TV cart broke her fall. "Ouch," she said. She got up and dusted herself off.

Maggie thought of bronc riders dusting themselves off after a fall in the arena. Her knife clipped a rhythm against the wooden cutting board as she chopped vegetables. A hill of neat chunks appeared on the side of the board. "Be careful over there. I'm making a stew for supper."

Hannah loped back into the kitchen. Her limbs seemed to have lengthened in the short time she'd been here.

"I'll make yours meatless, okay?" Maggie asked.

Hannah stood beside Maggie, chin-high to her mother. Agile as a thief, she reached around and snatched a carrot slice. She popped the carrot into her mouth. "He's pretty cool. But that's really awful about his kid."

"Those kind of accidents happen a lot out here," Maggie said. "Unfortunately."

"I'm going to ride all over this place."

"Just you be careful, my darling." Maggie tossed the vegetables in the Dutch oven and covered them with water. She found a chunk of cedar in the wood box, placed it in the stove, then, as the heat rose, added her seasonings and stirred the pot. She offered a wooden spoon for the girl to taste. "Here. Do you think it needs anything?"

"Tabasco," her daughter pronounced.

"You're absolutely right," Maggie said.

SEVENTEEN

Tommie's townhouse perched in a row of renovated Victorian apartments opposite a hillside park. She'd put off this visit, but Tommie had persisted, and her calls finally persuaded Maggie to come by. She didn't know what to expect or what Tommie needed from her after all this time. She felt obligated though, as if called on to pay a visit to a distant cousin, tugged by ties to a mutual distant past. So what if they knew some of the same people? That didn't guarantee a conversation that went beyond dim recollections and polite pleasantries.

Maggie saw no point in confronting her old friend with the past. The entire melodrama wearied her, and she'd had enough of trying to straighten it out with Roger. As Lucy would say, digging up the past does no good. Nothing would change it. She wished it would just go away. She rang the chiming doorbell of the neat, green-shuttered dwelling.

"Thank you for coming, Maggie." Tommie wore a tangerine velour warm-up suit with a v-neck that offered a hint of generous cleavage. Her dark hair was tied back with a pastel chiffon scarf, the ends draping down her back. Tall and graceful, she looked more like a model for a Caribbean cruise ad than a nurse who'd spent the day dealing with mortal illness in the intensive care unit.

The two women stood back and assessed each other. Time told the truth about Tommie. Her origins showed more clearly now: her almond eyes looked almost Chinese. Her high Indian cheekbones shaped a face with the planes of an ancient mask, and her thin, refined lips suggested a Spanish epic.

Wreaths of beribboned dried flowers and grasses decorated walls painted pastel mauve and green. Sinking into the overstuffed cushions of Tommie's flowered chintz sofa, Maggie accepted a cup of mint tea sweetened with honey. A calico cat jumped on her lap.

"Get down, Gitana," Tommie ordered. "That cat thinks she's a dog, she's so friendly. And completely spoiled. She was just a scrawny stray I couldn't resist feeding. To look at her now, you'd never believe how timid she was when I found her. Or when she found me."

Maggie stroked the cat's silky fur. "It's all right. She can stay." The cat began to purr, stretching its neck to receive her touch.

"How is Lucy doing?" Tommie wanted to know.

"About the same. Struggling to talk, to move. Eating enough to keep going. The visiting nurse comes every other day. That's a blessing. You know more about these things. What can you tell me?"

After a moment, Tommie said, "How long has she got, is that what you mean? That's what people usually want to know. Could be weeks or months. Could even be years."

Maggie placed her teacup on the scarred antique chest that doubled as a coffee table. "Maybe I better think about subletting my apartment in San Francisco."

"At least until you have a better idea how Lucy is recuperating. Otherwise, buy airline stock. You'll make them rich, flying back and forth," Tommie said, pushing up her sleeves. "I like your hair like that. You used to say you'd never cut it."

Maggie combed her fingers through her drooping curls. "I need a perm, that's for sure."

"Get yourself over to the Crowning Glory. Esperanza would love to get her hands on you." Tommie examined her own manicured oval fingernails.

"Guess I better make plans to stick around. I've got enough saved so I won't have to worry about the bills for a couple of months. Plus a bad case of city burnout."

"Monte Alto's not so bad," Tommie said. "You'll see."

Maggie gave her a half smile. "Sure," she said. "I don't see you around town."

"That's different." Tommie creaked back and forth in her bentwood rocking chair. Her apartment, with its pastel splashes of pink, blue, and yellow, ruffled curtains, and silk flower arrangements, looked like a page out of *House Beautiful.* A lady's refuge, it was so different from Maggie's chic North Beach apartment, with its gleaming wooden floors and oversized unframed abstract canvases electric with intense color.

"I don't know how to say I'm sorry about Jesse," Maggie said, studying the silver-framed photograph of a handsome young man posed as though for a yearbook picture. "I feel like a fool, letting all those years go by." She replaced the photo on the end table next to the sofa.

"I only wish you had known my boy. You have no idea how I miss him." She sighed. "And it doesn't get any easier. What about your daughter?"

"She's suffering from the divorce. And she's angry at me. She's convinced I'm to blame for the breakup. And maybe I am, but not the way she thinks. Her daddy walks on water. If he strayed, it had to be because I wasn't a good enough wife. I drove him to it. That's her version, anyway. And I wasn't there for her the way she wanted, so any amount of anger she feels is justified." Maggie shook her head. "Where did our perfect families go? Nothing turned out like we thought, did it?"

"Whose life does?" Tommie offered her a plate of bizcochitos.

Maggie bit into one of the anise-flavored cookies. "Where did you find bizcochitos this time of year?"

"I made them. Jesse loved my bizcochitos." Tommie's face brightened. "I couldn't bake enough of them. I used to pretend to be angry at him every Christmas for eating them all. I tried to hide them. Imagine."

They sat in silence as twilight enveloped the city. Traffic noise quieted to a distant hum. When a siren screamed through the dusk, Tommie rose and switched on lights.

"Maggie, for years I thought about you—every day. I wondered: Should I write? Should I call? What if she tears up the letter? What if she hangs up on me? Meanwhile, years went by and I did nothing."

"What did you want to tell me?" Maggie asked.

Tommie twisted a hanky in her lap. "I missed you. All the time."

Maggie resisted this revelation. She hesitated. "You had Roger and Jesse."

"I didn't have us. How could anyone take your place?" She set her teacup down with a clatter. Liquid jolted into the saucer. "Do you have a picture of your daughter?"

Maggie opened her wallet and pulled out Hannah's past holiday snapshot. She handed Tommie a wrinkled photograph of a smiling child in a plaid skirt and red reindeer sweater. She needed some new pictures of Hannah. But she didn't want to show off her spiked hairdo, dyed some wild color that didn't exist in nature.

"I can't believe it. She looks just like you at that age."

"Does she really?" Maggie asked. "I don't see it."

"She's got your spirit. Look at those eyes."

Maggie waved this observation away. "Actually, she's got Momma's eyes."

"Maybe the color, but not the depth. Or the fun. She's you all over." Tommie returned the photo. "I was thinking about Lucy today. Do you remember how she used to surprise us after school?"

"How she used to show up in the truck and take us downtown?"

"And buy us ice cream sodas at the Rexall?" Tommie continued.

"I haven't thought of that in years. I'd completely forgotten about it."

"Your mother loved surprises," Tommie said. "That's one of her endearing qualities."

Maggie's tension punctuated her words. "For other people, you mean. She hated being surprised. Particularly by a rattler."

"Don't talk about her in the past tense, Maggie."

"I don't see much hope in the situation. I'm trying to resign myself and just keep her as comfortable as I can. Isn't that what you're telling me to do?"

"We'll have to wait and see. It's not impossible for her to improve." She poured them each another cup of tea from the blue-and-white-flowered china pot. "Have you seen Roger?"

The question caught Maggie off guard. "A few times. Why?"

"How did he seem to you?" Tommie asked.

"All right." Maggie considered her words. "He's got his troubles. He's still grieving for Jesse, that's for sure."

Tommie stood. She paced the room. "Things were never right with us," she said. She shook her head. "Never. Everyone in town thinks I kicked him when he was down; that I should have stayed and ridden it out. Every woman there believes that's what she would have done. But they don't know. I had to leave." Tommie faced Maggie. "You know, he never stopped thinking about you."

"I don't believe that." Tommie's statement shocked and embarrassed her.

Tommie stood, her face flushed. "I'm going to tell you everything. Right now."

"I don't need to hear your confession, Tommie."

"But you're still angry. And I still feel guilty."

Maggie stared. Her problems seemed trivial when weighed against Tommie's loss. "I'm the one who ought to ask your forgiveness," she said.

"Whatever for?"

"For letting old hurts stand between us."

"Please listen, Maggie." Tommie spoke slowly. "You were going off to Berkeley. Roger and I felt left out. Sorry for ourselves. You can understand that, can't you?"

Maggie nodded. "I suppose."

"One night Roger and I went down to the train station. To talk. I started crying. I needed something—comfort, reassurance, to know I wasn't going to be completely alone after you left. I'm the one who turned to him. It wasn't the other way around. Just so you know." Her voice fell to a whisper. "I've never been able to forgive myself."

She raised her fists in the air. "I got pregnant that night. I didn't even know that could happen. Guess I thought the first time wouldn't count." Her arms fell to her sides. "We thought we had to get married."

"That's the way it was then. I have to give him credit. Roger did the right thing by you."

"Yes. He did. We even talked ourselves into believing we were in love. So it wouldn't all seem like such a big mistake. And so we could overlook what we'd done to you. A week before the wedding, I had a miscarriage. But we decided to go through with it anyway."

"You stayed together all those years."

"Roger and I were friends, Maggie, remember? We went to State and got our degrees. We learned to rely on each other. I got pregnant again during senior year. Then Jesse was born, and he kept us together." She stared into the whirlpool of her memories. "Without him, it all fell apart."

"You were my best friend!" Maggie couldn't help herself. She didn't want to carry on, but the emotion she'd held back for so long poured out. "We were raised like sisters!"

"You're right. We were like sisters. You have no idea what it was like, watching you walk away with every prize, with every honor. And if that wasn't enough, you had the best guy. I felt like your sidekick. But then, Maggie, you left us!"

"I left. I left. That's my crime. Well, you all made it real easy never to come back!"

"Nobody could have stopped you. We wouldn't have dreamed of getting in your way. You had all the opportunities we didn't. We wanted to see you succeed."

"You're right. I made my choice. And I'll have to live with it."

Tommie reached out her hand. "I wish we could start over."

Unable to respond, Maggie stood and began to pace.

Tommie's voice followed her. "Jesse played guitar. We'd just gotten him a new one for Christmas. He was in a band, a few of his friends who got together on Saturday afternoons. One night, he said he wanted to go out and practice with his band.

'Not on a school night,' Roger insisted. It was the end of senior year, but Roger didn't want Jesse to think he could slack off. But Jesse was determined. They fought. Roger finally let him go." Tommie choked on her words. "That was the last time we saw him."

"I am so sorry," Maggie said, "that you lost him."

"I still dream about him. When he was a baby. I've never loved anyone so much."

"What was your life with Roger like?" Maggie asked.

"Like most marriages. Work, church, TV, Sunday dinners, school meetings, fights. You know how he can get."

Maggie nodded. "He can be moody, all right."

"Try living with it. But all in all, you couldn't tell us apart from any other couple you know."

"It could have been worse."

"Don't I know it! But I could never be you, Maggie. All along, I knew it was wrong. I knew Roger and I weren't meant to be together. He never got over you."

"If Roger thinks he's missing something, it's only because he hasn't seen me in the morning before I've had two cups of coffee. And I've never yelled at him to pick up his socks."

"Roger and I are through, Maggie."

"So you're handing him over to me. And it's not even Christmas."

"Maybe you're the one who can help him." Tommie's gaze was hypnotic, impossible to turn from. "Maybe you're the one he needs."

"You're the professional. Do I look like a social worker to you? Besides, he seems about as much on track as anybody else."

"You look like somebody with a heart. Somebody who knows what counts."

Maggie was not about to reflect on the state of her own

heart. She quickly changed the subject. "What are things like for you now?"

"Work at the ICU. That's about it. Not much time to think about myself. I can only sleep when I'm exhausted. If I have a day off, I clean the apartment, walk around the mall, see a movie. Thank God I'm in the city."

Maggie stood. She rubbed numbness from a leg that had fallen asleep.

"Last door down the hall." Tommie tilted her head in the direction of the bathroom.

Maggie passed three closed doors.

The same magazine-inspired decorator's touch dominated the bathroom. Light-blue color-coordinated towels matched the seashell-print shower curtain and the soft rug; baskets of potpourri scented the room with rosebuds and cinnamon. The face in the mirror looked more than tired. Maggie slid the bathroom cabinet open, looking for Advil. She searched through the prescription bottles jamming the shelves. Lots of medication; none over-the-counter.

Maggie wondered if Tommie kept the Advil on her bedroom dresser. She walked out of the bathroom and opened the next door in the hallway.

The stifling smell of burning beeswax filled the darkened room. In a corner, votive candles flickered on an altar bedecked with flowered scarves. The shrine was crammed with a quartz-crystal rosary, a teddy bear, a red rose, the statue of the Santo Niño that had graced Jesusita's altar, a color photograph of Jesse—a smiling boy in a Little League uniform—and a white porcelain figurine of praying hands.

In the center of the altar rested a plate of bizcochitos.

Candlelight played shadows over the tin-framed Lady of Guadalupe hanging above the altar. Standing on her crescent moon, supported by an angel, wearing her blue mantle studded with golden stars, she presided over the shrine with her look of complete serenity.

Jesse's things, his team pennants, posters of rock stars, his guitar, kindergarten paintings, baseball caps, report cards, and class pictures were posted about the makeshift chapel.

She struck a match and lit a candle. Then she closed the door and returned to the living room. "Tommie," she said, standing at the threshold.

"Yes?"

"I'm sorry. I don't know if we can go back to the way it used to be. Probably not."

"That's all gone, isn't it?" She sat quite still, her face in shadow.

"But I'd like to know you again." She put her arms around Tommie. They embraced. The little calico cat jumped down from the sofa and rubbed against their legs, purring, until they had to laugh.

EIGHTEEN

Giving up on a night of broken sleep, at 4:30 a.m. Maggie hauled herself out of bed. While coffee perked, she paced the kitchen. Then, tackling one of the jobs on her long list, she removed dishes from cabinets and stacked them on the table. Two hours later, she'd finished lining the shelves with fresh yellow-checked paper and replaced the dishes in neat order. The house breathed along with the peaceful inhalations and exhalations of her charges as they slept.

She poured another cup of coffee and watched day break in the eastern plains. A jolt of aquamarine fractured the violet horizon. Slowly, a fortune of golden light suffused the sky. That magic glow lasted only moments, then drained away, leaving an endless ceiling of polished porcelain blue.

She picked up a pen and began to doodle on the yellow pad in front of her. The thick stem of a letter formed on the page. Her hand finished shaping an "R," then surrounded the letter with a circle of arrows pointed toward it. As she scribbled, a plan came to her. She spent the morning bathing Lucy and cleaning the house, then she got ready to go out. The sight of Hannah and Lucy playing Chinese checkers was her reward for the morning's endeavors.

Maggie got in her truck and headed toward town. First she picked up the groceries. Old Mr. Branson insisted on helping her out with her grocery bags. Tall and stooped, he struggled with loading the bags into the truck, but to offer assistance or refuse his help would never do. Next she went to the bank, then on to the post office, exchanging greetings with folks along the way.

People knew her now. As she went about her business, she received tips of the hat and hellos. Everywhere she went, people inquired about her mother's health and asked how Hannah was getting along. People she didn't even recognize asked if there wasn't something they could do. They told her to call if she needed a hand with anything, anything at all. And if they couldn't get whatever she needed done themselves, why, they'd get their son-in-law from Sherlock over here after work to fix it. And they meant it.

She returned to the truck and headed out toward the new neighborhood on the edge of town. She drove around look-alike houses with shingled roofs, brick fronts, well-watered lawns, and rose gardens until she found the house she was looking for, one as immaculate as a real estate ad, a place so orderly it appeared uninhabited, and, to her eyes, haunted.

Only one piece of the picture wasn't magazine perfect. Roger had a car up on blocks in the driveway. Whether he was taking it apart or putting it back together, she couldn't tell. But she recognized that car. She knew his '56 baby-blue Thunderbird.

She sat in her truck parked across the street and recalled the day he'd gotten that car, during the spring of their junior year. The afternoon had been one of brilliant May light, that famous crystalline light that brought artists to New Mexico. Wisps of cotton from the cottonwood trees swirled through the air. She'd been in the barn grooming her horses, and walked out just as he drove up. If there was ever a frame of her life she'd like to freeze forever, a moment she'd choose to return to and live in, that was it.

She stood and watched him cross the front yard. When he reached her, he leaned over without a word and kissed her. It wasn't the first time, but it was the first kiss done as part of an everyday greeting that confirmed they were now "boyfriend and girlfriend." He took her hand and led her to his car. Then he opened the door for her. She slid over the seat and rode close beside him.

They drove west to Abo. There they watched the sun set behind the standing wall of the three-hundred-year-old San Gregorio mission church. Shafts of light smoked through the clouds like pillars to heaven, a backdrop for three stories of red sandstone rising out of the desert. It was an awesome view, and the place also had a reputation as a make-out spot. If you looked too close, you could see empty beer cans, cigarette butts, and other garbage left by those who came here to park in secrecy. There was something more than a little scary about this isolated ruin where the Franciscans had erected their religious monument atop the ancient pueblo, its dwellings and gravesites and sacred kivas. And the place was crawling with snakes. Her mother had always warned her away from here. Local superstitions backed her up. Ghosts were sighted here, and so were fireballs, believed to be departed spirits, usually around Halloween, the time of year when Spanish people celebrated their Día de los Muertos, the Day of the Dead.

"Everything was fine until the Spaniards came and made the Indians their slaves," she said.

"You know those Spaniards. Always hunting for gold. Always needing help finding it. Always searching for those magical Seven Cities. Wouldn't want to get in their way," he said.

"What do you suppose is in those mounds?" Maggie mused, though she had a pretty good idea.

"Bones. Mummies. Pottery. Beads and feathers they traded from Mexico and Peru. That's what Uncle Albert told me. He always wanted to hunt the stuff up."

"How come nobody's dug them up yet?" she wondered.

He placed his hand on the back of her neck and moved it caressingly under the collar of her blouse, sending wild shivers down her the length of her back. "They're waiting, baby," he said.

"What for?" One hand explored her shoulder, while he slipped the other inside her blouse at the waist and began a slow, excruciating journey upward. She couldn't bring herself to ask him to stop.

"For us to go inside. Want to Maggie? We'll be the first to get at all that loot," he whispered, breathing into her hair, making her his with small, gentle circles of his fingertips. She was awed by a sudden realization of the power of his maleness. No longer was he the familiar friend with whom she felt so comfortable. Gold and lavender clouds darkened into night. They kissed hungrily, unable to stop, then drove each other crazy as brilliant galaxies of stars lit up the night. Afterward, connected to him in a new way, she found out what fear was. She believed she would die if she couldn't be with him.

She covered her eyes with her hand. Her mind went blank. Why was she sitting parked outside this man's house in the middle of the afternoon? What was she supposed to do next? A yellow pad lay on the seat beside her. She picked it up and wrote him a note, signed her name, then folded it in half, got out of the truck, and crossed the street. She tucked it into his mailbox.

Then she got back in the truck. She sat and waited. Not a car passed. A cat ambled across the lawn. Two people walked across her memory. She saw her mother and Elias, out in the pasture, working the cows together. That's how she remembered them, all the years she was growing up. They were always together, yet always distant. She never understood how they could work together every day, yet never really talk to each other.

At night, Lucy came into the house and Elias stayed in the bunkhouse. Maggie missed him, his jokes and his warm presence. She wanted Elias to sit at the table with them, she wanted to hear his grumbly voice. She worried about him out there all alone. She couldn't understand why Lucy didn't invite him to eat with them, but she never dared question her mother's decisions. Meals were flavored with loneliness.

Again, Maggie got out of her truck. She slammed the door and ran across the street. She grabbed the note from the mailbox, tore it into pieces, then stuffed the shreds in her pocket. She headed back downtown.

At the hardware store, Roger was busy with a customer, a thin, elderly fellow who needed a particular piece of pipe. She watched Roger search for the item. He showed the man several variations, but none of them would do. Throughout the interaction, Roger remained patient. He looked tired. When the man left, finally, with a $2.85 piece of pipe he thought might work, Maggie stepped forward.

"Hi, Roger," she offered.

"Maggie," he greeted her. "What can we find for you this afternoon?"

"Nothing in the way of hardware," she said. "Though it looks like you've got everything here a person could use to fix things or keep them running. I want to talk to you. I wanted to apologize for the other day."

He raised his eyebrows. One always lifted higher than the other. "What for?"

She recognized that look. It revived the memory of the boy-man she'd once been so crazy about. "I think you know. For what I said."

He waited, thumbs tapping.

She took a deep breath. Her words came out in a rush. "It was so good of you to bring Zia. That horse has made all the difference for Hannah. She's so much happier now." She hated her words. They sounded like a speech.

"I'm glad. Glad to be of help." He waited.

"Are you busy?" she asked.

"Look around. Not specially." He tinkered with the old-fashioned scale on the counter.

"I don't know why I said what I did. When you questioned the way I handled Hannah, I just snapped. I obviously have a problem there. I guess I can't handle anything that sounds like criticism when it comes to her."

"It's okay, Maggie. Not a problem. Apology accepted." He didn't bother looking her in the eye.

"Look. I don't want it to be like this between us."

"Well, how do you want it to be?" he asked, facing her finally.

She didn't want to be the one to say. The fan whirled above, clackety-clack, over and over.

"Look," he said, "can you meet me at the Seven Cities tomorrow night?"

"Fine. Good. Yes." Inside, something broke free and soared.

"About eight?"

"Sure. See you then." She waved a hand as she backed out of the store. She just missed knocking over the paint display.

~ NINETEEN

MAGGIE, WEARING A CORAL SWEATER, brushed a blush called Dusky Rose on a face that makeup hadn't touched for months. She could see the changes in her face. A willingness to be amused brightened her eyes. Tension lines around her mouth had relaxed as her strained face had filled out, and the shadows under her eyes were almost erased. She had taken an odd beauty cure of hard physical work and caring for those who needed her.

She had been wearing a mask so long she had forgotten she had it on. The wind had sheared it away, but once she knew she could stand up to the wind's force, once she stopped resisting it, it had gotten under her flesh and into her bones. It stripped away self-consciousness and left only what was true and necessary. It had revived her.

The mirror also reflected a pile of discarded clothes on the bed, including a little black dress, a silver glitter top, and a royal-blue silk blouse. She had tried on just about every item she owned in an effort to look as though she weren't trying. Maggie brushed her hair and fastened it back with a silver and turquoise barrette. That didn't look right. She tried pinning it up. She unfastened it. She pulled it into a pony tail with a black clip bow. She brushed it loose again. A pile of earrings lay on her dresser. Opals, pearls, turquoise, lapis, silver, gold—she couldn't decide which ones to wear.

Hannah slouched into the room. Her shirt was imprinted with the famous picture of the earth taken from outer space captioned "Love Your Mother." She flung herself on the bed and pulled a pillow over her head. "Too blatant, Mother," she said.

"What are you talking about?"

Hannah rolled off the bed and stood beside her in the mirror. She pointed to the bit of black lace that topped the camisole Maggie wore under her sweater. "Ooh la-la."

"That's just for fun. I think it's pretty."

"That's not what *he'll* think," Hannah said.

"Since when did you become the expert?"

"Everyone knows these things, Mother. When was the last time *you* went out on a date? You're not supposed to look like you're asking for it."

Maggie pulled up the black lace edging to make sure it covered any hint of cleavage. "I'm not asking for anything," she muttered.

Hannah continued the sarcasm she found so funny. "Then what are you doing? Hot fudge sundaes at the soda fountain?"

"How's grandma? Has she had supper?" Maggie quickly asked.

"That's it. Change the subject, why don't you." She grabbed a pillow and clutched it to her face. "Oh, my darling," she breathed. She smooched loud kisses all over the pillow case.

"It's time you looked in on your grandmother."

"Fine, Mother. Ignore my instructions at your peril." She flung the pillow on the floor and flounced out of the room.

As soon as Hannah left, Maggie reexamined her outfit. She pulled off the sweater and replaced the lacy camisole with a black turtleneck. Definitely not, she decided. She slipped the camisole back on. She let her hair fall loose, down to her shoulders. Then she sprayed some Chanel on her wrists, the back of her neck, and above the edge of black lace. She decided pearl-drop earrings provided the right finishing touch.

She picked up the brush and curled the ends of her hair under. When she clipped on a barrette to hold the sides back, the final effect was familiar, but not one she was accustomed to seeing in her own mirror. She recognized in her own face the faces of women she'd grown up around, those distinctively Western ladies who always kept their lively prettiness. All their lives, they wore their hair curled under, in the same style they had worn as young women in the 1940s. Their faces made no secrets of their strength or their tender feelings. They liked to laugh, and they never failed to show you they understood whatever you were going through. They looked real, and they were.

Maggie went down the hall to say good night. Hannah and Lucy were engaged in a game of cards. "What are you playing?" she asked.

Hannah looked up at her. "Spite and Malice."

"Where did you learn how to play that?"

"Grandma taught me."

"So, Momma. You've finally got you a bridge player. Guess it just skipped a generation."

Lucy managed a half-grin and a croak.

"This isn't bridge," Hannah said.

"It soon will be," Maggie replied.

Hannah shuffled the cards. "So tell me, Grandma—what did

you wear when you went out on a date with Grandpa? Did you go dancing? Did you ever have other boyfriends? Did you go out smooching?"

Maggie locked eyes with Lucy. The room went completely still. She could swear she saw her mother blush. Hannah saw it, too.

"Sorry, Grandma! Didn't mean to embarrass you," Hannah laughed. "Guess you were pretty wild in your time."

The hand in which Lucy held her cards was trembling. "Are you going to give your grandmother a hard time when I leave?" Maggie asked.

"We're going to have some serious girl talk," Hannah said. "And you're going to miss the really good stuff."

Maggie walked from the doorway to the bed to give her mother a hug. Then she hugged her daughter. "You take care of Grandma," she said. "I'll be back by 11."

"Yeah, right," Hannah said.

"Here's the phone number where I'll be." She handed Hannah the slip of paper. "Call if you need anything."

"We won't," Hannah said.

"Are you sure you're okay here?" Maggie asked.

"Bye, Mother. Have fun," Hannah waved.

As Maggie walked to the door, she heard kissing sounds behind her. She turned and blew a kiss back at Hannah. She was reluctant to leave them.

Roger waited in a booth at the back of the Seven Cities. The saloon was the only place in town that was free of memories for them. They'd been too young to be allowed in back when they'd been seeing each other. An empty suit of armor greeted patrons at the doorway.

"How do you like my conquistador?" Lukie asked from behind the bar. "His name is Don Juan," he giggled.

Maggie patted the statue's arm. "Don't you think he'd be better off in a museum someplace?"

"Nah. He likes it here. I got it off one of those lost Spaniards myself. Had to peel it off him."

"What does he like to drink?" Maggie asked.

"You wouldn't know it to look at him, but he's a whiskey drinker. I leave him one straight up when I close the place. Keeps him happy. Don't you know the glass is empty by morning."

Roger watched her approach in the dim light. She met his gaze as she walked toward him. He slid over to make room for her. "Hi," he said. He'd ordered her a margarita. It sat in her place beside him, next to his glass, glistening, with a thin slice of lime balanced on the neatly salted rim.

"Hi." She hesitated. Sitting next to him meant one thing, sitting across from him another. She slid over the brown vinyl next to him, just beyond range of his body heat. Brenda Lee crooned on the jukebox. Aside from the regulars at the bar, the place was empty.

"Slow night," she said.

"You look great," he said. "I like your hair that way."

He was trying to shift gears that were on the rusty side. "Thank you," she responded. She clinked her margarita with his Jack Daniels and took a sip of the salty-sweet-sour drink and gave his hand a squeeze. "Tonight feels kind of like the old days," she ventured. "Like meeting somewhere after school."

"Better," he said.

"How's that?"

"I'm smarter." He smiled. "And you're more beautiful."

A woman would do some awfully stupid things to sun herself in the light of that smile of his. "Your lines sound just as good as ever."

"Oh, I've even got some new ones. Might surprise you yet."

"Such as?" She smiled at him.

"Like this: 'I'm sure glad you came back, Maggie.' How's that sound to you? Or 'I don't know where my sorry self would be if you hadn't come home.'"

"Don't know if I can buy that one."

"How come my great lines don't work on you?"

The air between them started to heat up. "What do you mean?"

"How come, no matter what I say, or do, you're always pushing me away?" He placed her hand between both of his.

She looked him in the eye. "I'm here, aren't I?"

"You sure are." He brushed the ends of her hair. "What's the deal, Maggie? Do I strike you as a one-night-stand kind of guy?"

"I know you're not," she said.

"Do you think I have any less to lose than you? How many chances do you think I have left?"

"I don't want to make any more mistakes," she said.

"Then you might as well hang it up right now." He placed his hands flat on the table.

"Maybe I already have. Maybe I've taken one fall too many."

"I'm not willing to buy that." He took her hand again. "I want to hear you say yes to me."

Her hair swung back as she tilted her head toward the glowing jukebox. She smiled. "Want to dance?"

"Thought you'd never ask." They slid out of the booth. He stopped at the jukebox and made a selection.

He put an arm around her as Merle Haggard's knowing, tender voice wrapped them in a guaranteed-to-break-your-heart, you're-never-gonna-make-it-out-in-one-piece-alive love song.

They glided around the tiny dance floor in the rainbow glow of the jukebox. She inhaled the tang of his skin. They danced song after song. Neither of them wanted to stop. "What time is it?" Maggie asked finally.

"Quarter to ten," he said.

"I've got to be getting back," she said. "I'm more nervous than I thought I would be about leaving my ladies at home."

With a hand on her shoulder, he guided her back to their booth. They sat in silence. She had no compass and no notion how to navigate this territory.

"Maggie," Roger began at last. "I've been thinking about what happened. With us."

She looked at him, holding her breath. In slow motion, she leaned toward him. She grazed her lips over his. He sat still as stone, simply receiving her touch. She sat back. Even in the shadows, she could see his face had gone chalk white.

"What is it?" she asked.

He tried to speak, but no words came out. He shook his head. He clasped her shoulders. "I want to tell you," he whispered.

"Tell me, tell me," she responded.

He looked behind her. His face broke into confusion. She turned. Lukie stood beside the booth. *Why was he intruding? Couldn't he see?*

"Phone for you, Maggie."

She tensed. "Is it my daughter?"

"Yes," the bartender replied. "Your mother's not well."

"Not well" was the going euphemism for "expect the worst." When somebody was "not well" around here it translated as "too serious to say." Maggie sprang out of the booth. She ran to pick up the phone behind the bar.

"Hannah! What is it?"

"I don't know," the girl cried. "Grandma was fine. Then she started choking. Now she can't breathe!"

"I'm on my way. Will you call 911?"

"I already did." Hannah's voice was on the verge of hysteria.

"Good girl. I'll be right there." Maggie slammed down the phone.

Roger held out her coat. "Let's go," he said.

"It's Momma."

"I know. We'll get you home as fast as we can." He opened the truck door for her.

"I should never have left them alone."

His knuckles were white on the wheel. "Don't," he said. "Going there is pointless. Believe me, I know."

Cumulus clouds, the high pillow clouds of summer, drifted across a three-quarter moon that backlit the indigo sky. He took the road as fast as he could. His eyes scanned the edges of the woods for the startled deer that might leap out at any time, for the porcupine lumbering in front of the truck.

When they burst in the front door, they found Hannah curled in a ball on the couch, sobbing. "She's dead!" she screamed at them. "Grandma is dead!"

"No!" Maggie cried. "That can't be! She's just had another stroke. We'll get her right to the hospital." Her arms went around the trembling girl. "She's going to be all right. You'll see." Lucy couldn't have chosen this time to die, not when Hannah was alone and she was gone.

"No, no. Really. Go see. It's true," Hannah cried.

Roger stayed with Hannah as Maggie walked down the hall to Lucy's room.

One look told her Hannah was right. Lucy was gone. Her face finally relaxed, her mouth slack, her skin already tinted with a blue-gray cast. Maggie lifted the friendship quilt folded on the rocker. She approached her mother's body holding out this flag of simple loyalty, of beauty made of scraps by hands that didn't know how to stop working.

Maggie had grown up with death. She'd seen it often, and it didn't surprise her. No place to hide it out here. Cows died. Calves were born dead. Men hunted; that's how most people got Sunday dinner. They dragged home dead antelope and deer and elk. Then they told you about the kill—where it happened, and how the animal died. She'd put her own horse, old and blind, to sleep with a shotgun. She recognized this rigidity, this finality.

She unfolded the quilt and covered her mother's still body. That done, she stood beside the bed, lost, beyond thought or speculation or memory. Then she bowed her head. She offered a prayer. *"Please God, bless her journey. Let this good woman, this good mother and grandmother and friend find peace. Thank you for bringing us all together here. Amen."*

Maggie returned to the living room. She sat beside her daughter and embraced her. Gently, she said, "What happened, baby?"

"I was asleep," Hannah said. "I mean, I think I was. I was in bed. I know that. Then I was having this dream where Grandma got up. So I went to her room. I saw her walk over to this man. He was standing at the foot of her bed. He was holding out his hand. She took his hand. Then they disappeared. It's like they melted away."

Maggie bundled an afghan around the girl's shoulders. "What did the man look like?"

The girl's voice trembled. They strained to make out her words. "He was kind of little. He wore a cowboy hat pulled way down on his forehead and a buttoned-up brown jacket." Hannah couldn't stand still. She bounced around the room, practically hitting the walls.

Maggie locked eyes with Roger. They both said the name at the same time: "Elias!"

"So that's when I called you," Hannah said, beginning to sob. "Who was that little man?"

"Somebody who used to live here. He and Grandma worked together on the ranch a long time."

"It wasn't Grandpa?" Hannah's eyes opened wide in disbelief.

"No, honey. It wasn't your granddad."

Hannah seemed to accept this fact, then her curiosity prevailed. "Where is Elias now?"

"He passed away a few months ago."

Hannah looked from Maggie to Roger as they all struggled to take this report in. "So I saw ghosts?"

"Spirits. You and Grandma were very close," Maggie said. "She wanted you to see what you saw."

"It really happened. I saw them. I really did."

"We believe you," Maggie said.

Roger spoke. "Your grandma wanted you to know she had a friend on the other side. So you wouldn't feel so bad about her leaving."

"Do things like that really happen?"

"They just did," Roger said. "You'd be surprised. Around here, it's not so unusual. When you've been here a while, you'll hear plenty of stories like what happened tonight."

"How come?" Hannah asked.

He took her to the window. "Just look outside," he said.

"So?" Her usual diffidence returned.

"So what do you see?"

"It's just empty." She waved a hand, dismissing the view.

"That's right. Looks empty, doesn't it? But there's space out there. And the more you look, the more you can see. All that emptiness, that sky and desert, gives dreams and memories and spirits a place to be."

"What was Grandma's friend like?" Hannah asked.

"He was the sweetest man," Maggie said. Tears came to her

eyes. "I only wish you could have known him. He was like a father to me."

"Does that mean she's happy?" Hannah wanted to know.

"I don't think you have to worry about her," Roger said. "Your grandma was a strong woman, as strong as they come. I have a feeling things happened tonight just the way she wanted."

A siren screamed. The window glowed red as the ambulance pulled up to the house.

Roger stayed until dawn, helping Maggie fill out the coroner's forms and the death certificate. He handled the officials who showed up with clipboards and kept the coffeepot going. Before he left, he tucked Maggie into bed, then checked on Hannah, who had fallen asleep in her jeans and tee shirt on the sofa. He found a quilt and covered the sleeping girl.

TWENTY

On the morning of Lucy's funeral, the Wednesday Club gathered in the parlor of Findlay's Mortuary. They each wore their best funeral clothes—neat, predictable belted black dresses with jet buttons, pearls, pillbox hats topped with veils. Details distinguished their outfits: a pinstripe on one dress, a pattern of embossed roses on another, the texture of raised dots on the third.

"Will you look at that sweet smile on her face," said Ruby, tallest of the assembled group, as she leaned over Lucy's open coffin. "They've done a lovely job. I'm real impressed." She looked around the room. "And how about these flowers? It's like a jungle in here! Hasn't been a display like this since Doc Caul passed on."

"Doc brought most of the town into this world for better than forty years," said Elvira.

"And saw quite a few of 'em depart," Ruby said. "Lorraine

swears to it: the night he died she took the shortcut home across the field behind his office. Do you know she saw a fireball rolling along like a tumbleweed."

"There were quite a few reports of rolling fireballs that night," said Elvira.

"Doc always was real good about his house calls," Ruby said.

"I know Lucy wanted to be buried in this blue lace dress," Mercedes said over recorded organ chords. "She kept it wrapped up in tissue paper for years. But she looks a smidgen bewildered, don't you think? Not quite herself, to be honest."

"She doesn't look quite right to me, either," said Elvira. "But I was out to the ranch earlier. Found these things in the drawer of her night table." She untied the knot in her floral handkerchief. Several small objects fell out.

"Did you ask Maggie if it was all right?" Ruby wondered.

Elvira stared. "What do you mean?"

"Nothing. Nothing at all," Ruby said.

Elvira raised her eyebrows. "Well good." She shut the curtained French doors. "Let's get to work then, ladies. The whole town's gonna be here before we know it."

Mercedes pushed her walker over the burgundy carpet to stand beside the coffin. She reached in. She lifted Lucy's hand. "Look at this. They even gave her a manicure. Her first, I'll bet." She addressed the corpse. "Wherever you're going, dear, you're going to look just fine. We're here to see to it." She patted Lucy's hand.

She fitted white gloves between the hands. Elvira raised Lucy's head from the pillow. She arranged the short veil of a blue straw hat over the forehead.

"Let me do that, will you?" Ruby teetered over and realigned the veil. "Been to so many funerals lately," she sighed. "Last week I had two on the same day!" She centered the hat and tucked wisps of white hair under the brim. "There. Isn't that so much better? Surely you agree."

"I hope she appreciates the trouble we're going through to get it right for her." Elvira removed a bolo tie from her purse. She laid the turquoise and silver ornament alongside Lucy's skirt and tucked it under a fold. She glanced at the door. "Golly. The smell of those flowers is enough to knock you over."

"What's that, dear? One of her husband Billy's bolos?"

"Not exactly," Elvira replied. "It is a bolo I found on Lucy's nightstand."

"Then how do you know it's not Billy's?" Mercedes asked.

"Because it has 'To E. R. from L. C.' engraved on the back," Elvira hissed.

"I see," said Mercedes. "Do you really think we should leave it with her?"

"I'm positive that is exactly what she wanted," Elvira said. She hid the black strings from view.

"Elvira, how can you be so sure?" Mercedes said. "Are you saying that Lucy and Elias..."

"I'm not saying anything of the sort. They worked together for better than forty years. That ought to amount to something, don't you think? A little tribute isn't out of line here."

"I'm not so sure about this," said Mercedes. "What if somebody notices? We don't want to be setting off rumors at this stage of the game."

Elvira faced Mercedes. "Since when did you turn all hat and no boot?"

Mercedes's oxygen tank wobbled. "This is for eternity, Elvira."

"That's right. And I expect Lucy to be there waving us in with a smile on her face when our time comes," Elvira said. "That's why we're going to do this little thing for her now."

Ruby poked Mercedes. "Maybe Elvira knows more than she wants to say about Lucy and Elias," she whispered.

"I know they were extremely fond of one another," Elvira said. "Let's leave it at that, shall we ladies?"

"Let she who is without sin cast the first stone," Mercedes said.

"Amen," said Ruby and Elvira.

"Do you think she would have chosen that color lipstick?" Mercedes asked.

"It is a tinge on the orange side," Ruby said.

"Could be that yellowish light they've got in here. It'd make anyone look sallow," Mercedes said. "Where's her glasses?"

"Right here." Elvira slipped the silver-framed bifocals on Lucy's face.

"Now that just makes the whole outfit." Mercedes clasped her hands together in satisfaction.

"Do you think so?" Ruby wondered. She smoothed a wrinkle from Lucy's sleeve. "She didn't always want to be seen wearing her cheaters."

"They make her look like herself," Mercedes said.

"She'll need 'em for cards, that's for sure." The lenses flashed as Elvira straightened them over Lucy's eyes.

"She looks so happy. Just like she was going out to play bridge," said Ruby.

"And planning to take home the winnings," said Elvira.

"She couldn't ask for anything more," said Mercedes.

"No, she couldn't," Elvira touched a hanky to her own eyes. "She had her ways. She did. I remember how she beat gas rationing during the war."

"She rode her horse into town every Saturday for her supplies."

They all laughed. "I can see that," Ruby said. "I remember how she'd brag about that snake that had the nerve to crawl into her kitchen. 'Got him dead center,' she always said."

"She was worse than some old fisherman," Elvira said. "Every time she told the story, that snake got bigger."

"She always wanted to see Yellowstone. Too bad."

"She never took a vacation."

"That's right. 'I can't afford to take two weeks out,' she'd say. Nobody could look after things but her. She didn't like to be away for a single night."

"But she had Elias on the place," Mercedes said.

"He did so much," Ruby said.

"Now she's ready. Not a minute too soon. People are here to see her."

The volume of organ music went up. The ladies stepped back behind pillars of russet and gold chrysanthemums and ivory lilies. They nodded as mourners filed in.

"Where's Maggie?" Ruby wondered.

"You can be sure she's not just leisuring this morning," Mercedes said.

"Last I saw her, she was trying to round up that daughter of hers. Hannah had taken off on that palomino," Elvira said. "The one that belonged to Jesse."

Seated at Lucy's vanity, Maggie straightened the white collar and buttoned the top button of her black suit. Her one Neiman's outfit. Simplicity—how expensive it could be!—was what it had going for it. She'd gone everywhere in this understated garment: to court, to publishers' meetings, to interviews with legislators, and she never had to worry about how she was dressed. Today it would again provide the armor she needed. The soft crepe of the jacket pricked the sensitive, raw-feeling skin of her arms. She ached from the inside, as though she'd taken a bad fall. She wished she could climb into a hot tub, close her eyes, and stay there all afternoon.

She was cried out, wrung out. Her throat was raw from sobbing and light hurt her eyes. Yet a certain peace had come over her since last night, perhaps from the knowledge that Lucy didn't suffer any more, that she was truly at rest. And Maggie wouldn't have to stand by and watch a strong, proud woman become increasingly helpless and dependent.

She picked up Lucy's alabaster brush and ran it through her hair. She missed Lucy already, more than she would have believed possible. True, her mother hadn't provided her the warmth and affection Maggie craved. But now those lacks and the lifelong resentments they had sprouted weren't so important. Lucy's enduring presence had meant something more, something Maggie was, in her grief, just now beginning to understand. Lucy had been a solid rock wall, a sheltering oak. She had been a steady, reliable presence in her daughter's life. Whether she liked it or not, Maggie always knew where she'd stood with her mother. And she couldn't argue with the things her mother stood for. Lucy's unwavering love of her land, her tradition, her community, her uncomplaining dedication to hard work and the belief that her survival was in her own hands made her a model of womanhood Maggie had to respect.

The mirror suggested, with no subtlety whatsoever, that she had aged a dozen years. No makeup mask would disguise the facts. Lines around her eyes and forehead creases seemed to have become full-fledged, no-doubt-about-it wrinkles. Welcome to a preview of coming attractions, it told her. Get used to it. She put on her dark glasses to cover her puffy red eyes. That would just have to do. Her patent leather pumps beat a sharp rhythm along the empty hallway. It was almost time to leave for the funeral. She knocked on the closed door. "Hannah? Are you almost ready? We need to be going."

She knocked again. When no answer came, she opened the

door. There was no time to fool around. "We need to leave," she said. But she spoke to empty air. A breeze at the open window tugged the curtains eerily. She hunted for Hannah all over the house—up in the attic, in the living room, the closets, behind every closed door.

Maggie walked outside, her stomach registering fear. Zia wasn't in her corral, either. She got in the truck and started driving. She wasn't sure what direction to head. She followed the faint trail behind the barn. Hannah was fond of that path. She drove slowly, scanning the fields. She caught a movement at the edge of the trail. It could have been a deer, or an antelope. She drove toward the flash of movement. As she approached, she recognized Hannah on horseback. She caught up to the girl. Then she got out of the truck, stomping mad.

She picked her way over the dusty ground in her good shoes. Hannah sat three feet above her in the saddle. Her toxic green hair stuck out at an odd angle. Natural roots poked up from the scalp in wild contrast with the unnatural color the girl had chosen. Maggie saw both the child she was and the woman she would become. But she was dealing here with neither of those. Hannah stared down at her mother with cold eyes that shut her out.

A tremor shook the girl's chin like the trembling of a wounded bird. If Maggie had found a quivering a creature lying hurt on the ground, nothing could have stopped her from scooping it up and cradling the frightened critter against her breast. She'd have done whatever it took to set it right so it could fly again. But right now, she could not reach out to her daughter.

"What do you think you're doing?" Maggie asked angrily. "Why aren't you back at the house and ready? We need to get going!"

"I'm not going," said the girl on horseback.

"It's your grandmother's funeral! What do you mean you're

not going?" She had to restrain herself from yanking her daughter out of the saddle.

"I know it's my grandmother's funeral, Mother," Hannah said in a monotone. "Thank you for that information. Is there something wrong with your ears? I said: I-am-not-going."

"We have to go!" Maggie shouted, provoked by Hannah's insolent response.

"You mean you have to go." Hannah turned the horse and began to ride away. "And don't you dare try to make me. If you think you can."

Maggie took a deep breath. "Hannah, please," Maggie called after her, struggling to gain some calm. "We both need to be there."

Hannah rode away without looking back. Maggie got in the truck and put her head down on the steering wheel, too heartsick to drive. Neither screams nor persuasion were any use. Dealing with her daughter had taken her last kernel of strength and will. Mechanically, she put the truck in gear and headed back to the house. She walked to the kitchen sink, turned on the faucet, and splashed water on her face. "All right then." Tears knotted her heart and burned her throat, but she was too worn out even to cry. She gathered her gloves and handbag and stepped outside.

From across the field, Hannah came galloping toward her. "Wait! Wait for me!" she cried. She dismounted and walked up the steps. "I changed my mind," she said. "I want to say goodbye to Grandma," she whispered.

Maggie decided to forget about her own emotions and put her arms around the sweaty, sticky, heartbroken girl. All Hannah had needed was a chance to make up her own mind. "Thank you, sweetheart. I'll wait for you in the truck."

The ladies at the mortuary exchanged a knowing look. Ruby spoke. "I guess the little girl is taking it hard. Wasn't she home alone when Lucy passed?"

"Too bad Maggie was out," Mercedes murmured. "At a time like that."

The ladies looked at the floor. They nodded in unison.

"You can't very well expect her to stay locked up in that house day and night," Elvira said.

"But what was she doing out after dark? At the Seven Cities?" Mercedes asked.

"She is a grown woman," Ruby said.

"Give her some waggin' room," said Elvira. "If you expect her to stay in the neighborhood."

"Well here she is now," said Ruby.

Maggie took her place beside the coffin. She began to shake the hands offered her. Tommie walked in stiffly, wearing a black mantilla, her hair pulled back in a twist. The two women embraced, then looked each other wordlessly in the eye.

"Heavens. Nobody ought to arrive at a funeral looking so good. That Maggie could stand up right next to Jackie Kennedy."

"Leave the poor child alone, will you? It's not her fault black suits her," Elvira said.

"I didn't say she looked happy. She's properly pale. Done her share of crying, I'm sure," said Ruby.

Mercedes spoke. "Lucy shed her tears, too, but she went right on and kept the ranch running."

"Maybe Maggie will do the same. She's been hard at it in that garden. She's got her hands full with that girl," commented Ruby.

"Will she stay, or will she sell out? That's the sixty-four-dollar question," said Elvira.

"Maggie will do the right thing," Ruby replied. "That's what Lucy always said, anyway."

"She is her mother's daughter, after all," Elvira said. "So it won't be long 'til we're rubbin' off on her."

An hour later, Maggie stood in the middle of the crowd on the sidewalk outside the funeral parlor. Hannah, in a white blouse and navy skirt Maggie had no idea she owned, stood by her side. This day would be remembered for its heat. Here it was, only May, and the sun already blazed to eighty-six degrees. Overnight, what little spring they'd had had turned to summer. Weeds already shot up along edges of the buckling sidewalk.

"Ah yes. Yerba la negrita," said a woman shrunken like an ancient doll. Wrinkles inscribed every inch of skin on her face. She took note of the path of Maggie's eyes. She waved her cane in the direction of the weeds. "Makes the hair grow! Make your black hair shine, real pretty."

Maggie struggled to remember her name.

The woman responded to her lapse. "Fabiola Gutierrez. I was a friend of your mother's. I will miss her."

A safety pin where three tiny golden angel medallions jangled was fastened to her blouse. Maggie remembered. Fabiola stood outside the post office each afternoon for years. She talked to anyone who happened by. It's what she did for company. She had no one. She faithfully stood at the post office, invited everyone who went inside to mail a letter to visit her in her little house across the street. No one ever did, that Maggie knew of. The kids thought her house was haunted.

"Your mother was very kind to me," Fabiola said. "She brought me bread, fruit, eggs. No one was ever so good as your mother."

"Thank you," Maggie said.

"Your daughter?"

"Yes. This is Hannah."

"Que bonita. You had a wonderful grandma, 'jita," Fabiola said.

Hannah took her hand. "Thank you."

"Be good to your momma. She needs you now." The old lady backed away into the crowd.

Car doors slammed. Motors revved. The caravan to the cemetery lined up. Tommie and Roger stood together out of the way of the crowd in the shadow of the mortuary. The intensity of their conversation was unmistakable. Each listened to the other, completely absorbed, then fired back another passionate round of words. *What if they got back together?*

"Miss Chilton?" A frail gentleman leaning on a walker asked for her attention. She held out her hand. "We're so glad you came back to be with your mother," he wheezed. "I'm sure it meant the world to her to be able to count on you." He shook his head. "You probably won't remember me. I'm Milo Burch."

She glanced up. Roger and Tommie were still talking. What in the world did they have to carry on about all this time? Roger, arms folded, leaned against the front wall of the building. Tommie touched his shoulder. Her hand lingered there. Was she straightening his lapel?

"Your mother came and looked after my two babies after my wife passed on. Lucy came over every day 'til I got back on my feet. She never would take anything for her trouble. She'd turn her pocket out for you. Even in the droughty years."

Maggie tried for a smile. "People have some wonderful things to say about my mother today."

"Oh yes. There's nobody who didn't think very highly of her. No finer lady in town. You have a lot to be proud of." He hit the pavement with his cane to emphasize his point.

"And a lot to live up to, I'm afraid." She wished she could go and hide.

"What's wrong with that, Miss Chilton?" the stooped gentleman asked.

She shrugged. "Not a thing, I suppose. I just don't want to be a disappointment to anyone."

"You couldn't be." He placed a kindly hand on her shoulder.

"Well, thank you. Thank you for coming." Impulsively, she hugged him. The frailty of his dry bones shocked her.

Roger had left Tommie and now stood beside them. "Can I give you a ride over?" He knew she needed to make this last ride with her mother, but here he was, offering what small comfort he could. She wished she could tell him that his presence was the only bright spot in the day.

"No thanks. We're going to ride up front." She nodded toward the large black hearse.

He squeezed her shoulder. "How are you doing?" His touch pushed her shakiness away. She immediately felt stronger, taller, just standing next to him.

"As well you could expect. Which means about as well as somebody who's landed in a burning barrel of kerosene." Her tears started flowing again. "Thank you for staying the other night," she told him.

"I sure know how all that goes." He nodded toward his ex-wife, who was chatting with the minister. "Tommie and I still have a bit of old business to settle. Listen, Maggie." He took her hand as he spoke in a low voice. "I'm glad to be there for you however I can." He took a handkerchief from his pocket and wiped the tears from her face. Then he leaned down and gently kissed her forehead. "See you over there, Maggie."

Hannah turned to Roger. "I'll ride with you," she volunteered.

"No, Hannah. You go on with your mother." He tipped his hat and walked away. To Maggie's relief, he didn't get in the car with Tommie.

An hour later, Maggie stood with the mourners at the Hilltop

Cemetery. A plain, dusty place on a rise overlooking a scraggly bunch of piñon and juniper trees, the old homesteaders' burial ground had an air of abandonment. Tilted wooden crosses, simple stone slabs, dates and names fading, homemade picture frames, marked the gravesites. The place emanated humble dignity.

The family plot stretched across an entire row. As the preacher began speaking, Maggie read the gravestones. There were her aunts, the infants, an uncle killed in the war in France who'd flown into a cloud and never flown out again, her grandmother and grandfather, her father, and now, beside him, the freshly dug grave prepared to receive her mother. The plot stretched many yards farther, empty earth willing to receive her bones. Along the edges, blue cornflowers and garnet and yellow Mexican hat sprouted, the most common, toughest wildflowers, the kind that grew best in deserted fields and along dusty roadsides.

Maggie had come here often with Lucy, who'd had to badger her to get her here. The humble cemetery seemed a place distant in time, a place that had nothing to do with her. As a little girl, she placed a plastic poinsettia or a new wreath on the grave of the father she had never known while her mother weeded the plot. She watched as her mother stood silent a long time before the grave. She could now imagine her mother's silent dialogs with her absent husband as she stood there.

A strange place for a cemetery, some might say, outside a schoolhouse. But maybe not. The little community could only afford to keep up one building, and it wasn't a church. It was a school. All the community activities—the quilting bees, the pie socials, the cakewalks, the dances, the weddings, and the funerals, were held in this little schoolhouse. So they buried people in the same place they'd done their living.

The minister opened his Bible. Maggie recognized the poetry of Psalm 126. Lucy had so often recited it aloud that Maggie knew it by heart. The words were a source of faith to her mother: *"When the Lord brought back those that returned to Zion / We were like unto them that dream / Then was our mouth filled with laughter, / And our tongue with singing."*

Maggie looked up. A hawk circled above. She watched the raptor inscribe a circle in the faultless blue sky. She bowed her head.

"Then said they among the nations, 'The Lord hath done great things with these / The Lord has done great things with us; / We are rejoiced."

Maggie looked up again. The hawk ascended straight up to the sky. In his beak dangled a snake.

At last, she understood the sign.

"Turn our captivity, O Lord, / As the streams in the dry land. / They that sow in tears / Shall reap in joy. / Though he goeth on his way weeping that beareth the measure of seed, / He shall come home with joy, bearing his sheaves."

With creaking of ropes, Lucy's coffin was lowered into the ground. Maggie threw the first shovelful of earth, then passed the shovel to the circle. She'd done the right thing by coming home. Thank God she'd been able to make amends with her mother. She turned to leave the cemetery. Tommie waited for her at the weather-beaten picket gate, her arms wide open. Maggie walked into the offered embrace. She laid her cheek against Tommie's warm rose velvet skin.

"I give up," Maggie sobbed.

"It's all right querida," Tommie said. "It's all right." As Tommie smoothed her friend's hair, Maggie swore she heard the low accented voice of Jesusita, the midwife, the curandera, her mother's best friend.

TWENTY-ONE

The third day after Lucy's funeral, Maggie did something new. At four P.M., she stretched out on the couch and watched the Oprah Winfrey show. With daylight burning and plenty of chores waiting, she stared at the TV screen. So long as her mother had been in the house, even half-paralyzed and flat on her back, Maggie never dared slack off. If Lucy walked in now, she'd scold: "What do you think you're doing leisuring in the middle of the day like the Queen of Sheba? Last time I checked, that garden wasn't watering itself!"

And the place was getting away from her already. Dishes piled in the sink, weeds choked the garden, growing taller by the hour, yet here she sat, like a child home sick from school.

Oprah's guests were animated and sincerely irate. Maggie couldn't quite grasp what they were so upset about. Their mouths opened and shut and words came out. Their problem, no doubt, was relationships. Today the topic was infidelity. You could count on drawing an audience for that subject.

Like a confused butterfly, her mind flitted about as she tried to absorb the fact that Lucy was gone forever. That's what death ultimately means to the living, she reflected. Mixed with the sadness was the struggle to accept the hard truth of permanent absence. Maggie had so recently dealt with the death of Ramona, and already, time had tuned down the ferocity of her feelings. She was moving away from the sight of the girl's blood and her screams for help. She had acquired the dubious peace of distance. These days she replayed that brutal tragedy only once every hour or so, instead of obsessing on those events day and night, on into her dreams.

But it was different with Lucy. Her mother had inhabited this house, and she was no longer anywhere Maggie expected to find her. Maggie just couldn't get used to her being gone. So she stared at the television.

She turned to Hannah, huddled in the wing chair. "Are you getting hungry? All you had for lunch was some potato chips and a few nibbles of cheese."

The girl shifted. She uncurled her legs and refolded herself. "Not really." Her eyes also remained fixed on the television screen.

Was a two-word reply an improvement over the usual monosyllabic response? Hannah had worn the same torn jeans and stained tee shirt the past three days. She must be sleeping in those clothes, going without a bath all that time. Oily spikes of two-tone hair protruded from her head at odd angles. She had the surprised expression of a stranded chick.

As a baby, Hannah had given her that wide-open look, that slight raise of her half-moon eyebrows. It looked like surprise. She had been a happy baby with a sweet disposition, easy to care for. Back then, Maggie had been able to figure out what her baby needed and get it for her. Food, cuddling, or sleep had usually quieted her. Not any more. Hannah let Maggie know whatever she could offer was unwanted, useless and beside the point. What the point was, Hannah kept to herself, but Maggie was supposed to know. The game was set up so she could never win.

"I'm not hungry, either. But we should eat something." She stood. "How about if I fix us some pasta?" She had to at least try to take care of this child.

"Okay. Doesn't matter. Whatever you want." A stream of tears ran below the surface of her words.

"I know you miss Grandma," Maggie attempted. "I sure do. She loved you very much. You're a lot like her, you know. She loved your spunkiness." She chanced sitting on the arm of Hannah's chair. Sensing Hannah would allow it, she stroked the girl's tense back. "I wish you could feel how much I love you," she told her. Hannah didn't reply. Maggie actually felt her heart sink to the pit of her stomach. Trying to talk to her daughter worked about as well as talking to her mother had.

Afterward, Maggie walked down the hall to Lucy's room. She hadn't entered it since she'd placed the quilt over her mother's body, and she had to go in sometime. She opened the door. Might as well get started clearing it out. She could still get something done today. She raised the shade and opened the window. The mattress had been stripped bare, but otherwise, the clutter was thick as ever. She went to the closet. Old shoes, handbags, garter belts, boxes of God knows what crammed every inch of space. She wouldn't be able to wedge a dress off a hanger without the whole mess tumbling down.

She ran her hand over the tightly packed clothes then pressed her face to them. Her mother's scent, a compound of talcum powder, camphor, and rose water, lingered there. As she rubbed her cheek over textures of wool, rayon, and cotton, heartache seeped through her body.

How desperately she had loved her mother, and how unrequited that love had been. She had tried every way she knew, turned every somersault she could dream up. She'd knocked herself silly. But Lucy had been too wrapped up in her own worry ever to appreciate her efforts. Feeding her, clothing her, educating her, teaching her how to work: that's how Lucy had perceived her job as mother.

Was this a bad mother? No. But Lucy's lack of affection had created a hungry, frightened child who learned early the dangers of revealing her hunger and fear. The only way to hold her mother's respect was to stand up for herself and win. Winning that never-ending contest was how Maggie had managed to keep some kind of equilibrium in this house.

Afternoon sunlight warmed the room, carrying the sweet breath of lilac from the big hedge on the south side of the house, laced with the itchy scent of pollen. The lilacs were especially profuse and long-lasting this year, thick with heavy cones of gorgeous blossoms. That hedge, almost up to the roof now, got started with twigs Aunt Lorna carried all the way from Oklahoma. Did the plants come from Virginia before that? Aunt Lorna's grandfather had run a nursery in Richmond. If Maggie could trace the path of those lilacs, she could trace her own origins, back to the colonies, maybe, and all the way back to the clans of Ireland, Scotland, and Wales. They always moved west, looking for something better than what they'd left behind, and she'd gone farther west than any of them. Could now be the time to retrace her own steps home?

A meadowlark called from the field of rabbitbrush outside the window. Between the blue-gray bushes of sage, a roadrunner darted. The longer she looked, the more she saw. She belonged in the living landscape framed by the window. The silhouette of serene blue Monte Alto consoled her like a medicine woman's healing prayer, with the beat of the drum synchronized to her heartbeat.

She shut the closet door. "Hannah?" she called down the hallway. "What are you doing? Will you talk to me?"

She stood beside her daughter. "Talk to me, please." She took Hannah's hand. She wrapped the small palm inside her own. "Tell me what you're feeling. Scream at me if you want. Anything. Just don't go away."

Hannah withdrew her hand from Maggie's grasp. "I miss Grandma," she said in a small voice.

"Is there anything I can do?"

"Leave me alone."

The words stung like a slap across the face. "Don't do this to me," she pleaded.

Hannah looked away. "I can't make you feel better."

"All I ask," Maggie said, "Is that you don't push me away. Don't put up walls between us. I need your help here."

"I can't help," Hannah said. "Why don't you ever care about how I feel?"

Maggie placed her hands on her daughter's fragile, narrow shoulders. "All right. I understand. I'm here. No matter what. Just give me a chance."

"A chance for what?" Hannah muttered. She clicked the TV to another station. The earnest weatherman predicted high winds for southeastern New Mexico, including Monte Alto, with the possibility of funnel clouds in the east.

A knock sounded at the door. Neither had heard anyone drive up. When Maggie opened the door, Roger stood before her, his angular shoulders blocking the sun, outlined by an aura of golden light. "Just wanted to see how you all were getting along." His shirtsleeves were rolled to the elbow, and the muscles of his forearm flexed as he removed his hat.

Maggie wiped a hand across her eyes. She waved him into the living room. "Come on in," she said. She lacked the energy to put a smile on her face or a lilt in her voice.

He glanced around the room and nodded at Hannah. "Maybe it's not such a good time. I can come back another day."

Hannah rose from her chair. She went to Roger and put her arms around him. Maggie had witnessed this little drama before. He placed a hand on her head. "You growing your hair out?" He ruffled the funky locks.

"I guess."

"We've got to get you a hat," he said.

"So I can be a real cowgirl?" she asked, trying for swagger with her sarcasm.

"Why not? Say, I have to pick up some supplies in Sherlock. Thought you ladies might want to ride up there with me. We can grab some Mexican food at Montoya's."

"Thanks for the invitation," Maggie said. "But I don't know if we're up to going out."

"Gotta get out sometime. How long you gonna stay cooped up in here like this? Besides, it's a beautiful afternoon. Some fresh air and sunshine'll do you both good."

"You go ahead," Hannah said.

"Oh, no," Maggie said.

"Really." Hannah looked her straight in the eye for the first time that day. "I mean it, Mom." She hugged Maggie. "Go do something else besides fight with me. I can take care of myself. You don't have to babysit me forever."

"What do you say?" Roger gave Maggie a wink. "We'll only be gone for a couple hours."

Maggie thought a moment. "Well, all right. If you're sure."

"I'm sure, Mother," Hannah said. "Now go change your outfit."

Maggie looked down at her coffee-stained tee shirt. "I'll just run and put on a clean shirt."

"What would you like us to bring you from the Mexican restaurant?" Roger asked Hannah.

"A smothered bean burrito."

"Red or green?"

"That's the big question around here, isn't it?" she pouted.

"You bet it is," he grinned. "There's people put money on which is better."

"Red then."

"You got it," he said.

Maggie reappeared, wearing a light-blue denim shirt tucked into her jeans and her Tony Lama boots, her hair tied in a ponytail with a red ribbon clasp. Her energy had returned with the prospect of getting out of the house and going somewhere, anywhere. Even Sherlock. Some decent Mexican food and a beer and she'd feel better. She'd be like Scarlett O'Hara and worry about the rest tomorrow. The fragrant afternoon spread its golden wings for her. "You're sure you'll be all right?' she asked Hannah.

"Omigosh, yes. I'll be fine. Honest," she replied, sprawling her long legs up on the couch.

"We won't be back late," Maggie said. "Before dark."

"By eight," Roger said.

"Don't worry about me," Hannah said. She lifted her hand in a goodbye wave, a trace of a smile on her wan face.

Outside, in the truck, Roger turned the ignition. Maggie glanced back at the house. "What is it?" he asked.

"I don't feel right leaving her alone."

"We won't be gone long. She'll be fine. Why shouldn't she be?"

Maggie shook her head. "I don't know. No reason, really."

Along each side of the two-lane road to Sherlock, bright new leaves clothed the gnarled limbs of venerable cottonwood trees.

Drifting puffs of cotton caught the light as they twirled and glistened like tiny prisms. Spiky heads of purple thistle poked up through grasses that shimmered like feathers of light. The air was full with the scent of green new life and the hum of insects. Roger drove slowly, in no hurry. They didn't speak, but marveled as the gorgeous afternoon unfolded around them. Maggie stared at the miles of wooden fenceposts as though hypnotized.

"So Maggie." Roger kept his eyes on the road ahead. "Now do you think you could be happy here in Monte Alto?"

She faced him. "That's not the question."

"Well then, what *is* the question?"

She smiled. "The question is: Can I *be* here? At all?"

"And the answer?"

"The answer is yes," she said.

"What about the happy part?"

Her arm described an arc that encompassed the world they moved through. "This is it."

"It is?"

"There's no such thing as 'happy' all the time. You just have to stay ready for the moments. You can't hold onto it any more than you can get your hands on a redwing blackbird."

"The redwing always was your favorite bird," he said. "Maybe because they live in marshes, and there's not a whole lot of wetlands where we can find them around here."

"I'm amazed you remembered that."

He shifted his hands on the wheel. "I remember more than you think. But it's not that I remember. I just never forgot."

She gazed out the window. Faded ads on a passing barn read MEAD'S FINE BREADS and AERMOTOR WINDMILLS: PUT THE WATER WHERE YOU WANT IT.

"By the way, what's happening with your real estate deal?" she asked.

"It's dead," he said.

"Who, or what, killed it?"

"Doesn't matter. Other things are moving. The old Irby place sold last week to a developer who's done a lot of work in Santa Fe. They're gonna divide it into forty acre ranchettes. Blue Grama County is changing, whether or not you and I approve."

"What about the water?"

"There's enough for now, the hydrologists claim. And when they need more, they can truck it in and store it in tanks. That's one thing you don't have to worry about, with your good well and your springs."

"Our water also makes our land a prize for any developer," she mused. They continued past several mile markers in silence. "They'll be after us all the time. They'll look at our old corrals and see a golf course."

"What are your plans, Maggie?" he asked, at last.

"I'm staying on for now. It's a struggle, but me and Hannah are slowly finding our way." She thought out loud. "Being on the ranch, where we have to work together, gives us a better chance to learn to appreciate each other. Even if she's only here for vacations, I want to give us the best chance."

"And what'll you do?"

"Work with Ivy on the paper, I suppose."

"What'll you do with the ranch?"

"Everybody'll say I'm a cup and saucer short of a place setting. But I want to grow the old seeds Ivy and the Wednesday Club give me. Even though I keep refusing their invitation to join the bridge club, they keep handing me those seeds." Her voice rose with excitement. "Roger, between the old well and the springs, with a few improvements, we've got enough water on the place to manage some small farming. There's quite a market for fresh basil, baby squash, and heirloom tomatoes at the farmers markets and those Santa Fe gourmet restaurants now. I might even put in a greenhouse and grow salad greens and those edible flowers they use to decorate the plates year-round."

"Sounds good to me. Better than ostriches or emus, anyway. Seeds have their points. They don't eat while you're asleep."

"What about you? Where does it put you with Randy?"

"Randy can jump in the Rio Grande gorge as far as I'm concerned. He's not worth the powder it'd take to blow him away."

"Oh my. What can have brought about this change of heart?"

"I've found out one or two things I don't like."

"Mister, you've been holding out on me. Afraid you might give me the chance to say I told you so?"

"Go on and say it. You earned it."

"Not 'til you give me a good reason."

"How's this: He was behind that break-in at Ivy's place."

"How'd you find this out?"

"Told me so himself. He wanted to see what she was planning to write about him. He thought it was funny. Then he insulted me by thinking I'd share the joke. Only one thing to do though."

"What's that?"

"Make sure he's gone for good. He left town with the promise he'd never set foot in Monte Alto again."

"What's funny is he thought he could intimidate Ivy," Maggie said. "Does she know?"

"She will."

"Because she'd go after him like . . . "

"A duck on a june bug?" he asked, with a crooked smile.

"Something like that."

"No way a lowlife like that will hang around our town for long."

"You sound more like sheriff than mayor tonight. Come to think of it, you'd look good with a silver star on your chest."

"I don't need Randy Bradford's money. Nobody around here does. You were right. He'd milk us for every drop, then leave us."

"High and dry."

"Thank you."

"You're welcome. Just don't go getting the idea I'm opposed to growth. We need development. But finding the right kind isn't easy."

"Where's your Bible?"

"Is there a verse you want to read me?"

"I want to swear on it: I am not now, nor will I ever be, a fanatic environmentalist."

"Keep that up, you'll be voting Republican before long."

"Dream on." A flash of color caught her eye. "Roger, will you look at that? Over there?"

"What do you see?"

"Those trees." She pointed. "Back there."

Behind the cottonwoods was a small grove of apple trees in delicate pink and white bloom. "Pull over," Maggie said.

He slowed the truck, steered it off the road, and killed the engine. "Let's go see," he said.

She followed him through the dappled shade. Fragrant flowers of the gnarled apple trees were alive with the hum of honeybees and the whirring wings of ruby-throated hummingbirds.

"I bet heaven smells as sweet as this," Maggie said. "Those trees look like they've gone wild. Whose old orchard is this, anyway?"

"This isn't just any old orchard," Roger said. "These are trees the first friars brought from Spain in the seventeenth century.

"My grandfather said they used to cut the shoots and leave them in the ditch until the new ones rooted. That's how they kept them going all that time. They say the last ones died out in the thirties, when some government expert came in and fed 'em some special fertilizer. Ended up killing 'em instead. But

I'd always heard there were a few left someplace around here, growing near a spring."

"Manzanos. Sweet little golden apples," Maggie said. "Incredible they're still here."

Roger snapped off a sprig and brushed the pale petals across his lips. Then he tucked it in Maggie's hair. Then, as easily as he had given her the flowers, he drew her to him and kissed her. His lips met hers gently and tenderly.

She drew back and tucked her head under his chin. Her lips brushed the exposed skin beneath his unbuttoned shirt collar. His steady pulse kindled her old ache. Instinctively, she put her lips to the hollow of his throat and savored the taste of his skin—wild grass, burnt sugar, salt.

She looked up at his face. The perfection of its planes and angles dazzled her. She kissed him, hard, full and open. He tightened his embrace. Their breathing synchronized. He took her hand and led her into the darkness of the cottonwood grove. He stopped beside a tree and pressed her against it. Rough bark dug at her back. He unbuttoned her shirt. The wind blew across her bare breasts and time shifted into slow motion. They lay together, limbs entwined, in the shelter of the tree. He covered her face and her hair with kisses as he chanted her name. He traced her form, up and down, back and forth, gently at first, then gradually increasing his demand, until she opened to him completely. She ran her hands up and down his back, learning him as he moved within her, slowly, deeply, with a deliberate passion that gave way to abandonment, rousing her beyond any sensation she had ever known. She knotted her fingers in his hair and screamed into the wind as finally, he met her desire.

Unwilling to separate, they drifted together for an unknown time. Suddenly, he flinched. Then he turned from her, distracted by a sudden sound. "Maggie, look," he whispered.

She struggled to see what he saw. "What?"

He pointed. "Over there. What do you see?"

"Just trees."

"It's a bear. A black bear."

"How can that be?" She strained to perceive the shape emerging from the woods: the triangular head on the low-to-the ground body. The bear lumbered closer in the falling darkness. With a single swipe, it rolled over a ten-foot log as though it were a twig and clawed its underside for grubs. Then the bear stood and let out a roar that seemed to come from the belly of the earth. The bear swiveled its head in their direction and sauntered toward them.

"Lie still." Roger covered Maggie's shoulders with his arm, his gesture emphasizing their nakedness and vulnerability. She fought the urge to bolt. The bear stopped about twenty feet away. Again it stood, and looked around blindly. It turned and sniffed in another direction, then disappeared into the forest with a snort and a rustle of leaves.

When they were sure the bear had left, they dressed quickly and cautiously walked back to the truck.

On the drive home, they held hands but did not speak. He walked her to the door. Moths beat their wings against the front porch light. Chastely, he kissed her forehead.

"Can I call you tomorrow?" he asked.

"Maybe that's what I like best about you," she smiled.

"What's that?" He angled his hat back on his head.

"Your sense of humor, cowboy."

He grinned. "Sorry I got you home so late."

She grabbed his wrist. "Call me," she whispered. She reached up and kissed him once more on the cheek. She turned to open the door. "'Night, baby," she heard him say.

The house was dark and still. She walked upstairs and tiptoed into Hannah's room. In the ray of light shining from the hallway, she saw that Hannah lay asleep, breathing peacefully. Maggie straightened the blanket Hannah had tossed aside.

"Where's my burrito?"

Maggie jumped. "I thought you were asleep."

Hannah sat up, wide awake. "Did you forget it?"

"I can fix you something if you're hungry. How about an omelet?"

"How was the Mexican restaurant?"

"We never got there."

"Why not?" Hannah perked up at the chance to tease her mother.

"Something else came up."

"Yeah, right, Mom." Hannah started to giggle. "Like I can't imagine what."

Maggie frowned, at a loss for words, as Hannah ducked under the covers and drew them up to her chin. "Oh, Mom! Your shirt's on inside out."

"Goodnight, honey-child," she said, and left.

Downstairs at the sink, Maggie splashed water on her face. She was too agitated to sleep. She was hungry, but not for food. She felt her face, her throat, her breasts, the places Roger had touched. She paced the kitchen floor. She looked out the window at the constellations, wheeled around to their summer-sky positions. She'd become a cat ready to prowl the night. She jotted a note for Hannah: "I'm right next door if you need me. Love, Mom."

She grabbed a jacket and went outside into the starry night. She opened the creaky door of Elias's bunkhouse. She struck a match and lit the candle on the bedside table. Candlelight glowed on the hand-carved santos and the well-worn cast-iron pots of the simple sanctuary. She crawled under the rough woolen blanket on the cot. She thought she heard Elias's voice, the beloved male voice of her childhood, come to her out of the flickering shadows.

"It's all right, 'jita. He is a good man. He loves you. Do not be afraid."

In moments, she was asleep.

TWENTY-TWO

MAGGIE AWOKE DEEPLY RESTED AND SERENE, her mind free of scattered dreams. By the angle of light, she gauged the time at around eight, which amounted to serious oversleeping. She stood and stretched until her fingertips grazed the low ceiling. With a single motion, she swished open the green-checked gingham curtains above the bed. Sunshine washed the room, revealing the bunkhouse's cobwebs, cracked paint, and scratched floors. Sometime soon she needed to get in here with a mop and bucket. Like so much else around the place, there was nothing wrong that couldn't be fixed with several hours of well-applied elbow grease.

She wanted to spend more time here. The handmade pine table in the corner would make a sturdy desk. She could spend hours there, watching the play of wind over sage and mesquite and an ever-changing endless sky framed by the window.

She hadn't had a real meal in days. She decided on a big

breakfast: eggs, bacon, home fries, green chile, and pancakes for Hannah. She lifted a cast-iron skillet off the shelf. It was time to put Elias's pots back to work.

On the path back to the house, she stopped still as yesterday's events with Roger began to replay in her mind. A cricket's chirp punctuated her thoughts as she inhaled the land's calming morning perfume. Her footsteps released the scent of mint growing wild beside the path. She bent to pick a few leaves. As she continued to the house, she brushed the length of a juniper branch. Fine needles pricked her fingertips. Each sensation registered with fresh clarity.

Truth was, if you didn't pay attention, you didn't make it out here. If you wanted to stick around, you couldn't afford to get lost inside your own head. There were snakes, bobcats, and lightning to contend with, and they didn't fool around.

Back in the kitchen, she glanced at the weather instruments by the door. The barometer's pressure was low and falling, as was the temperature. On the wall nearby was the National Bank calendar where Lucy had recorded each day's reading and temperature. The squares were blank, as they had been for weeks, since Lucy had become ill. With the pencil dangling from a tacked-up string, Maggie inscribed the morning's numbers.

As bacon sizzled and warmed the house with its fragrance, she cracked eggs one by one into a chipped crockery bowl and beat them with a fork. She heated Elias's skillet. She would make Hannah's pancakes with crushed pecans, the way she liked. Maybe later on they'd go into town, visit at the café. She poured the beaten eggs into the skillet and slid bread into the toaster.

When breakfast was ready, she went upstairs. She knocked at Hannah's bedroom. "Breakfast is served. Come and get it!" she called. She waited. No answer. She called again. She knocked again, loudly. It was past time to be up. No sense lying tangled up in sheets all day. It was a beautiful clear day. Hannah should be out enjoying the morning, and she should be getting to her chores.

Slowly, she twisted the tarnished brass doorknob and pushed the door open. Patchwork quilts were piled in a jumble on the empty bed, as if a scuffle had taken place there. She slid the closet door wide, but her daughter wasn't hiding there, either.

A fresh breeze coming through the open window swayed the organdy curtains. Maggie scanned the yard below, through branches of lilac bushes under the bedroom window. She ran out of the room. "Hannah!" she screamed. She raced down the stairway. "Where are you?" Deliberately, she searched the house: the pantry, the closets, the empty rooms with shut doors. As if Hannah were a four-year-old playing hide-and-seek, Maggie expected to find her, wearing a mischievous smile.

Finally, she retreated to the kitchen. There, on the counter, she found the note, in purple ink: "Mom—went riding—want to see those old ruins. See you later. xxx H.

Maggie sat down to breakfast, but her appetite was gone. She munched a few bites of toast then flipped on the radio. Between reports of lost pets, trailers for sale, and the daily reading of the obituaries on the local station, the weather report forecast sunshine this morning, changing to thunderstorms by afternoon. Hardly unusual for this time of year, she told herself. She cleared the table and put everything up. She'd better see how much she could get done before the weather changed. She put the dishes in the sink to soak and pulled on her gloves and straw hat.

She opened the makeshift chicken-wire gate to the garden. Right away, her sense of balance returned. She knelt. The ground was soft. Her seedlings had sprouted and grown new leaves while her back was turned. She had never seen anything come up so fast as those Ghost Ranch calabacitas or any corn so healthy as that

Acoma blue. And the Quarai beans Ivy had given her were taking off like magic, with little assistance and less water. With her trowel, she loosened the earth around the rows. Meticulously, she extracted each weed by the roots, then applied a new layer of mulch. She remembered something she had once heard—Indians buried *ollas* in the garden, and water dripped out of the porous pottery water jugs at exactly the right rate for the beans. Maybe she ought to give it a try. She could take down Grandpa's old ollas and plant them between the rows.

A blanket of dark cloud drifted across the face of the sun, blocking its warmth, as an engine hummed up the road. Stepping down from her old Chevy beater, Ivy landed with a bounce. Draped around her neck was a loopy crocheted rainbow creation, the lightweight version of her six-foot purple scarf. In her arms Ivy held a squirming bright-eyed ball of fur. The puppy wriggled down from Ivy's grasp and ran to Maggie.

"No doubt about it. Border collies are the most intelligent dogs," Ivy said. She took in the orderly garden, the respectable pile of weeds, the woman with dirt streaked on her face and arms and mud on her shoes. "Well, well," she mused. "Looks like you've become a real hand!"

The puppy jumped up and licked Maggie's face. She embraced the warm, lively bundle of delicious softness. "If she wags that little tail of hers any harder, it'll break."

"Where's Hannah?" Ivy asked. "This is her puppy."

"Out riding. Toward Abo, she said."

Ivy's eyebrows shot up. "They're predicting thunderstorms, don't you know." She nodded toward the sky where thunderheads were already piling up into towers on the horizon.

"They do that most afternoons, don't they?" Maggie asked. "So how come it never rains?"

"It rains someplace, all right. It'll rain, here, too," Ivy answered.

"Always does when it comes from the east like this. And we're overdue for a big one."

"Thanks so much for coming by. I'm sure glad to see you." Maggie hugged her. "Hannah will be back soon, I hope. Just wait until she sees this little sweetheart."

"I thought, well, this puppy of Annabelle's will give Hannah one more reason to think about sticking around. Besides, you need a dog. She'll make you a fine companion. Best security system you could want."

"Thank you, Ivy. She's adorable." Maggie looked at the bright eyes, fuzzy ears, and perfect tiny paws.

"This here's a cow dog deluxe," Ivy said. She turned and unhooked the pie safe and gently removed a latticed rhubarb pie sparkling with beads of sugar.

"What's new with you?" Maggie asked.

"Now that you ask, I do have an item to report."

Maggie gave her a thumbs-up sign. "Good news, I hope?"

"I suppose most people would look at it like that." She drew a breath. "I've got me a new friend."

"Of the pants-wearing variety?" Maggie smiled.

"Yes, ma'am. Do you by any chance remember Aubrey Redwine?"

"The music teacher? Who played the guitar?" Maggie reached back into her memory and recalled a tall, quiet redheaded man in suspenders.

"That's the one. Except since he's retired he turned full-time cowboy poet. He goes all over to perform. He even got invited to the Smithsonian Institution. Back East, they call him a 'folk artist.' So we've been packing up on weekends and traveling around to his performances. Been to Silver City and Tucson in his big old Airstream."

"Are you telling me there's dating after seventy?"

"Of course there is, my dear." Ivy sounded as indignant as if she'd been asked if she knew who wrote the Gettysburg Address.

"We need to talk." Maggie put her arm around her friend. The border collie puppy scampered underfoot. "You're a pretty sexy woman, Ivy."

"Go on!" Ivy ducked her head and tried to push Maggie away.

"It's true. I mean it," Maggie laughed. "Don't try to get out of it."

All spunk and sparkle, Ivy's straight-talking earthiness declared to the world that she knew what was what. Ivy continued the conversation. "So, Maggie, did you hear? We found out who broke into the paper."

"I heard."

"I figured. I could have made a pretty good guess, but that wouldn't have been fair, now, would it?"

"Didn't have much to go on."

"That weasel Randy! He can go to hell, but the devil wouldn't have him."

"He's one character we're not going to have to worry about running into at the Seven Cities."

"He's so rotten salt wouldn't save him," Ivy spat.

"Don't worry. He's gone back to where he came from."

"So?" Ivy folded her arms. "So what? We got rid of one of the professional leeches. They're lined up from here to Santa Fe. What about the next one?"

"Don't worry, Ivy. We'll cross that bridge when we come to it. The next one won't have a chance against us," Maggie said. She felt more confident about her statement knowing Roger was on their side. She set out a dish of milk on the floor for the puppy. "Does she have a name?" she asked, spreading newspapers next to the stove.

"Figured I'd leave that to Hannah." Ivy sipped her coffee. "You know, the schools here aren't half bad."

Maggie shot her a look. "Yes. I know."

"School bus stops out here at the end of your road."

"I know that, too."

"Well?"

"Where Hannah goes to school isn't really up to me, is it? She's been out here a month longer than her spring break because of her problems in school. She begged Paul to let her stay so she could be with her grandmother. He agreed, hoping it'd keep her out of trouble, so long as she promised to make up the work she missed this summer. Sometimes I think he'd be only too happy to keep her here, out of Robin's hair. That way he doesn't have to be constantly playing referee between his daughter and his wife. Other times, I get the idea that now since we've put her through rehab, he'd do whatever it took to get her back."

"You're the mommy, Maggie," Ivy said.

Maggie looked out the window. "Maybe I'm trying to figure out what that's supposed to mean. I can't keep Hannah here unless she wants to be here. I'm no salesman for Monte Alto."

"I think you know what it means. You had a mommy."

"Sure did." Tears burned her eyes. She reached for a napkin. "Sorry."

"What for? You just buried your mother not even a week ago. You're entitled to be a little weepy."

"I miss her, Ivy."

"I should hope so."

"I'm not the same person as Lucy." Maggie blew her nose.

"You say that because you know how good your mother was at getting her way. She wasn't afraid to grab a hold and hang on, if she believed it was right."

Maggie's voice shook. "Getting her way wasn't always the best thing."

"Nothing is always the best thing. That's why all you can do is trust yourself to do right."

Maggie went to the stove and reached for the coffeepot. She refilled Ivy's cup and her own. "I'm listening, Ivy. I just don't see that I can make Hannah stay."

"That child has lived in the city all her life. This place would do her a world of good."

"I wish she would stay. It'd be good for her. For us."

"Now you're talking. How about a piece of that pie?"

Maggie sliced two pieces. "Strawberry rhubarb. That's what spring tastes like to me."

"Cut the rhubarb and stewed it up early this morning."

"I wish Hannah would get back."

Ivy shook her head. "Well, have a little patience. She's a good rider, isn't she?"

"Fair, I'd say. But she has no idea about how fast the weather can change out here. I doubt she's prepared for rain."

The phone rang. Maggie jumped to pick up the receiver. "Hello?"

"Hey, baby."

"Hi, Roger." A twang of dismay played through her greeting. She twisted the phone wire around her wrist and met Ivy's gaze across the table.

"What're you doing?" he asked.

"Having coffee with Ivy."

"What's going on?"

I miss you, she wanted to say. I'm scared, and now I have to admit it. Her voice wavered. "I'm a little worried about Hannah. She's been gone all morning. With Zia."

"Gone where?" His deep voice resonated over the wire.

"Over toward Abo, she said in her note."

"They just announced a thunderstorm warning."

As his words sank in, the calm façade she'd been busily constructing all morning crumbled.

Roger repeated the warning. "Did you hear what I said, Maggie? We better pay attention. It's been dry."

The ground was so dry that any heavy rain would hit it hard and bounce off without penetrating. It would rush into the arroyos, transforming them instantly into raging rivers.

"The arroyos could run," Maggie said.

"I'd say so," Roger agreed.

She peered out the window. While she wasn't looking, a gray curtain of cloud had been drawn across the sky. A steely gleam lit the fields, and a lone meadowlark's call, sounding melancholy, pierced the stillness. "It could start up any minute over here. I'm going out to look for her."

"Wait for me. I'll be right over," he said.

She hesitated. "How soon can you get here?"

"I'm leaving right now. I don't want you heading out alone. They spotted a funnel cloud in Milagro County."

Milagro, one county east, was usually the first to catch rough weather coming in from Texas. "I'll be ready when you get here." She hung up the phone.

"What can I do?" Ivy asked.

Maggie went to the window. Granite clouds massed in the southeast shut out the sun. "You ought to get home before this storm hits. Unless you want to wait it out here."

"Call me if you need me." Ivy stood. She took Maggie's hand. "Be careful. Looks like we're in for a frog strangler." She removed her rainbow scarf and placed it around Maggie's shoulders.

"We'll do that." Maggie started taking rain gear off back porch pegs—long slickers, blankets, sweatshirts, flashlights, rope.

Her mother's rubber boots fit her fine. She filled canteens and stuffed them in a pack with chocolate bars, dry socks, and a first-aid kit. Outside, cottonwood leaves rustled sharply as tree branches bent in the wind.

Static garbled the voice of the radio announcer: "Heavy storms are predicted this afternoon for all of Blue Grama County," he said. "The storm watch has been upgraded to a storm warning. Repeat: a severe thunderstorm warning is in effect for Blue Grama County until four P.M." A crack of lightning interrupted his report. As the lights in the house flickered and dimmed, the puppy whimpered. Maggie wrapped her in a blanket and tucked her into a cardboard box. A cannonball of thunder boomed and a sudden chill filled the house. She ran and checked the porch thermometer. The temperature had plunged more than twenty degrees in two hours, and the red line of mercury was still falling.

TWENTY-THREE

AS THE FIRST RAINDROPS HAMMERED on the tin roof of the house, Roger pulled into the driveway. Maggie ran to help him unload the horses from the trailer and found him focused entirely on their mission. He said an abrupt hello and kept working. She watched him until he took a moment to grab her by the shoulders and pull her close, kissing her once, quick and hard, before returning to saddling the horses and checking gear.

"What kind of a mother am I?" she wailed.

"Blaming yourself is no use," he spat. "You need to keep your mind clear. That's the best thing you can do."

Working with him through the falling rain, Maggie packed saddlebags with ropes and flares, a radio, a first-aid kit. They had to be ready for whatever they might find—and for the worst.

He flung a saddle over his pinto's back and cinched it, then looked up and placed a steadying arm on her shoulder. "Maggie," he said, "We're going to find her. Hannah's a smart kid. She'll be all right."

Dismayed, she said, "She doesn't know the terrain. She has no idea what these storms are like, how sudden they can turn. She's not that strong a rider. She'll be scared to death, and she won't have any idea what to do."

"Did you explain about the arroyos?" he asked.

Maggie shook her head. "I never did. And she wouldn't have listened if I had. She thinks she's invincible." The subject hadn't actually come up, and they'd had so much else going on. But now she wondered how on earth she could have been so careless.

He thought a moment. "Probably doesn't make a bit of difference. Until you've seen one run, you wouldn't believe it anyway. How could a little old dry streambed turn into a river before you can turn around?"

He took his horse's reins. The animal raised his head, alerted. "Do you know that back trail to Abo?"

She raised her voice to be heard over the rain. "I used to ride out that way, but that was a long time ago. I hope I can remember the way."

"Don't think this old Indian trail has changed any," Roger said. "It's wound through here at least a thousand years."

Lightning fractured the sky. The storm's cold breath blew dread in their direction.

"This is exactly how my father died," Maggie said. She was shaking, and not only from cold.

"...and he didn't come back and he didn't come back. And there was a big bolt of lightning and I knew what had happened..."

She thought she remembered her father's death, but that was impossible. It had happened before she was born. But she recalled every detail. She knew where her mother had ridden out in the rain, and how Lucy's horse had led her mother to her father's body in the dark.

Maggie whirled in a circle. Her vision blurred. Sky, horizon, llano, mountain—the home that she knew as well as she knew the shape of her own body now revealed its sinister aspect. Its familiarity had turned deadly dangerous.

"I know a storm killed your father," Roger said. "That storm was over a long time ago. We have to pay attention to this one." He handed her the reins of a gray mare. "Let's get going."

Any other time, Maggie would have savored the opportunity to ride alongside Roger. Now she hesitated. She hadn't ridden in so long. She placed one boot in the stirrup and swung her other leg across the saddle, then settled into place. The animal sensed her anxiety. She whinnied and pawed the ground, then backed up into a half-circle.

"She's a little spooked," Roger said. "Are you going to be all right? I can go alone, if you'd rather stay here."

She came close to snapping at him. "Of course I don't want you going without me." She'd never been out in weather like this. Whenever a summer storm came up, her mother bolted the doors and locked the windows. No one was allowed to talk on the phone, watch television, iron, or even take a bath so long as lightning flashed. Her fear for Hannah played out against a background of primal fear she'd absorbed even before she'd learned to talk. Then there was the guilt—for leaving Hannah alone while she indulged in her own pleasure. She knew she shouldn't have gone out with him!

"I'll be okay in a minute," she said, struggling to gain command of the horse. She was already out of breath, and they hadn't even gone anywhere. They cantered across the field, and at its edge, they found the crooked trail leading through unruly stands of piñon and juniper. "Look," Maggie said. "Here are her tracks." Sheltered from the rain by the tree cover, the tracks were only starting to disappear.

"Let's go then." Roger led the way.

Abo. The name meant "water bowl." The pueblo mission with its ancient springs had offered precious water in the desert to all who passed by. Horses had smelled it from miles away, leading their parched riders straight to the source of their survival. It had been a place of hope and renewal as surely as any shrine or temple. The thought kept Maggie's spirit going. The rain beat down harder. The horses kept a steady pace through the downpour. "Let's hope we don't get hailed on," Roger said.

Maggie continued on, all the while taking a pelting from heavy raindrops. Images of her daughter's broken body, flung like a rag doll's across the desert floor, revolved in the kaleidoscope her mind had become.

She remembered the raging arroyo she'd witnessed when she was eleven years old. She and Lucy had gone out in the pickup just after a storm. Her mother insisted on touring the ranch to make sure none of the dogies was in trouble. But Lucy knew storms, and she could've charted the wild behavior of the arroyo. She saw to it they were parked on top, a safe distance from the water when the flood came. They watched the push of debris, tree trunks, tires, old shoes, and fenders rush past. The boulders made an awful grinding sound as the fast water tumbled them downstream.

They turned toward the ruined pueblo mission, San Gregorio de Abo, its stones the red of dried blood, three stories high against the stony sky. Here Ice Age nomads able to bring down a bison with a pointed spear had turned their attention to cultivating the earth, growing maize, beans and squash, making pottery from the same earth that gave them their food, making ritual, creating home. They accepted the earth's hospitality and honored her with their respect. As they learned from her, their civilization took root along with their bean plants. Then raids and drought had driven them away. They had vanished and never returned, leaving behind still walls reeking with abandonment.

Stormy darkness obscured the rock walls of Abo. The draw would run. Lightning continued to flash as the rain fell in sheets. Maggie took the lead as if charging into battle, saber aloft. She called Hannah's name and received only echoes answering from the walls. The sky brightened to pearl gray. In the distance, fountains of rain descended in every direction.

The horse stepped onto a narrow sandstone ledge and carried her past spirals, bear paws, and arrows. Maggie could almost remember the language of the petroglyphs. If only these images carved and painted in stone could tell her what she needed to know right now: Where was Hannah?

Beneath the petroglyphs, soot marked the wall. Ancient fires had scorched this curvilinear red rock, a shelter of sorts. Maggie rode on, soaked with perspiration beneath her slicker. Every muscle ached. Lightning flashed to the south, the direction of the storm on Monte Alto. They were only inches from the edge, where the jagged precipice dropped off forty feet to the basin below. Her horse shied. Maggie grasped the reins while she struggled to keep her balance.

A lone petroglyph on the wall beside her caught Maggie's eye. Longer than the rest, a zigzag of lightning sliced across the rock face. The sign for lightning and the sign for snake were the same—a bent line with a pointed arrow. Maggie followed the arrow's direction. Behind the crevice, she saw the deep arroyo with six-foot walls. She waited for Roger. "You go on ahead," she told him. "I'm going over this way."

"Are you sure you want to split up?" he asked.

"We've got a lot of ground to cover, and there's only the two of us."

"I'd feel better if we stuck together," he said. "Maggie, I don't think this is a good idea."

"Don't fight me!" The hysterical edge in her voice frightened her. She checked herself. She took a deep breath. "I'll be fine," she added, with deliberate calm. "Don't worry about me." She placed her palm against his cheek.

"You know that's impossible," he said. He took her hand and pressed his lips to her fingers.

"All right, Maggie, if that's the way you want to go. We'll meet back here after we've searched both sides of the mission."

She watched him turn and ride away.

Her horse trod carefully on the downward slope. She picked her way between cobbles to the edge of the arroyo. She called Hannah's name, over and over. "Where are you?" she pleaded. Fear and exhaustion had unplugged her everyday connections. She was ready to trust something else: A burning bush. A dancing kachina. The Virgin of Guadalupe.

Heading downhill over slippery stones loosened by the rain, her horse had a bout of nerves. She urged her to move ahead. Still, the reluctant creature moved slowly, much too slowly. How would they ever reach Hannah in time? Her anxiety mounted. The horse pulled her ears back and snorted. She wasn't accustomed to being out in this kind of weather. "Come on there, girl," she said. "You can do it."

The horse tested the stones, suddenly clumsy. Her weight shifted awkwardly as the ground moved out from under her. As she slipped, Maggie heard the sickening scrape of hooves on stone. They were falling, and there was nothing she could do about it. She looked for the best place to land. There was no time to engineer this crash. The split-second it took stretched into slow-motion. A collage of sky and mountain spun across her vision. The horse's knees gave way as she bowed low. Maggie tugged on the reins when she should have given her a moment to right herself. The mistake cost Maggie her balance. She fell off the horse's back and landed on the rocks. The sky went midnight black.

A figure approached her. A man in coveralls, with the kindest face, so familiar. Though she'd never seen him before, she knew him. He held out his hand to her. She had been searching for him all her life.

"Daddy," she said, so grateful.

He placed his hand on her shoulder. He lifted her to her feet.

"Maggie. You're going to be all right."

"What about Hannah?"

He removed his hand and looked at her with love. She blinked. He was gone.

When she opened her eyes, she was lying on the rocky ground, cold and soaked, looking up at a stone gray sky. The rain had let up. She scrambled to her feet. She shook her arms and hands. She turned her head from side to side. Everything still worked. Nothing was broken. She wasn't even hurting too badly from the fall.

Then she remembered her father's visit. She had been warned. Time was up. "God," she prayed, "I know I'm not in any position to bargain with you. But if you're planning on taking anybody today, I ask that it be me."

Ten yards away, she saw her horse. She took the reins and tried to mount, but she skittered away. She spoke to her in a low voice. "Come on, girl. We still have work to do." She continued coaxing, until the horse stood still and waited while she climbed cautiously back in the saddle. They rode on, slowly.

A shape emerged from the mist. As if stepping out of a misty dream, the figure of a riderless palomino materialized before her.

"Zia!" For a long moment, the woman and the horse gazed at each other.

TWENTY-FOUR

THE PALOMINO STOOD STILL. WHITE-SMOKE breath swirled about her eyes. Following the horse's alignment, Maggie searched the foggy landscape to the west. There dark water, heavy with sediment, trickled down the arroyo floor.

An unearthly, metallic glare lit the canyon, and a faint electric smell singed the chilly air. She scanned the embankment. Thirty yards away, on the opposite side of the ditch, an elfin black-clad figure huddled against the canyon wall, one arm wrapped about herself.

"Hannah!" Maggie shouted. "What happened?" Her words ricocheted along the canyon walls. What in God's name was Hannah doing down there? What the hell had happened to her arm? Had Zia's bad eye caused her to take a fall on the narrow ledge? Water continued to seep down the arroyo from shrouded Monte Alto. By her best calculation, she didn't have time to outrace the flood.

"Hannah!" Maggie screamed. "Get out of there! Get away! The arroyo's going to flood!"

A crack of thunder rumbled down from the mountain. Rain swept down in a rush behind. Should Maggie try to run to Hannah along the bank, or could she find some way to pull her out from up top? She studied the red sand, the tangles of brambles and vines, datura, gourds, and boulders that crowded the arroyo floor. The bank above was steep in places, uneven, corrugated by tree roots and erosion, a trap where she could easily trip and fall. Quick dodging back and forth between the trees was required to keep a footing and avoid getting slapped in the face by low branches.

From here, the arroyo looked to be the faster route. However, if she went that way and miscalculated, neither she nor her daughter would stand a chance against the torrent. They'd be swept away and dragged under in no time.

Cold, wet, and exhausted, Maggie didn't know if she had what it took to save her daughter. Who was she, anyway? A forty-two-year-old woman, just starting to get back in shape after years in a city at a desk job. Her muscles had turned to mush.

She screamed to Hannah to climb out of the arroyo. The girl shouted back, but her words were lost beneath the approaching roar of water. Hannah sat unmoving, directly in the path of the flood.

Maggie tore off her slicker and lowered herself into the floodway. At the edge of the six-foot bank, she dug in her heels and slid down the nearly perpendicular arroyo wall. Halfway down she jumped and landed hard, scraping her hands and knees. She grabbed onto brambles to pull herself upward. She ran toward Hannah, her steps slowed by the effort to keep her balance in the slick red caliche.

Trying to move faster than the mud would permit, Maggie

stumbled on a half-concealed chunk of sandstone and went down face-first. The thick mud sucked her body down, holding her sprawled on the ground. Groping blindly, she found a tree root no thicker than her own wrist poking out of the arroyo wall. She used it to pull herself up, but she only made it to her hands and knees.

A lizard scurried past, leaving a squirm of tail-print behind. She hoped any snakes would get out of the way as easily. Her cheek burned. Maggie touched her hand, with its fingernails broken below the quick, to her face and her fingers came away bloodstained. She struggled again to stand. Pain shot through her left knee. She had to get to Hannah before the flood arrived.

As she sloshed through the rising water, Maggie scanned the side of the arroyo for a way up, perhaps just a chink in the earthen wall where she might gain a foothold or an eroded incline she could scramble up with Hannah.

Hannah, twenty feet away, cried out, "Mom! Hurry!" The flood was midway up the child's legs. The roar of oncoming water, reverberating within the confines of the arroyo's walls, sounded as though the earth was splitting.

"Get out of the canyon!" Maggie yelled. "Move up the side!"

"I can't!" Hannah moaned. "My foot hurts! I think it's broken. I can't move!" She looked down at the water now swirling as high as her knees.

The stream surged, carrying sticks and brush and the stink of mud. A wave of water six feet high snaked around the last remaining bend and charged at them with the speed of an oncoming train. Exhausted, out of breath, and almost out of hope, Maggie took one last step. She grabbed Hannah's shoulder, then gripped her. Hannah clung to her tightly, almost choking her.

Maggie planted her feet as firmly as she could in the ooze below. Inky water was already up past Hannah's waist. "Grab hold of that ledge above you," Maggie shouted.

"I can't, Mom, I can't," Hannah wailed. "It hurts too much!" Maggie screamed, "Yes you can! You have to!" When Hannah would not let go, Maggie pried her daughter's arm from its hold on her own neck and placed it on the ledge. Then Maggie put her hands under Hannah's bottom and shoved her upward. Hannah found a crack. She dug in and clutched with her remaining strength. "That's the way! Pull yourself up!" Maggie called over the water's roar. Hannah gained a toehold and moved a few inches higher. Maggie gave her another ferocious shove, then glanced at the encroaching froth. She had used all her remaining strength to push Hannah upward along the incline of the bank. She watched as her daughter reached safety on solid ground above.

Above the roaring, Maggie thought she heard a voice. She looked up. Roger stood on the bank with a coil of rope in his hand. For a moment, she thought she must be imagining him.

"Hang on," he shouted. He threw an end of the rope down the embankment and he started toward her. He stretched an arm out to Maggie. He inched closer. She reached for him, but slipped backward into water, now chest-deep, pulling her downstream. Somehow, Roger was able to take hold of her waist. He half-dragged, half-carried her to the top. She fought her way up, barely ahead of the waters closing over them. Once they had crawled to the top, they looked down, where two feet below, fence planks, rocks, tires, and branches swirled past in the thick mud flow.

"You picked one hell of a day to go for a swim, Maggie," Roger shouted above the roaring flood. Winded, he held her close for a moment before turning to Hannah, whose bluish lips trembled in her sheet-white face. He pulled dry blankets from a saddlebag. "Hypothermia is the first thing we've got to worry about," Roger said. "Then we'll see what's broken. You too,

Maggie. Get yourself into something warm and dry." He placed a woolen blanket over Maggie's shoulders. She wrapped another blanket around her shivering daughter and hugged her as though she'd never let her go. Hannah relaxed in her arms. The feel of her daughter's perfect, fragile bones and the scent of her wet hair nearly overwhelmed Maggie. Nothing could ever be as beautiful as the way Hannah's eyelashes curled against her exquisitely soft cheek.

Roger poured a cup of steaming cocoa from a thermos. Hannah sipped from the cup Maggie held to her lips then asked for more. The scalding brew had an immediate effect. Color began returning to her ashen face.

"Good girl," Roger said. "Maggie, let me see that cut on your face." He poured peroxide from the first-aid kit on a piece of gauze and dabbed at her cheek. She winced and turned her face from his fingers. "Pretty nasty gash you got there. May need some stitches," he said.

"Rock tried to bite me," she joked. She clutched his hand. "Lucky you found us. Thanks for not following my directions."

"I don't always do exactly what you tell me," he said. He turned to Hannah. "Let's see that foot, cowgirl," he said. He pulled off her boot and peeled the sock. A ghastly swollen purple bruise covered the ankle. Gently, he tested the foot. Hannah winced and let out a yelp.

"Looks like a bad sprain, but we can't tell for sure," he said. "We'll splint it until we can get you to the doc for an x-ray." He quickly prepared the splint. When he was through, he elevated Hannah's leg on a folded saddle blanket.

"Storm's passing," Roger said, looking up. Monte Alto was again visible, blue and serene in the rain-washed air. "But we're stuck here until the water goes down and we can cross the arroyo. Hannah, do you think you can ride back?"

"Sure I can," she hiccoughed.

"Good. I'll be right back."

A few minutes later, he returned with an armload of cedar.

"How do you light a fire when it's rained?" Hannah asked.

"Watch now," Roger said. He constructed a pile of dry twigs within a quickly arranged rock circle. He took a match from his pocket and struck it on a rock, then placed it in the twigs. A tiny flame ignited. He held his hands close to the wavering flame to keep it alive.

As the fire grew, he fed it bigger pieces of kindling, one by one. Hannah reached her hand out toward the warmth. Her eyes reflected firelight, and slowly she stopped shivering.

Roger put one arm around Maggie and the other around Hannah. "Maybe next time you decide to take Zia for a ride, you'll check the weather report first."

"I promise I will," she said. "Look!" Hannah pointed.

Arched across the darkened sky, a perfect rainbow gleamed.

October, 2000

COTTONWOODS BLAZED A GOLDEN LIGHT above the picnic tables covered with red-checkered cloth in the front yard of the ranch. Jars of fall wildflowers and pumpkins wreathed with garlic and red chiles served as centerpieces. Maggie and Hannah had worked all morning to get everything ready for this Sunday afternoon harvest feast.

At the fire pit, Maggie used a wooden spoon to stir the beans laced with chile and garlic that simmered in Elias's biggest Dutch oven over the glowing coals. With the *gancho*, the old branding iron, she lifted the lid on the arroz con pollo. An appetizing burst of steam wafted out of the pot. Then she checked the brisket cooking in a third pot. She rearranged white-hot coals on the lid of the pot in which peach cobbler bubbled. She had gotten the knack of keeping four or five pots going at once over the fire. She expected all the food would go—she had invited half the town.

She shaded her eyes from the sun and watched Hannah, tall and graceful, run across the field with Winnie scampering right behind, as usual. Amazing how that black-and-white puppy had grown in just a few months, just as Hannah had. And talk about smart! Winnie already had the schoolbus schedule down. Every afternoon exactly at 4:30, she trotted off to wait for Hannah. The two were inseparable.

Only last week, right after Hannah got her cast off, she announced she'd decided to stay on for the school year. Paul immediately agreed to her remaining in Monte Alto, so long as she returned east for Christmas vacation.

Maggie unlatched the garden gate, where blue morning glories still bloomed. They'd had a good crop of tomatoes, cucumbers, beans and potatoes, mustard and okra all summer. The squash wanted to take over, with so many of those calabacitas ripening that she had set them to dry on screens. Those old seeds produced well, and they didn't take much work or water. There'd be plenty to eat as well as seeds to save for next year. Not bad for a first harvest, everyone said. They'd had no hard frost yet, but they expected one any time now. The cedarberries were thick this year, causing old-timers to predict a tough winter.

The ladies from the Wednesday Club arrived first. They stepped out of Elvira's old Mercury, each carrying a covered dish. "Looks mighty nice what you've done," Elvira said.

A table quickly filled up with pies, cakes, casseroles, and salads. Each lady had brought her specialty today. The Wednesday Club took seats under the big cottonwood, where they had the best view of the doings.

"That Maggie. She's something else," Elvira observed, as Maggie began to welcome the guests.

"She's done Lucy proud, that's for sure," Mercedes agreed.

"Fixed this old place up real neat," said Ruby.

"What a pretty girl that Hannah's turning out to be," said Lola. "Since she's grown out that scarecrow hair and put a little flesh on her bones. Guess Esperanza finally got her hands on that one."

"Looks just like Maggie at her age, don't you think?" Mercedes said. "With those long legs."

Ruby chimed in, "Hannah's turning into a fine bridge player, isn't she? And who would have thought it? She's the youngest member the Wednesday Club ever had!"

"What do you mean?" Elvira piped up. "She's already beating us forty percent of the time!"

"At least we didn't have to change our rule," Ruby replied.

The ladies nodded. "And did you hear Roger's teaching her to shoe horses?" said Elvira. "That little gal can do anything she sets her mind to."

"Will you look over there. It's Tommie. Who's that good-looking fellow with her?"

"I hear that's a Dr. Padilla. A fellow she works with at the hospital."

"And will you look—here's Ivy McGrath," said Elvira.

Gravel crunched as Ivy's Chevy turned in the driveway. A hand-knitted crimson scarf was wrapped around her shoulders. "Something smells awfully good," she said. A lanky bearded fellow with red suspenders, red bandanna, and straw hat followed her out of the truck carrying a guitar case.

"What this party needs is some music," Ivy declared. "Aubrey, let's get tuned up." She took out a harmonica and sounded a few chords.

"Will you look at that Ivy," said Elvira. "She never quits."

"Don't you know she's on Easy Street now she's got Maggie working for her over at the paper. She's got all the time in the world to do as she pleases," Mercedes said, "and she gets to call herself publisher."

"I've noticed that the paper has gotten more interesting since Maggie's been working over there as editor," Ruby said.

Elvira tapped her toe to the music. "Ivy and that Aubrey fellow make a nice duet," she said.

A white pickup pulled into the driveway. "Looks like the mayor has arrived," Mercedes said.

He came over to greet them under the trees. "Good afternoon, ladies," he said. "How pretty you're looking today!"

"Hello, Mr. Mayor," the ladies fluttered. Elvira giggled.

"Where's Maggie?" he asked.

"I think she went inside," Elvira said. "She came by and said: 'It'll be easier if we can run into the pantry to get water. I'm going to get that stubborn tap working.'"

Maggie locked the wrench around the stuck tap, gripped it with all her strength, and turned. The tap obliged with a whoosh of rusty water just as she heard footsteps approaching.

Roger got handsomer every time she saw him. "Hi there," she said.

"Hello. Quite a party you've got going out there." He shut the pantry door behind him.

"Hope you're hungry," she said. "The ladies will be disappointed if you don't taste every dish they brought."

He stepped closer to Maggie and took her in his arms, pressing her against the pantry wall. Golden sunlight shone through a small, high window. The room was filled with the scent of cinnamon, cloves, honey, and sweet drying apples.

His lips met hers softly at first, then they kissed as though they would never stop, as they had when they were teenagers.

"Mom? Are you in there?" Hannah pushed the door open.

"You guys!" she said with an unusually piercing voice. "Everyone's waiting for you. Come on, break it up."

Maggie turned to her. "You're sure bossy for someone who's just become a teenager herself." Hannah had survived her first rough test on the land with good humor, but she had a hell of a lot of challenges still in front of her.

Under his breath, Roger said to Maggie, "Sounds like Lucy for sure."

They looked at each other and burst out laughing. Hannah opened the door, and looked back over her shoulder, saying with gravity, as she exited, "I'm going to learn to have the last laugh if it takes me my whole life."

The two lovers stared after Hannah in contented silence and followed.